Praise for
Marie Lamba

Drawn

"Marie Lamba's *Drawn* is a wonderfully spooky tale of romance and discovery. It's a magical exploration of the unconquerable power of love. Highly recommended!"

—Jonathan Maberry, *New York Times* bestselling author of
Rot & Ruin and *Dust & Decay*

"In *Drawn*, Marie Lamba deftly entwines romance and mystery, past and present, into a page-turning adventure. Buy it today and I promise you'll be finished reading far too quickly!"

—Joy Nash, *USA Today* bestselling paranormal
romance author of *The Immortals* series,
The Grail King and *The Unforgiven*

Over My Head

"Marie Lamba brings a fresh, new, and very authentic voice to this fabulous young adult novel. Coming of age has never been done so well!"

—LA Banks, *New York Times* bestselling author of
The Vampire Huntress Legends series

"Marie Lamba strikes gold with *Over My Head* — a funny, touching, and at times heart-breaking Young Adult novel about the search for love. Gorgeous prose, deep insights and a wonderfully rewarding read."

—*New York Times* bestseller Jonathan Maberry

What I Meant...

"Lamba makes an impressive debut with this contemporary novel introducing Sangeet, a 15-year-old Indian American girl who at times feels like the whole world is against her."

—*Publisher's Weekly*

"...spies and secrets make for great drama, and many readers will not be able to get enough of Sang's hilarious, angry, hip narrative about her diverse family and friends."

—*BOOKLIST*

DRAWN

DRAWN

Published by

Lamba Associates, Inc.
P.O. Box 415
Doylestown, PA 18901

Copyright © 2012 Marie Lamba
Cover copyright © 2012 Marie Lamba
Book design and layout copyright © 2012 52 Novels

http://www.marielamba.com

Email with inquiries to: marielamba@hotmail.com

First Edition: January 2012

Books by
Marie Lamba

Drawn

Over My Head

What I Meant…

DRAWN

Marie Lamba

Love is forever....

Marie Lamba

This one's for my wonderful girls
Adria and Cari Lamba
and Louisa and Jacqueline Busterna

1

I pull the zipper up the back, sealing myself into the dress. All maroon velvet, with lace along the low neckline. Long, full skirt and tight sleeves ending in a point over each hand. This is *so* not me.

I cast a longing look at the soft jeans I'd tossed onto my bed, and at my sketchbook. Especially at my sketchbook. On it is a quick drawing I did of some imaginary guy seen from the back. He's wearing a loose shirt and his dark hair reaches his shoulders— shoulders that seem almost alive with tension. Even though the sketch is just a few strokes of a pencil, there's something about it. I find myself looking at it over and over again.

If only he'd turn around.

Okay, that's a weird thought.

It's also pretty weird that I'm playing dress up for some party.

"That's it. I'm done." I try to yank down the zipper. It doesn't budge. Crap. "Dad? Could you come here a minute?"

We're in a two-story house, part of a twin, or a "semi-detached" as the British call it. I hear the creak of his steps along the floorboards leading to my room. Dad enters and I feel a flurry of panic. With me in this ridiculous huge dress and now my dad hovering, the bedroom feels much too full. I *hate* small spaces.

"Oh, Michelle." Dad takes my hands in his and tilts his head to the side. "You are an absolute vision."

I roll my eyes. A dad sees what he wants.

"I mean it." He squeezes my fingers. "You look so much like your mother."

I twirl toward the mirror standing in the corner and I expect to see staring back at me Madame Florabunda, psychic extraordinaire (AKA my mom). But it's just me. Mousy brown hair with unpredictable waves and curls. Plain brown eyes, just like my dad's (except mine are a little too large for my face). Not that I wouldn't kill to be as beautiful as my mom. She's got jet-black hair and intense hazel eyes and a gorgeous, curvy figure. Oh, and she's nuts. Did I mention that?

At once I remember how Mom held my chin in her hand and said, "Shelly, honey, you are so like me. You've got the power, just like me. Just like your brother." She's wrong. I don't. I never will. I want to be as unlike her and my older brother Wayne as I possibly can. It's kind of my life's goal.

After that little chat with my mom, she left to answer "a calling." And hasn't called us for over a year.

Suddenly it's like the heavy fabric is pressing in on me, as if the dress is becoming smaller and smaller. "Dad, help with the zipper. Please."

Dad squints. "But I think it's up all the way."

"I need it *down*. I'm not wearing this thing. Maybe I'll just stay here."

"Shelly, come on. I brought your mother's dress especially for this." He sinks onto the bed, his knees cracking and the duvet poofing around him. "You know we have to go to this dinner. Anyway, you'll finally get to see the castle. That's got to appeal to the artist in you."

"Maybe." Instead of just having the dinner at the school, the Academy rented out the town's castle for the night.

"And most of the students will be there. Everyone will be in period costume."

"Oh, yeah? What time period is that from?" I nod at his tan slacks and white button-down shirt.

"I'm changing in a minute. Headmistress Hunter's secretary dropped off a costume for me."

"Well, then, why couldn't she drop off one for me so I wouldn't have to wear this?" I tug at the zipper again. No luck.

"Actually, she did drop off something. Hang on." He springs off the bed and leaves, returning a moment later with a large maroon cone that has a bit of purple scarf hanging from the tip.

"What is *that?*" I ask.

"Your hat."

"No." I cross my arms.

"Please, Michelle. The Headmistress sent it over special. We don't want to upset her."

I bite my lip. From what my dad's told me, this Headmistress is a real stickler for rules and for upholding the traditions and reputation of the school. If she likes my dad enough, she might offer him a permanent teaching position at the Academy, which would be amazing. The two of us have only been in England for a few days, yet I'm already convinced it's the best place in the universe. Not because of the quaint little shops or everyone's adorable English accent, or even because of this supposedly grand castle on the edge of town. No. This place is perfect because here no one knows that back in New Jersey my family, the De Freccio's, are called the De Freak-o's.

My dad's eyebrows are drawn together. He looks almost lost, like he has so many times over this past year. I'm not the only one who needs a new beginning.

I sigh and stick out my hand for the hat. As my dad gives it to me, my eyes again stray to the drawing of that guy. In the sketch I can now see the very edge of his cheek. It's as if he's just turned ever so slightly toward me.

But that's crazy.

2

"Oh, God." Dad clutches the steering wheel of our tiny orange car. He veers toward our exit, then back into the roundabout traffic, passing the castle sign for the third time. Horns sound. "Sorry!" he shouts, as if the drivers can hear him.

Dad's dubbed this car our "Clockwork Orange" because it's like a little wind-up toy. But right now it feels more like an instrument of death. He has definitely not mastered the art of driving on the wrong side of the road from the wrong side of the car.

"Dad, you have to get off this circle." My stomach makes an unpleasant sound. "Or just stop." My window is open but the fresh air doesn't seem to be helping. I look at the cone hat in my lap. It'd make a fancy barf bag.

"I'm doing it this time." The car points toward the exit at last. "See?" He gives me the thumbs-up.

A horn blares. To our right, a rusty brown truck appears seemingly from nowhere. Dad swerves to the left. The truck zooms by. The driver leans on his horn and holds out a finger. It is most definitely not a thumbs-up.

Our car veers sharply onto the exit's shoulder and rolls to a stop. I hear the unmistakable hiss of a tire letting out its final breath. Behind us, a car's doors slam. "Need some assistance?" a refined British voice calls.

"Yes!" Dad cuts the engine and opens the door.

I grab his arm. "Where are you going?"

"Somebody's got to change the tire."

"Dressed like that?" He's wearing green tights and a black tunic, along with knee-high black boots. It's supposed to be a nobleman's costume but he looks more like a drag queen.

"Afraid I'll get a run in my stocking?" He steps out. In the rearview mirror I see an older gentleman dressed up as a thinner version of King Henry VIII and another younger guy in a blue Prince Charming-type outfit approaching. Horns toot. Someone shouts from a passing car, "Oi oi, nice pair of stems."

"Hello." It's Prince Charming leaning down to my window. He's even more charming—gorgeous, in fact—up close. Long black lashes surround his sky-blue eyes.

I tuck a ringlet behind my ear. "Uh. Erm." I'm completely incoherent. Those eyes. That accent. It's too much.

"Are you all right?" he asks.

I gulp and shake my head.

"You're not all right?"

I nod. Then I shake my head again. Then I want to disappear.

"Right. Well, my name is William."

"Michelle," I say. It sounds like a gasp.

Long, awkward pause.

"William, lend a hand," his father orders.

"Yes, sir," he says, waves to me and walks away.

And I put the cone hat over my face.

With William and his father helping my dad, we're soon on our way. We pull out after their sleek black car and follow them toward the castle. Dad fills me in on all the gory details. How William is actually William Wallingford, as in the Wallingfords of Wallingford Academy. "His father is obviously a terribly important man. He's a big solicitor—that's a lawyer."

"So he owns the school?"

"I think his family helped found it or something. It was started several hundred years ago on the philosophy of 'The Best Win,' and we definitely want to be one of 'the best.'"

Our car turns a bend, and rising above the trees is a stone turret connected by a wall to another turret, then another. It's huge. I had no idea.

Dad parks the car in the nearly full lot. "That sure is impressive," he says, nodding at the castle. "Nothing like that back in New Jersey. Unless you count the Trenton Prison."

As I get out of the car, I pop the hat on my head. My vision travels up the steep wall to the top where blue and red flags snap in the wind. I have to sketch this. Do a painting. Or maybe I'll do a block print instead to emphasize the castle's simplicity. The black and white starkness of my print starts to form in my brain.

"Milady," William says, suddenly at my side. He grins, does a ridiculous bow and offers me his arm. I smile and take it, trying my best to act casual. "I've never been to America," he says.

"I have." No duh. My cheeks sting.

"Ever been to a castle before?"

I shake my head.

"Well, mostly they're just a gloomy pile of rocks. Quite dull. Quite for tourists, Americans such as yourself, to be amused by. But this one is a real beauty." He stares at me. As I feel a blush rise on my cheeks, I quickly look away.

My dad and Mr. Wallingford are a few yards ahead of us when Mr. Wallingford turns. Even from this distance I can see that he has glittering blue eyes lined with black eyelashes, just like William's. He says in a sharp voice, "William, don't dawdle. We are late as it is."

"Yes, sir." William raises his chin. I notice our pace slow and my dad and Mr. Wallingford are soon out of sight.

We pass a rusty brown truck. "Look, that's the one that cut our car off."

William's face contorts into a sneer. "That's Roger Mortley's piece of rubbish. Well-suited to him."

"Is he a student at the Academy?"

"A charity case," he says with obvious distaste.

"Huh." I let go of his arm and step back.

"What is it?" He gives me a puzzled look.

"It's, well, nothing. Go on without me. I forgot something in the car."

"Oh." He glances toward the castle as if expecting his father to pop back into view. "You're quite certain? I *could* wait."

"Go. Please. I'll be fine."

He nods and quicksteps ahead, following the red crushed stone path.

I collapse against the truck. What if he knew about my own family's past financial woes? My brother Wayne's outrageous medical bills? The free holiday dinner delivered to our house from the Lion's Club? I imagine William's gorgeous face contorting with disgust. My family is clearly not one of 'the best.' Fortunately, my dad is one of the best when it comes to literary criticism. His article on Edgar Allan Poe definitely got the Academy's attention.

I take a few more moments to try to get my act together, reminding myself over and over that no one will know anything about my past unless I'm stupid enough to tell them.

Okay. Be brave.

I follow the path and cross a stone bridge over a dry moat bed. Enter a high arched gateway where the stone flooring is worn into grooves, probably from centuries of carts rolling through. The passage is dark and chilled. I hug my arms, hurry toward the brightness beyond and arrive at a vast open courtyard. It's grassy and surrounded on all sides by the massive walls with various styles of stone buildings attached to them. The late afternoon sun slants over the top of one wall, casting a gloomy shadow on half of the green.

It's quiet. It's like I'm the only one in the entire castle. A gust swirls around my dress and stirs the lace hanging from my hat. There's a tingle along the back of my neck.

My heart starts to race. I am not alone.

3

I swallow hard. Someone or something is behind me.

"Welcome to Blanchley Castle!"

"Ohmygod." I clutch my heart like I'm doing the pledge.

"I'm Roger and I welcome thee." Roger has stringy blond hair and a sarcastic smile. He's wearing brown leather leggings, knee-high boots, a coarse white shirt and a red hat stabbed through with a feather. He removes his hat and takes a deep bow.

"Wait, Roger? As in brown rusty truck Roger?"

"She runs well," he says, a bit defensively as he puts his hat back on. He's tall and his cheeks have an underfed gaunt look. "You're new." He holds out a hand. "And you are…"

I'm about to shake his hand and introduce myself, but suddenly I say, "I'm the one you ran off the road."

"Ah." He drops his hand. "Well, I'm paid to welcome all guests to the castle, even if they are crap drivers and practically kill me." He glares.

"You gave us a flat." I glare back.

He smirks. I clench my fists. I could so punch him. Instead I give him the finger, march to the nearest building and tug on the door. It's locked.

"Try the next one," he says and laughs.

Furious, I stride to that door and my anger ebbs the instant my hand touches the large tarnished handle. Did I really give the finger to somebody I just met?

Roger watches me, hands on his hips, looking like a very cocky Robin Hood. "Right about now you're probably wondering why you got so angry." He walks over to me. "I should have warned you. It's that spot." He points his thumb over his shoulder. "It's cursed," he says in a dramatic whisper. "It makes people extremely irate. Some people, such as yourself, are more sensitive to the spirit world than others."

"I'm *not* sensitive to the spirit world," I practically shout.

"Whoa. See that? And you're not even close to the spot. Anyhow, legend has it that the third Earl of Blanchley was murdered right there. It was a savage and bloody killing, and his spirit lingers, looking for revenge."

I hold up a hand. "Save the spooky stories."

"Hm." He seems disappointed. "Most American tourists eat this stuff right up and beg for seconds."

"The only stuff I want to eat up is dinner. The banquet's in here?" I point to the rough wooden door.

He nods. "Down a hallway, then right up the steps."

"Thanks." I turn to the door. "Look, my name's Michelle and I'm sorry about giving you the finger."

"Like I said, it's not your fault. Sorry about giving you the puncture. That's all on me. I'm a first-class prat. Just ask anyone."

I turn back to see his pleasant smile.

I follow the sound of music and laughter upstairs and enter a giant hall. On one side there's a massive hearth with logs sputtering flames. The head of a roaring bear is mounted above. Stained glass windows make up the opposite wall. It must be beautiful when the sun streams through it, but now the daylight is just about gone. Suits of armor stand guard in the corners.

The costumed students of Wallingford Academy sit around three rows of long tables covered with white cloths and candelabras. A chubby man who should definitely not be wearing those striped tights strolls past me strumming what I guess is a lute.

I scan the room for my dad and find him at the head table, chuckling. He's sitting along with the other twenty or so teachers who are dressed as monks, nuns, queens or wizards. It all reminds me a bit too much of Hogwarts. I look at the ceiling half expecting to see clouds flitting overhead but only find rough wooden beams.

"Where did you get that dress?" a pretty girl says to me. Her shoulder-length hair has the sheen and color of copper wire, and her dusty gray eyes are almost cat-like.

"Oh, hi. I brought my dress from home."

She smiles and is instantly elevated from pretty to stunning. "You're the new American student, aren't you? Michelle? I'm Constance Hunter."

"As in Headmistress Hunter?"

"She's my mother." She rolls her eyes. "I'm glad to hear you didn't get your costume here. Farley's Fancy Dress always promises me the best rental. I was afraid they'd cheated me with this rag." She flicks her hand at her outfit, an elegant pale green gown that accentuates her narrow waist and shows off just enough cleavage to grab any guy's attention. "Honestly, I feel like a fat-arsed cow in it."

"But you look gorgeous."

Constance rests her hand on my wrist. "You know, I believe we are going to be grand friends. If you'd like, my William and I can show you around the school a bit this week. Help you get sorted."

"Your William?" A bad feeling edges up my throat.

"William Wallingford. As in Wallingford Academy." Her nose rises a notch. "I can introduce you if you'd like."

I swallow. "Oh. I've met him. He's...nice."

"You've met him? He didn't say." Her hand slips from my wrist. "Well." Her eyes scan me for an uncomfortable moment. "I'd best sit. I'd ask you to join us but the spots are all taken. You understand."

One other table still has free spots, so I go to it and say to an Indian girl, "Do you mind if I sit here?"

Her name is Guncha, she's really friendly and she quickly introduces me to everyone at the table. I relax and someone sets a plate filled with steaming roast beef and mashed potatoes in front of me. I pull off my hat and place it in the middle of the table next to the other hats the girls have dumped there. Picking up my fork, I crane my neck looking for William. Sure enough, he's sitting beside Constance. Her hand rests possessively on his arm and he's whispering to her. Why did I ever think someone like him would be interested in me?

"You're admiring the perfect couple," Guncha says.

"I wasn't—"

"It's alright. Constance Hunter and William Wallingford won't mind." She pushes her long black hair back over her shoulder and leans closer. "They'd probably love that, actually, like a pair of preening peacocks. You know the sort. You eating that?" She points to an untouched roll on my plate.

"No. Here." I pass the roll and say in what I hope is a nonchalant voice, "So, how long have those two been together?"

"Seems like ages." Guncha scrapes some butter onto the bread. "It's pretty sickening, actually."

"Careful, Guncha," Justine says. She's a heavy girl with short blonde hair and a wry smile. "I'm seeing some envious green appear."

"Well, why not?" She leans her chin on her fist and sighs. "Life's unfair."

"The best win, right?" Justine nudges me. "School motto, you know."

Later there's free time to wander around the castle. It's too bad Roger isn't around to give me some background on what I'm seeing. Since he works here, he might know who slept in this four-poster bed. Who prayed in this cute little chapel. What treaties were discussed in the grand paneled study.

The crowd thins as I move on, until it's just me. I avoid visiting the small dark dungeon and enter a wing filled with stern portraits, their paint thick and darkened with age. To the right is a cracked leather seat mysteriously labeled "The Mating Chair." In the next room a tapestry of a unicorn in a field of roses hangs on the wall. It reminds me of the rose print on the travel bag my mother had, or probably still has wherever she is…

The smell of cinnamon fills the air. Past the tapestry, a very narrow flight of stone stairs leads toward a dim light. I immediately decide I won't go up. It's too confining.

But the cinnamon smells even stronger here. It makes me think of warm cookies and my home from a long, long time ago. I change my mind and climb the steps. A small alcove is at the top and someone sits at a wooden table with his back to me. He studies a paper by candlelight. His auburn hair reaches his shoulders and he looks familiar.

With a jolt I remember the drawing of that guy in my sketchbook. To get his attention, I clear my throat.

In an instant, he stands, grabs my arm and shoves me against the wall. His face is close. His eyes filled with fury.

Sharp stones bite into my back. Tears spring into my eyes. "Let go!" I shout. I try to pull from his grip.

His glare softens, his grip loosens. "Forgive me. I thought…"

"You thought what?" I pull my arm from him.

He takes a step back. "I beg your pardon. I was taken by surprise. There have been dangers…"

I'm rubbing my arm. Blinking away tears.

"I have hurt you." His voice is surprisingly gentle. He's around my age and wears a brown woolen cape over an emerald-green tunic that fits him better than most of the rental costumes I'd seen tonight. His square jaw and strong chin add ruggedness to his face, and his eyes…

His eyes are studying me. I feel my cheeks burn. "It's okay," I say. "I'm fine."

"Let us begin anew. I am Christopher." He bows his head.

"I'm Michelle."

"Please, join me." He pulls out the only other chair.

"Oh." The space around us feels tight. "I don't think—"

"Please," he says.

So I sit. He shakes back his hair and sits beside me. I notice the fine gold embroidery around the wrists of his tunic, the bear-shaped golden clasp that holds the cape around his shoulders. "You really look authentic."

"Do I?" He seems confused. His eyes are a strange pale green. Like the color of a glow stick just before it fades. Then again, maybe this is just from the reflection of the candlelight.

"Yeah, this is great." I wave my hand toward his outfit. The candle flickers. "Much more authentic even than the prince or the king."

His jaw tightens. "Be careful of what you speak, Milady."

"Careful? Why?"

He rests his chin on his fist. "You are obviously a newcomer, and a delightful one at that."

"Really?" I rest my chin on my fist too.

"And your words have a most unusual quality." He leans closer.

"It's just a plain old Jersey accent."

"Jersey? I think it is lovely."

"You do? Huh."

"I do," he says, very, very softly.

He leans in even closer.

It's crazy but I find myself leaning toward him, as if I'm drawn. My heart pounds. The smell of cinnamon saturates the air. I wonder if his lips will be soft like his voice, warm like fresh cookies. Sweet. He closes his eyes. My heart races. Our lips nearly touch when an icy blast blows through the room, ruffles the papers, snuffs out the candle and leaves us both in the dark. The smallness of the room seems to close in around me. I give a nervous laugh. "At least I'm not alone, right?" When he doesn't answer, I reach out my hand.

He's gone.

4

"No, no. Don't press so hard, Geoffrey," Miss Turner the art instructor says in a highly irritated voice. "You'll tear the paper to shreds." Her red hair is tied into a tight bun and she's wearing an immaculate gray business suit. Completely unlike the paint-spattered hippie teachers I'm used to back home. "Honestly," Miss Turner says, "you young men handle a pencil like it's a butcher knife."

William, who sits beside me, and who I'm supposed to be doing a profile of, holds up his pencil and pretends to chop at his drawing of the girl sitting in front of him. Guncha is to my left sketching my profile, her pencil moving fast. I can just imagine the mass of squiggles filling her page. Today, despite my best efforts, my hair includes some of those dreaded banana curls.

"You must loosen up your fingers," Miss Turner says. "Hold the pencil like it's breakable, delicate. You must hold it like…" She points across the classroom. "Like Roger. Roger, why don't you show the boys how it's done?" Roger looks appropriately mortified as he runs his fingers through his stringy blonde hair. Reluctantly he raises his left hand, which holds his pencil.

William pretends to cough while saying, "Poof. Poof." He smiles at me but I don't smile back.

Instead I turn to Guncha.

"Go back the way you were," she says. "I was finally capturing your scowl."

"I'm not scowling."

"You are. Don't you like it here?"

"What's not to like?" I'm determined to act like the prank somebody pulled on me last night never happened. Even though with every new class I enter I expect to find Christopher there, wearing the Wallingford Academy's charcoal slacks and black blazer uniform, and laughing his head off with a bunch of other guys over what a loser I am.

I get that familiar hot burn of humiliation. I always felt it whenever someone back in New Jersey would pull a trick on me, convincing me that I really was invited to a party, or that science class was actually meeting out near the woods on the edge of school grounds. I discovered I was an easy mark. Too trusting, too eager for friends.

I'd promised myself that those days were over. But here, an ocean away from New Jersey, it's starting all over again. It's like I've got a permanent "KICK ME" note stuck on my back.

I remove my school blazer, hanging it over the back of my seat. With a uniform, at least I *look* like I fit in. And the gray pleated skirt isn't so bad. But the black knee socks and clunky black shoes are another story.

I try to focus on sketching William, which, given his looks, shouldn't be too hard. He has classic regular features, but the key to a good portrait is to observe what is unique about a person and to be sure to capture that. From the side, I see that William's strong chin juts out just a bit more than average. It begins beneath his lip in a curve and ends more squared below. So that's where I begin. My lead rasps against the coarse paper.

My dad had told me Wallingford Academy is different from typical English schools. Run more informally like a college would be. I guess it's all part of being "the best." Before art class there was teatime in the cafeteria, which was pretty cute. Even though it wasn't fancy cups and teakettles and scones, but mugs and tea bags and plates of cookies.

During tea, I'd tried to see if Christopher was at any of the tables. I'd even asked Guncha if she knew anyone by that name, but she didn't. Maybe it was a pretend name. I wish I could pretend I wasn't humiliated. I wish I could forget how I panicked and stumbled down those dark stairs practically in tears.

Now I glance around the art room. Oh, God. What if someone made a tape of me puckering my lips like a love struck idiot? I'd be De Freak-o all over again.

I set my pad of paper down on the desk and swallow hard.

"Hang on," Guncha says. "That is seriously magnificent." Her dark eyes study my drawing. "He is an absolute stunner."

"Why, thank you," William says, while still looking at the girl he's drawing.

"It's not of *you*," Guncha says.

His head snaps around and the three of us stare at my notepad. At the guy with the long dark hair.

"Ooo, I'd sure like to meet him." Guncha taps the pad with her finger. "Anytime. Anyplace. Who is he?"

I tear off the page and stuff it into my book bag. "Nobody."

• • •

In the cafeteria, I take a tray and head for the salad counter. Guncha snags my arm, pulling me back.

"I'm just grabbing a salad."

"No, you can't. See that lady back there?"

I peer at a scowling matron with gray corkscrews of hair popping out from under her hairnet.

Guncha pulls my arm again and whispers, "Don't let her see you looking. That's evil Mrs. Crocker. She spits in the food."

"Seriously?"

Guncha looks queasy. "Trust me. Have the curry today."

I grab a bowl of sauce-drenched meat and follow her as she walks past several tables. Although everyone is in uniform, I can still see huge differences. The first long table is filled with beautiful slim girls, with Constance, her copper hair glittering, the most radiant of all. And there are also, of course, the good-looking guys. Strong, tall, confident. The rest of the tables seem to be occupied by the average, some more nerdy or awkward than others.

Guncha sits at a nearly full table near the end. Justine scoots over to make room for me.

"Hi," I say and smile but don't sit. There is one last table, with only one person sitting at it. "I'm going to say hi to Roger."

"Roger?" Justine wrinkles her nose. "Why?"

"Honestly," Guncha says, "you do *not* want to go there."

There's a mighty crash and the shatter of glass, followed by a hush. A tiny guy, his face dotted with acne, is sprawled on the floor with curry and milk splattered around him. William and a few of his buddies stand beside the mess. The cafeteria erupts into applause and someone high-fives William.

"Did they just trip that kid?" I ask.

"Probably," Justine says, seeming unconcerned. "Sit. Tell me all about America."

"I will. In just a minute." I walk over to Roger's table. He's at the very end, eating a salad. "I hope no one spit in that."

"You heard about Mrs. Crocker, then," he says. "She's not a bad sort."

"Does she really spit in the food?"

"Only if you're rude. Which I think only fair."

"Can I sit with you?"

"Dunno. Think there's enough room?"

I set my tray next to his and feel the pressure of many eyes on me. I look back and see that I'm right.

"Roger?" I push the icky curry around with a fork. "What is it with this school?"

"How do you mean?"

"Well, it's kind of cliquish, isn't it? And you're…"

"I'm?"

You're like I used to be, I want to say. "Having salad."

"I'm not rude to Mrs. Crocker."

"Right."

He crunches on some salad and swallows. "Look, Michelle, you're new here. Everyone's going to think you didn't know any better than to sit with the likes of Roger Mortley. So why don't you go before it's too late?"

"Um, Roger?" I say but then hesitate.

"Oh, it's okay. I won't mind if you go off me. Most people do. I'm a bit strange, is all. From the wrong side of Castle Road and all that. "

I shake my head. "No, that's not it. I want to ask you something. You work at the castle, right?" He nods. "Then I wonder if you know who this is."

I pull the sketch out of my bag and smooth it out on the table. Roger purses his lips. "You drew this? It's not half bad."

I blush. "Do you know him?"

"Hm." He considers the picture as he wipes his mouth with his napkin. "He looks familiar, but no."

"Do you think he works there?"

"I don't think so, but he might. There's a pretty huge staff, what with the reenactors and the ticketing folks, maintenance, guides and preservationists there. Why? Does he mean something to you?" He grins.

Now I can't help but wonder if Roger is the one who set me up. The entire school seems to hate him. Why?

"No reason," I say at last. I fold up the drawing and tuck it into my bag.

"I had your dad for American Literature this morning. He was really good."

"Was he?" I exhale with relief. He was so nervous when he left this morning and I hadn't seen him since. I guess the faculty eats in a separate room.

"Do you think he's got any stuff from the eighties?"

"Books?"

"No, stuff. Memorabilia. Clothes. Music. Anything like that. I'm kind of a connoisseur."

"I'll be sure to check. So, the art teacher seems to like you."

He pushes away his salad and bangs the table. Heads turn. "Damn that Miss Turner," he shouts. "She embarrasses the hell out of me."

"Imagine that," I say between my teeth. Okay. Time to go. I pick up my book bag. "See ya."

"Not if you don't have to, right?"

I'm not sure what to say. So I just take my tray and go.

5

"Michelle," Constance calls and points to the desk beside her.

I slide into the chair, feeling grateful I know someone in my history class. Feeling relieved that this first day is nearly over.

"At least this is the last class of the day," she says. "That's what you're thinking, aren't you?"

"How'd you guess?"

"Let's just say I know how you feel." She rakes her fingers through her copper mane. "Everyone staring at you. Everyone sizing you up. Welcome to my world."

Before I can even ask, she points to herself and says, "Headmistress' daughter here, remember?"

"No perks with that?"

"Oh God, no." We share a friendly smile and she says, "People tread so carefully around me. Like I'll turn them in for detentions. And the expectations! I'm to be nothing less than perfect at all times." Her smile quickly fades.

More students file in, including Geoffrey, the pencil-strangler from art class, who takes a seat behind me.

"So," Constance says to me, "tell me all about yourself. I need to know if you're the right sort, now don't I?"

"Oh. Uh."

"Don't look so terrified. I'm only joking with you."

"Right." I laugh but it comes out sounding shrill and less than normal.

"But seriously," she says and touches my arm. "What school did you go to back in the U.S.? I've got a distant cousin there and she knows everyone. I just bet she knows *all* about you."

"It's a big country," I say, mostly to reassure myself.

"I know that." She looks slightly annoyed. "I also know that you're from New Jersey. My mother said so. That's where this cousin lives. So, what school?"

"Uh, West High." Okay, so it was actually Westover Glen High. Constance raises an eyebrow and seems about to ask me more.

Thankfully our teacher Mr. Llywelyn takes this moment to say, "Off to work we go." His bulldog face is serious and there's a scuffle as students yank notebooks out of their book bags. "English history," he says, "starting at the War of the Roses. Term paper required. Any questions?"

Yes. Lots. But before I can say anything, he raises his chalk and says, "Moving right along, then." He turns to the board and scrawls: Fifteenth Century Monarchy. "In the fifteenth century, who reigned in Britain?"

"The Wallingfords," a guy in the back shouts. Kids laugh.

Mr. Llywelyn cautions, "No calling out. And, yes, we are again studying the Wallingford family history as it intertwines with British history, including a deeper analysis of the world-famous Wallingford Papers."

William Wallingford. I immediately perk up with interest but others let out a groan.

Constance says, "Well, I think it's noble."

"Because you're shagging a Wallingford," someone from behind hisses.

Constance and I both turn. Everyone in the next row innocently stares at their notebooks. I notice Geoffrey smirking.

"You're jealous," Constance says, "because your lot has never brought down traitors." She faces forward and whispers to me, "So low class."

• • •

"Salvinegar?" a woman asks.

"Excuse me?" I say.

"Salvinegar with your chips?"

"Um, sorry. Could you say that slower or something?"

"Hi, Bessie," William says, suddenly appearing at the counter next to me. "This is Michelle, new from America and, yes, she would like salt and vinegar on her chips."

"I would?"

"You would." He smiles at me and his sky-blue eyes sparkle. "And, Bessie, an order for me too, if you please." He winks at her, unbuttons his cuffs and rolls up his sleeves. "So, Michelle, survive your first day okay?"

"Barely." I watch the lady expertly dump a pile of greasy fries, or "chips" onto a sheet of paper, douse both of the orders with salt and a few shakes of vinegar from a small bottle, then wrap them into two paper cones.

She holds the chips toward us like bouquets. "That's fifty P each."

I unzip my book bag and pull out a handful of odd-shaped coins. I pick up a silver one, which is worth how much? "Uh."

"I've got this one." William tosses a thick gold coin onto the counter.

"You don't have to."

"It's okay. I've got it." We take the cones and leave the shop together. "I'm impressed. You've already found the last remaining chip shop in town. Best-tasting food you'll ever come across."

I bite one of the plump chips and my eyes roll back in my head. "MMMM, this is unbelievable."

He laughs. "Told you. What do you think about the salt-vinegar?"

I lick my lips, enjoying the salty tang. "Surprisingly good."

"It's almost like sauce, without the tomato, if you think about it."

"Sauce? Really?"

"I believe you call it ketchup. Sorry."

He eats a few chips and wipes his greasy fingers on the legs of his charcoal slacks.

I lick my fingers. He looks at me and licks his lips.

The air is fresh and cool but suddenly I feel very warm. I take a deep breath. Remind myself he's just being polite to me, that's all. "So, where's Constance?"

"Out on the green at hockey practice, I imagine."

"She seems nice."

"She can be, when she wants."

I give him a puzzled look.

We wander along High Street, a wide road lined with shops. We pass the pharmacy (which the British call a chemist's), a butcher's (a real lamb's head hangs in the window, disgusting!), a laundromat called the Washateria, a small grocery store and a corner pub called the Castle Arms.

"It's so quaint here," I say. "Just like I imagined it would be."

"Quaint?" He does a mock shiver. "You imagined a town so stuck in the past it won't even allow a sushi shop to open? Don't go on thinking that Blanchford is a typical modern English town. All this is as modern as we'll ever be allowed to get."

"You guys have strict zoning for High Street or something?"

"It's called *the* High Street, never just High Street. And we *guys*," he says, drawing out the word, teasing me with a dreadful American accent, "have merely an understanding that this town must maintain its 'character' to preserve a certain feel. This is supposed to attract more tourists." He laughs. "But you don't see any motor coaches on the High Street seeking out the Washateria or the chip shop, now do you? They're all clustered around those tatty tourist shops near the castle."

"Well they don't know what they're missing." I bite into another chip.

William picks up a chip but sets it back into the cone. "It's not as if we have a lovely medieval village here. That's why my father has been trying to persuade the town to modernize the High Street for ages. He has a brilliant plan for it but it's like people here are afraid to move forward. We could really use a cinema and some decent restaurants and some clubs."

"And a sushi shop? And a Starbucks?"

"Well, yes, why not? And now there's a shopping area proposed on the Old Roman Grounds with a good amount of money being offered the town for the land, but there's a lot of opposition. Are you familiar with the Old Roman Grounds?"

"Is that where they keep the old Romans?" I cringe. I'm such a dork.

William grins. "No. It's an open space beside the museum of Roman history. It's a wild bit of land with ancient trees, and the preservationists want to keep it that way."

"And your dad's for building?"

"Actually, he's aiding the preservationists, helping them stage a fundraising fair in a few weeks. The plan is to raise enough capital to make a counteroffer on the parcel so that they can keep it as is. Sounds a bit hopeless, actually, but he knows how to play these things."

"Hm, I like that your dad is at least trying. He sounds like a good guy."

William shrugs. "He has his moments."

"What about you?"

He stops and smiles at me. "I suppose I have mine as well."

My throat suddenly feels full of sand. "I-I mean are you for building or do you want to keep that land as is?"

"Give me progress and hang the ancient trees. Sushi and Starbucks forever, right?"

"But once those ancient trees are gone, aren't they gone forever?"

"Oh." He studies me. "Of course. There are clearly no easy answers here." He walks on and I catch up to him.

"I heard something about your family's past in History today. The Wallingford Papers?"

"Impressed?"

"Well, it *is* pretty cool," I admit. According to my teacher, the papers are a medieval collection of personal letters between William's ancestors. Scholars all over the world have studied them. "It must be fascinating to read about family members from so long ago. To be sort of famous, even."

"Yes, there is much to be proud of there," he says, without a trace of modesty. "Well, this is my turn-off." William nods at an avenue called Rose Hill Way where the trees are large and grand, and the houses even larger and grander. "Sorry I have to hurry on. Apparently my father has something important he wants to show me. See you tomorrow, Michelle."

He winks and my knees get wobbly—I can't help it. And I feel a flash of anger at myself. I mean, he's going with Constance. Besides, even the chip lady got a wink.

6

"What do you mean, you aren't going to the castle? You're an artist." Mary, our neighbor, seems shocked. Then again, Mary always seems shocked, or outraged, whenever she isn't laughing hysterically. She popped by unannounced the very first day we'd moved in to be sure we knew how the electric kettle worked and to inform us what time she'd be by most days for tea. And here she is yet again in our kitchen, her round form somehow perched on the wooden stool by the counter, clutching a mug. Her hair is straight and black, cut short. Her cheeks have red spots on them like she's one of Santa's elves. And she's wearing her typical stretchy velour tracksuit and bright white sneakers. Today's green pants and red top make her look like a large and shiny Christmas ornament.

"Shelly," my dad calls from the front hallway, "come say a hello to your brother on the phone."

"Can't," I call back. "Busy. Send him my love."

Mary raises her brows at me and I avoid her eyes. After a few minutes, my dad comes in and picks up his mug.

"Donald," Mary says, "you must tell her to draw the castle."

"You heard Mary. You must draw the castle."

"I saw a pretty church on my walk home from school. I'm going to sketch there." I tuck my pad of newsprint under my arm.

Mary sets down her mug. "That'll be St. Paul's. Nice. Tiny. Not a castle, though. The castle's a bit farther but you could borrow me bike if I'm not using it for my rigorous exercise program. I'm quite athletic, you know."

I bite my lip and Dad buries his face in his mug of tea.

• • •

I like St. Paul's because you enter its yard through a little wooden gateway with a peaked roof. The roof leans to the left and the gate makes a horror-movie squeak when you open it. Best of all, the graveyard is filled with stones in varying stages of decay. Tall ones lean forward or backward like giant levers that have been pushed or pulled. And full-sized carved stone images of knights in armor on top of marble slabs look like they'd laid down for a nap and froze into place for a few hundred years. Closest to the tiny church are the oldest graves. Words washed away by time. Stones cracked and crumbling. My favorite stones are the ones that look like giant gingerbread noblemen resting on the ground. Their arms and legs are separated from their bodies as if they'd been soaked in milk for too long.

I can't decide what to draw first, so I pull open the wooden door and step inside the tiny chapel. Several elderly ladies kneel at various pews. I sit on a wooden pew in the back row, flip open my pad and lose myself in my sketch.

Things make sense when I draw. Everything is angles and texture and relationships. I sketch the pews and the rough wooden beams on the ceiling, which I hadn't noticed at first, and the bowed heads of the women praying, and the way the light plays against the rough stone walls, and I feel at home. I hear the whispered prayers, the creaks of the pews as the women shift from kneeling to sitting. The smell of smoky candles on the altar reminds me of campfires at Girl Scout camp. And the whiff of cinnamon—

I raise my pencil from my page. In the left corner of my drawing, behind the altar and amid the shadows, I've sketched a figure.

A figure wearing a cape. My eyes dart to that corner of the chapel. There in the dark, I'm almost sure I see a flash of movement.

I stand. It must be him. That Christopher kid.

With another flash, he's gone.

"Wait!"

The women gasp and turn.

"Sorry," I say and run up the aisle.

Behind the altar I see a door to the left opened a crack. I push it and daylight floods the church. The door leads outside to the grave-yard, which is empty, aside from the stones and sleeping knights and the soaked cookie nobility.

I race around the corner. No one but the dead. I lean against a monument and wonder what this guy's game is. The sun slants low. I know I'd better get home before Dad starts to worry. Before I find myself walking through dark streets with a caped lunatic on my heels. I shiver and notice the sleeping figure I'm leaning against. He wears armor and his arms are crossed over a sword, just like a lot of the other figures in the graveyard. The features are worn by time but one detail is very clear: he wears a cloak held by a bear-shaped clasp.

My heart speeds up. I look at the name on the side of the tomb. Most of it is illegible, except for the letters CHRI.

7

"So, are you saying this guy dresses like a tomb?" Guncha picks up a plate of cookies from the counter.

"That's disturbing," Justine says and blows on her mug of tea.

"No. Yes. I mean, I just think it's weird. That's all. A weird coincidence." I pick up a plate of cookies and a mug of tea and follow them across the cafeteria.

"But he's good-looking? Your fella?" Justine says.

"He's not 'my fella.'" I think of his broad shoulders. His light-green eyes. How I almost kissed him. Then I remember the force of him throwing me against the wall. "Anyway, that's not the point."

They laugh, and Guncha says, "That is *always* the point."

"Michelle, sit here," William says, waving.

I freeze. Warning bells go off in my head. Why is he being so nice to me?

He shoves over to make room for me, bumping into Constance. Her tea slops onto the table and her cat eyes lock on me with a less than welcoming look.

I decide it's best to just wave and keep walking. William's smile falters.

I set my tea and cookies at Guncha and Justine's usual table. They scurry over and sit and stare.

"What?" I say, and take a gulp of the too-hot tea, which scorches my mouth.

"Are you unwell?" Guncha blinks at me. "Seriously unwell? Did I not see William Wallingford offer you a spot at his table, where only the most privileged are ever asked to sit? And you turned him down?"

"But there wasn't enough room for us all."

"Wasn't enough—" Guncha takes a bite of her cookie and chews hard. With a full mouth she says, "You should think of your friends, you know. If you sat there, then maybe someday we could have sat there, too."

Justine snorts. "Not bloody likely."

"It's possible," Guncha says. "And at least the guys sitting there are a decent height."

Tiny Peter Nunnly, who is a few seats down from us, leans forward and shoots Guncha a poisonous look.

"Nothing personal, Peter," she says. "Michelle, you see my point, yeah? Opportunity lost."

I sigh, realizing I've disappointed my friends. I blink a few times, as this all sinks in. I've just turned down an "in" with the popular kids. And I actually *have* friends. It seems that by simply moving to a new place, I've somehow climbed out of my social wasteland. I think of all the high school kids in the world who are teased and shunned. They should all have the chance to move and start over— kind of like a witness protection program, but for outcasts.

I nibble on a cookie and look over at Roger, sitting by himself at the last table. "Maybe I should invite Roger to sit with us."

"No!" Justine and Guncha say, aghast.

"Look," Guncha says, "Roger's unpredictable. Frankly, he can be kind of creepy. It's better this way."

"Hm." I blow on my tea.

"I know. It sounds really bad, doesn't it?" Guncha grows serious. "But there is a definite order to things. Feudalism lives on." She shrugs.

I set down my mug. "But then why would William ask me to sit with them? I don't exactly belong there."

"Maybe he's falling for you. Maybe he really likes you." Guncha's eyes gleam.

Justine taps her chin. "Or maybe he's made a wager. See how quickly he can shag the new girl."

Now *this* I can believe.

"Stop it, Justine." Guncha's hands strangle her mug and her voice is surprisingly sharp. "Maybe he really likes Michelle. Maybe Constance isn't his soul mate. Can't that be true? Honestly, you are so cynical."

"And you, my friend, are a hopeless romantic," Justine says. "Maybe it doesn't mean anything and he's just being friendly. Ever consider that?"

Some guys break into a chorus of "Happy Birthday." I turn. A cluster of kids hovers around William. He faces a slice of cake with a candle on it. Constance has her arm around his shoulder and her head touches his.

What else did I expect?

Constance notices me watching and gives me a wave. I nod and turn away.

"Isn't William the lucky birthday boy?" Guncha says. "I heard his father gave him a Porsche. Must be nice."

"Yeah, nice," I mumble. I pick up another cookie and take a bite. Because it's a cinnamon cookie, I immediately think of Christopher. Again.

Is there no getting away from this guy? Last night I really wanted to relax, so instead of wearing my usual giant T-shirt, I put on my comfortable pajamas, ridiculous pink ones dotted with yellow chicks. I listened to music and sat on the bed idly doodling in my sketchbook. Relaxation time quickly ended when I found I had again drawn his face. His hair was wind-tossed. Surprise, like a fire, burned in his light eyes. I shoved the sketch aside and went to sleep. I dreamt he followed me as I got cereal for breakfast, and as I walked to school. That he sat at the desk behind me in math. And the entire time he stared at me with an intense, almost angry look. This morning the dream seemed so real, I actually turned around during math class just to make sure he wasn't there. My teacher deducted points from my grade because he thought I was talking during his lecture.

I drop the rest of the cinnamon cookie onto the plate. "Guys, I'll be right back."

When I sit next to Roger, he doesn't react. I realize he's wearing headphones and there's a cassette tape player on the table. I wave my hand in front of his face.

He hits a button on the player and pulls off the headphones. "What?" he says in a testy voice.

"Hi to you, too," I say.

"Sorry. Rough day." There are gray circles under his eyes.

"You sick?"

"Hey, I'm listening to 'Huey Lewis and the News.' Want to hear?"

I shake my head.

He holds up the recorder. "Vintage nineteen-eighties Sony Walkman. Great stuff. I've got three of these babies and some amazing tapes. Did you ask your dad if he has any eighties stuff?"

"Oh. No. But I will. Actually, I wanted to ask *you* something. Remember that picture I showed you? Of that guy?"

"Yeah."

"You said he looked familiar. So I was just wondering, did you happen to see him at the castle since we talked?"

Roger gives me a sly smile. "You'd like to see him again, eh?"

Again, a little voice inside me warns that Roger might be in on this whole disappearing guy hoax. But I can't care about this little detail now. Not when the guy's driving me crazy. And crazy is not good, especially for a De Freccio.

My mom wears her crazy with embarrassing pride. At back-to-school nights, she'd show up in a large floppy hat and a long Indian print skirt, and then start doing predictions by reading the worry lines on my teachers' foreheads.

My brother Wayne is being crushed by his crazy. He's twenty, and even though he's brilliant and kind, he can never keep even the lowliest job, even when he's on his meds. My dad and I had visited Wayne before we left for England, and I was shocked to see the weight he had lost, and the hollowness around his eyes, and the nervous tremble around his lips even when he tried to smile. It was as if his very spirit was melting away inside him.

"No, I don't want to see this guy again," I say to Roger now. "It's not like that. He's following me and stuff. I just want to tell him off. If you know anything—"

"Right." He drums his fingers on the table a few times. "Tell you what. I'm working at the castle on Friday. You stop by then and I'll see what I can do."

8

"Ticket, please," a stout guy with dark thick hair and a unibrow says to me. He sits at the admission counter by the castle parking lot.

"James, she's with me," Roger says.

"Now, Roger, there can't be any of that. You know I've applied for the assistant manager position." He puffs up a little. "Strictly by the book now."

"You've got that job in the bag."

"Not if I can't run the Ghost Tour smoothly." James shuffles some papers. "It all hinges on that, and I can't get enough staff to work the night."

"I'm working it." Roger thumps the desk. "So what do you say, James? Let Michelle in."

James frowns.

"That's okay, Roger," I say. "I got this." I dig through the art supplies in my bag for money, though I'm not sure I have the fifteen pounds required.

"No." Roger takes my hand and squeezes it. "No, sweetheart. That's rubbish."

I open my mouth, completely thrown off guard.

Still holding my hand, Roger says, "C'mon, James, old mate, don't show me up in front of my girl."

"But—" I say.

Before I can say anything more, Roger puts his finger on my lips. "Shh. Not to trouble yourself."

I'm briefly stunned into silence. Did I miss something?

Roger leans against the counter and, dressed in his Robin Hood-like clothes with his straw-colored hair peeking out from under his feathered cap, he looks charming and clever enough to con his way into even the most formidable of castles. "C'mon, James. Help a guy out."

James clenches his meaty fists and grumbles but then he whispers, "Ah, go on with you both, then. But if anyone asks, say she's applying for the Ghost Tour."

Roger tips his hat and tugs me past the desk. He squeezes my hand and guides me along the path toward the castle's main gate.

We go a few steps more before I pull my hand out of his. "Uh, Roger? I'm sorry if you got the wrong idea about me." I clear my throat. "About you and me, that is."

"You girls are all alike, aren't you?"

"Excuse me?"

"Think every bloke's after you if he shows you the smallest kindness."

"I didn't. I mean, I don't."

"Right. I was just getting you in free. Should we officially break it off so you can pay the entrance fee, then? Don't mind paying the fifteen pounds every time you set foot in here, then? You rich Americans can afford that, right?"

"I'm not a rich American, okay?"

"What are you, then? Exactly?" He gives me a nasty look and I again notice the shadows under his eyes, and the hollows beneath his cheekbones.

"I'm sorry. That's what I am. Thank you, Roger."

His look softens. "Okay, then. Look, I gotta lead a tour in about a half hour, so I'll take you to a few people who might know about this guy, then you can walk about on your own."

"And I won't get in trouble? I really don't want to get you fired or anything."

"No one will ask for your ticket now. And even if they do, just claim you are looking for the employment office to sign up to work that Ghost Tour."

"And what's the Ghost Tour, exactly?" We're at the foot of the gateway now and crossing the coarse stone bridge over the dry moat.

"It's a load of bullocks, really. They do it here twice a year. All night ghost hunting. Psychics come and bring special 'scientific equipment' and do séances throughout the castle."

Just the sort of thing my mom would get into.

"Costs a boatload of dosh," Roger is saying, "and attracts rich biddies looking for some titillation in their lives. Takes a ton of staff to run and most of the regulars beg off, since spending all night at work without earning overtime is not their idea of a thrilling Friday night."

We enter the shadow of the gate towers and reemerge into brightness in the castle courtyard.

"Don't you want to know what sort of ghostly activity they've found here?" he asks.

"No, thanks."

"I know loads of tales. Like the two headless—"

"Please. Not interested."

Roger stops and studies me. "Are you really not interested? Or are you too afraid?"

I suddenly fill with anger. "Roger, you are the most horrible—"

"Uh uh." He takes my arm and pulls me to the left. "That's the cursed spot again, remember? Where the Earl was murdered? There. Feel better now?"

I hate to admit it but the anger has evaporated like a dissipating storm cloud. "What crap."

He smirks. "Let's have a natter with the lady in the gift shop, shall we?"

We pass a door with a sign that cheerfully announces "Ye Olde Instruments of Torture!" and enter the next doorway, the Castle Shoppe, which is filled with things like plastic swords and bookmarks that have the castle name on them.

"Roger, love," a redheaded lady by the register says. "Come give us a hug." Roger walks over and endures a squeeze. She steps back from him. "Hm. You're exhausted and you're thin as a rail, love. You must eat. Be sure you load up your plate twice at the Castle mess tonight, all right?"

"Yes, Mrs. Reilly." He asks her about Christopher and even shows her my drawing, but she hasn't seen him before.

After this, we talk to Teddy, the lute player from the castle feast. He's again squeezed into those unfortunate striped tights. We also show the picture to a twentysomething college student in a serving wench costume. Behind the scenes in a workshop we see Mr. Bellamy, who restores castle artifacts, but he barely glances at my picture before he shakes his head. "Sorry. Can't chat now, Roger. Some twit sat on this today and I've got a bit of a job to do, fast."

"Tell me that is not the Earl's chair." Roger walks around the high-backed seat covered in cracked red leather. Its arm hangs limp at its side.

"The very same. Can't awe the tourists with tales of the Earl cavorting with maidens in his favorite chair without the chair for them to gape at. People are already lodging complaints it's gone missing." He frowns at a row of tools spread out on his worktable.

"This is the same Earl who was murdered in the courtyard?" I ask.

Mr. Bellamy looks at me over the top of his spectacles. "Exactly."

Back in the courtyard, a group waits by the sign announcing the next guided tour.

Roger takes off his feathered hat and runs his fingers through his hair. "That's my cue." He suddenly looks very tired.

"Mrs. Reilly is right. You need some rest. And some food."

"And you need to mind your business," he snaps.

"You okay?"

"Just go find this guy but don't let him bother you, got that? Sounds like he might be a little off in his head. If you see him, come find me. I'll be here in the courtyard or in the first set of castle apartments nearest to the dungeon."

I nod.

"Good." He sets his hat on his head, takes a deep breath, then strides over to the tourists and says in a cheery voice, "Hi-ho! Welcome one and all to Blanchley Castle, where history comes alive."

I enter the castle building, wander through some winding passageways and push past clusters of tourists crowding the corridors. I finally recognize the steps to the main hall where the Academy hosted the dinner.

The hall is empty and quiet. There is no lit fire in the fireplace now and a simple, brightly painted shield has replaced the bear head over the mantle. Daylight spills into the room through the row of stained glass windows along the opposite wall, covering the rough floor in bits of colored light. There is one raised table at the back wall with a few tall chairs, and in the middle of the room is a single long wooden table, with benches along its sides.

I turn and bump into someone.

It's Christopher. His glow-stick eyes are wide.

There's a moment of tense silence.

"Leave me alone!" we both say.

9

"Me?" I say. "Leave you alone? That's a laugh. You're the one following me."

"You deny bewitching me? Infecting my thoughts, my dreams?"

"Wait, dreams? You dreamt you followed me around my house
and at school, didn't you?"

"In the dreams it was you following me through the stables and
to chapel. No more. Be gone, witch."

I laugh. "You have serious problems, you know that? 'Be gone,
witch?' Who talks like that? And look at you? I don't even think
you work at this castle. I think you just dress like this to get your
jollies or something."

He briefly looks down at his green tunic, which is worn belted
over a white linen shirt, and at his knee-high leather boots. "It is
you who dress for jolly sake." He strides around me. Studies my
jeans, sneakers and jacket, and says with disgust, "Bedecked in such
harlotry. Showing yourself not a fine lady in the least but as the
witch you really are. And that waking vision I had of you haunts
me still. Of you dressed in garish garb of the most putrid pink with
yellow chickens upon it."

My pajamas. Was there a camera in my room? My stomach feels
full of ice.

He suddenly grabs my arm. Pulls me close. "You are the one who is not of this castle. No one knows of a Michelle from Jersey. Not one soul swapping the latest news in the castle courtyard has heard of you. What is your game?" When I don't respond, he says through gritted teeth, "Tell me!"

"There's no game," I say, my voice unsteady.

"Liar. For some reason you are sent to undo me. Or you plot about things far worse, far more traitorous. And fool that I am, I had thought you were the one who would..."

We are very close now. His intense eyes grow sad. I am all too aware of his fingers wrapped around my arm. Of his face bent toward me. Of his auburn hair falling over his forehead. Of his soft full lips. I again feel myself drawn powerfully to him. Feel my breath catch as his grip loosens and his hand slides up my arm. *This is crazy.*

I force myself to step back. "Y-you're crazy. Stay away from me, or I'll tell the police or the Bobbies or whatever the hell you people call them."

He seems stunned.

I run from the hall and down the steps.

"Michelle, I found him." It's Roger, striding up the steps, his hat in his hands. "That crazy bloke. You won't believe it." He takes my hand and pulls. "Come on. I'll show you before my next tour."

"But *I* found him. He's upstairs, right now."

Roger draws his brows together, races past me up the steps and into the hall. I scramble to follow.

I find Roger, hands on hips, surveying the hall. A room that is suddenly filled with ordinary tourists. No sign of Christopher. I notice that the bear's head is somehow again over the mantle. I look around wildly. In front of the windows are now suits of armor standing at attention—armor that definitely wasn't there a few moments ago.

"So? Where is he?" Roger says.

"I...I don't understand. He was standing right..." How could all the tourists possibly get in here so fast? "I must have been mistaken," I say.

"Well, I'm not. Follow me." He leads me out of the hall, down the stairs, through the courtyard where a fresh cluster of tourists waits by the sign for the next castle tour, and into another doorway. "I told you he looked familiar. I was leading the last tour when I spotted him." We go down a dark corridor lit with electric lights that are made to look like torches hanging from the walls. He turns left into a large arched entry, which opens into a long room richly furnished with Persian carpets and leather sofas. Roger says, "I was taking the group through this wing and just launching into an apology about the Earl's missing Mating Chair, when I saw this."

Roger points to an empty spot in the corner now occupied by a sign that reads "Exhibit Temporarily Removed." I notice the wall behind it and I gasp.

There, in a large gilt frame, is an oil painting. It's Christopher, complete with his long reddish-brown hair, his light eyes seemingly on fire. His bear pin gleams on his cape. The artist's technique is crude, the paint thickly applied and cracking, but Christopher's intense look is accurately captured.

I step closer. Read the plaque beneath the painting. "Christopher Newman of Watley Manor, circa 1460." My knees tremble. My hands start to shake.

"What's the matter?" Roger says. "You look like you've seen a—"

"Don't," I say in barely a whisper. Now my lips tremble. Tears stream down my cheeks. I back away from the painting.

"Michelle? What is it?"

I can't speak. Can only shake my head over and over again. And run.

I run through the bright castle courtyard, tears blurring the daylight into a rainbow of colors. I slam into a man taking a picture of his wife and kids and murmur an apology as I make my way past them and through the arched gateway. My shaky legs somehow take me down the path to the visitor's lot, where I fumble with the lock on Mary's bike.

Then I ride, my legs pumping hard, as if I can outride what I now know is happening to me. Wasn't my brother, Wayne, around my age when he started mumbling in class? When he got that crazed look and said, "They're talking to me. I'm just answering"? But he could never explain whom he'd answered. My mom had an explanation: he had the psychic gift. The doctor had another explanation: schizophrenia.

I soar along the road that passes St. Paul's Church. The wind whips at my face.

"Shelly, honey," my mom had said to me, "you've got the gift."

By the church's roofed gateway, I squeeze the hand brakes and throw the bike down. I drag myself through the graveyard, stumbling on bits of broken gravestones. I find myself at that tomb, wiping my cheeks and nose with the back of my hand. There is his figure. Christopher Newman of Watley Manor. I wonder if Wayne's delusions seem as real to him as this one did. I pant as if I can't breathe. As if I'm being buried alive. I sink to my knees, rest my forehead against the cold stone monument and whisper, "No."

10

"You're crazy, Guncha. We can't just sit there," Justine is saying, waving around a sandwich.

Crazy. All this craziness in my life and everything at school is going on like life is normal. And all I have ever wanted is to be normal...

It's been nearly a week since I'd been at the castle and beside that grave. I had wandered home and found myself sitting on my bed, again trying to sketch with the hopes that it would somehow calm me. With my drawing pad resting on my knees, I had let my pencil wander across the page in free-flowing strokes. An image quickly organized itself of that delusion named Christopher, his teeth bared, his face savage. His sword raised high, about to strike a man who cowered, waiting for the blow. I cowered. And I threw the drawing pad across the room.

I have become a trembling mess. I'm afraid to sleep at night for fear of dreaming about dead guys. I shuffle through my days like a zombie. I barely draw, even in art class, terrified of sketching faces that no one else sees. I'm hardly speaking, because what if I start muttering? What if the voices start and never stop?

"What do you think, Michelle?"

"Hm?" I turn to Justine.

"Guncha is under the mistaken impression that because William talks to you, we can all just sit at his table."

Guncha says, "Well, there's extra space there. Didn't you see Constance storm out a few minutes ago, followed by a few of her mates? Honestly, I don't think I've ever seen her lose her cool like that. This is the perfect opportunity. I just thought we could slide in and—"

"And they won't notice an Indian girl and her chubby friend?" Justine says.

"Actually, I'm hoping they will notice us, and you're not chubby. You're shapely."

Justine gives her wry grin. "We can't pretend we belong. Life doesn't work like that, yeah? Anyway, we're far too good for that snooty lot. Am I right, Michelle?"

I sigh.

"Still feeling poorly?" Guncha asks.

I nod. I've been telling everyone I'm just under the weather.

Guncha slips something into my hand. It's a little Cadbury's chocolate bar. "Always makes me feel better."

"Thanks," I whisper, grateful for her friendship. Wondering how long any of these friendships will last once my symptoms worsen. I chew on the chocolate and feel an endlessly deep sadness for my brother Wayne. He used to have a wide smile and a cute girlfriend, and he played soccer. Then he lost it all. He'd space out. Scare people with his ranting. He was so smart but never went to college. Now he lives in a special group apartment complex under the supervision of a physician. When he takes his meds, he seems almost okay, though there is a fearfulness that always lurks around him, making him cringe to the touch, or suddenly peer over his shoulder like he is being stalked by something unseen…

"You heading out?" Guncha says. I notice that she and Justine are standing now, holding their trays, and that a bunch of the other kids at our table have already left.

"Yeah. In a minute." I wave and they leave. And pretty soon it's just me all alone at my table. And Roger at his. My eyes fill as I think about my poor, sweet dad. First Wayne, then my mom, now me. After my mother had left, I found my dad leaning his head against the kitchen wall, tears silently streaming down his cheeks. It was the only time I'd ever seen him cry and it shook me to the core. I realized I was all he had left. And that I had to take care of him. But how can I now?

"Whatever it is, it'll be all right, you know?" Roger says. He stands in front of me, the shadows beneath his eyes looking as dark as mine must. He shrugs and follows the rest of the students out of the cafeteria.

I know it won't be all right. It'll be worse. Much worse.

11

"You like this place?" William nods at St. Paul's Church.

I'm leaning on the stone wall, staring at the graveyard, as he walks up to me. "I sketched it the other day," I say. I think about how excited I'd been to get lost in my drawing. "I liked that."

William leans on his elbows next to me. "You should have been out by the swan pond before lunch today. The boys tossed Nunnly in for a swim." He chuckles.

Peter Nunnly, the short, skinny kid who sits at my lunch table. "I bet he didn't think it was funny."

His brow wrinkles. "He did. Everyone did. It was just some good sport."

"Sure." I turn back to the church.

"Oh." He shifts from foot to foot. "Seems you disapprove."

I shrug in response.

After a long quiet moment, he says, "This church is nice enough, I guess. But what you're wanting is something grander. Something magnificent and inspiring. Don't you think? Why don't you let me take you to Gloucester Cathedral today?"

"Thanks, but I'm really beat. Anyway, you should take Constance."

"Constance? She wouldn't be interested. She's more about posh shops and impressing others. Look, I'll drive you to the cathedral and you'll be able to do some amazing sketches. Okay?" He gives me his Prince Charming smile and squeezes my hand. This is unmistakable flirting.

I pull my hand away, determined to not play the fool. "What about Constance? Your girlfriend?" And my friend. Well, maybe "friend" is too strong a word. After that first day of school, we've hardly spoken.

William shakes his head. "She's not my girl. I broke it off, actually."

"You did?" I remember what Guncha said about Constance storming out of the lunchroom.

"Come on, Michelle, let me take you to the cathedral. You'll be doing me a favor. I could definitely use an outing today. Been a bit stressful. And maybe this is just what you need too." He moves closer. Takes my hand again.

I find myself really smiling for the first time in days. I can't help it. He's so handsome. And even if this is all part of some bet he took on, or even if I ruin everything by transforming into a mental patient in front of him, right now his hand feels warm on mine. It feels nice. It feels *normal.* "Yeah, maybe this is what I need."

• • •

"Fancy that. Our Michelle going out with none other than THE William Wallingford," Mary crows from her perch on the kitchen stool. Today her velour tracksuit is bright yellow.

"Proves the kid has good taste," my dad says, raising his mug.

"Well, of course he does. She's a lovely girl."

"It's not like that," I say. "He's just being nice."

"Oh, is that all?" She winks. "You know, that father of his is a great and important man."

"We've met," my dad says. "He helped us change a tire."

"See that?" She waves a plump finger. "That's just what I mean. He's not too grand to help out the regular folk. He's been quite a supporter of our Council's Save the Old Roman Grounds efforts."

When we don't react, Mary says, "You do know about the Old Roman Grounds, don't you?"

"Isn't that where they keep the old Romans?" my dad says.

I snort.

"Well, it's no laughing matter, I can tell you. One hundred and forty pristine acres of ancient forest, all to be sacrificed to some greedy development corporation. And for what? A few tacky shops, a mini-mart and a lot of macadam. Mr. Wallingford takes it seriously enough, mind you. He's even helping us to raise money, and him such a busy solicitor. Was his idea to sell 'Roman General' decals. They're for your car, but you only get one if you donate ten thousand pounds. Would you like to purchase one?"

"Sorry," Dad says. "Fresh out of money."

"Oh, well, you can come to the fundraising festival, at least. That'll be in your budget for sure. They'll be rides and treats. Wonderful atmosphere for a date." Mary nudges me. "And what about you, Donald? Any friends of the female persuasion?"

"I'm married," he mumbles.

"Separated, he means," I say.

"Well, then, it's high time you engage in some activities, Donald."

A blush washes over his face. "Well…not appropriate…I don't think…" He swallows, making his Adam's apple bob.

"Goodness!" Mary's already rosy cheeks turn a deeper shade of red. "I'm speaking of a hobby. Of taking a cooking class at the community center. Getting out of the house. Not, well…"

There's an awkward silence and I bite back a smile.

William arrives and we zoom away in his new sleek black car with its smoked-glass windows and buttery leather seats. He's wearing khaki pants and a striped button-down shirt and a leather jacket, reminding me of those rich guys in the cologne commercials—the ones who toss around footballs on the beach while their supermodel girlfriends watch with delight. I can completely picture Constance in that scenario.

Self-consciously I pat down my hair. "Was this car really your birthday present?"

His mouth tightens into a line and he nods. "I'm really sorry but I seem to have forgotten my wallet. Mind if we swing by my house first?"

"Uh." I'm immediately very conscious of my shabby jeans and my Chucks. "No, that's fine."

He turns down Rose Hill Way and it's as if we've entered another world. A world of privilege and beauty and class. Wide lawns and grand trees and massive homes roll into view. An especially huge house is set behind a stone wall with turrets on either side of the drive. My heart sinks as William pulls in, the gravel drive crunching beneath his tires. He parks in front of the main entrance and gets out.

The house is faced with spectacular balconies and French doors. I close my eyes.

When I open them, I half expect a line of servants in the drive, curtsying and bowing to welcome the young master home. But it's just William. "You coming?"

Why didn't I dress better? *Why?* "Sure. Okay."

We step into the home's lobby, which is paved in highly polished marble. A massive urn on a side table overflows with spectacular fresh flowers and a wide center stairway with ornate banisters looks like it belongs in a palace.

"Make yourself at home," he says. "I'll just run up and get my wallet."

At home? I look at the antique chairs lining the lobby and suppress a laugh. I wander to the first open door and peek into a sitting room furnished in velvets and silks. I can almost picture gowned women there sipping tea from fine china. The next door opens to a library of dark wooden shelves loaded floor to ceiling with ancient leather books. Above a rose-colored marble fireplace is a painting that reminds me of a Rubens.

It occurs to me that this *is* a Rubens. An original, too, because people like the Wallingfords don't go around buying prints from Value City.

I walk across the Oriental carpet to see it better.

That's when I notice Mr. Wallingford beside a long mahogany desk with his hands holding flat a large roll of papers. They show architectural drawings and across the top it reads in large print: Proposed Roman Grounds Mall.

When he notices me he immediately rolls up the papers. "I beg your pardon." His face is indignant.

"Oh, Mr. Wallingford. I'm sorry. I was just waiting for William and I saw the painting and, well, I am sorry."

His expression relaxes. "Of course. Miss De Freccio." He turns to an open wall safe, which is filled with a stack of browned pages, and quickly places the roll into it. He closes the safe, which is behind a still-life painting of fruit arranged around a dead rabbit, and places his hands on his desk. "So, is Wallingford Academy living up to your expectations, then?"

"Uh, yeah. The Academy is great. Really. So, I'd better go find William."

"Of course. Lovely to see you."

I turn and bump into William.

"Ah, William," Mr. Wallingford says. "I've just been chatting with your charming friend."

"Another one of your 'frank discussions'?"

"Miss De Freccio, would you excuse us while I have a word with my son?"

William's gaze drops to his feet.

"Oh. Sure."

As the heavy door closes behind me, I hear Mr. Wallingford whisper, "I know this is hard. My father was hard on me as well. Some day you will see the wisdom…"

I walk around the lobby feeling awkward. What am I doing here, anyway? And what will Constance think about me hanging out with William? Sure, they've broken up and she and I aren't exactly close, but still. Just as I wonder if I should leave, the door to the study bursts open and William comes out, fists clenched.

Mr. Wallingford calls, "William, pay heed to what I've said."

William pauses, then strides toward me.

"William?" Mr. Wallingford steps into the lobby. "The family is depending on you."

William pauses again. He looks pale and nervous as he takes my arm. "Let's go."

"William?" Mr. Wallingford's voice is raised and his eyes spark with fury. "I'm warning you." He steps closer, fists clenched, and gives me a hate-filled stare.

William quickly pulls me outside and we get into his car.

Soon we're cruising along the road and the familiar shops of the High Street slip from view, replaced with wide Kelly green fields edged by tumbledown piles of stones. Jazz plays on the stereo like everything is cool but William's jaw is clenched.

After a few minutes pass I say, "Your dad doesn't really approve of me, does he?"

"What?" He laughs. "What are you going on about?"

"No, it's okay. I'm not like Constance. All proper and perfect and well bred. I get it."

He looks me up and down in a way that actually makes me blush. "No, I don't think you do. Anyway, I've had enough of the whole 'proper and perfect and well bred' charade to last me a lifetime. That pretty much sums up why I've broken up with Constance."

I glance out the window, not knowing what to think.

William says, "I'm sure you just startled my father. He's not upset with you." He starts talking about how he's looking forward to visiting France for winter break. Soon his accent and his perfect profile combine with the music and the car's soft leather seat to relax me, and then lull me into a peaceful dream…

"We're here," he says, his breath tickling my ear.

My eyes open. "Already?"

"Apparently I bored you into unconsciousness."

I stretch. "Sorry. I just haven't been sleeping much lately."

The cathedral is all tall spires and tortured gargoyles on the outside. Inside it is hushed, narrow and long. My gaze travels far far up toward the high stone pillars. At the head of the church is a large stained glass window of mostly blues and purples.

"You like it?"

I nod.

"Well, come on then." He guides me up the wide aisle. Our sneakers sound like taps on the tile floor. "If you want to draw it, I don't mind just watching you."

"Really?"

"I can't draw at all, or didn't you notice that in art class? It's kind of fascinating watching someone who has talent…unlike anyone in my family. We're all useless."

"That's a bit harsh."

His brows furrow. "Not really, actually."

We sit in a dark oak pew and I pull out my pad and pencils, studying the window and the carved gray stone that divides its panels. Slowly, my pencil begins to shape the window. I pause and sigh with relief that it looks like just a window, and nothing more.

I feel William's eyes on me. I can't help but wonder what he sees in me. Of course Justine's explanation seems like the most logical: He's made a bet. The silence drags on. My eyes glued to my drawing, I gather my nerve. "William?" I say, my voice almost a whisper. "Why are we here? You and me, I mean?"

"I just thought you haven't seen much of the area yet and—"

"No, really. Why are you spending time with me like this? Because if this is some sort of a…" I set down the pencil and face him. "We are so different."

He raises his brows. "Wow. I've heard you Americans are direct. Okay, the truth?"

I brace myself.

"I find you interesting. And, well," he says, his gaze dropping to his hands, "you *are* different. You aren't like the other girls at all."

"I'll say," I whisper.

"Besides, I enjoy a challenge." Now his cool blue eyes slide back to me with confidence.

A challenge? Me? I blink and look around. My voice is wobbly as I ask, "How would Constance feel about me being here with you? Everybody still thinks you two—"

"Suddenly I'm not so interested in what everyone thinks. I'm more interested in what you think."

"Oh." I return to my drawing, which doesn't turn out very well. William said I'm a challenge. Like a great lady whose hand must be won through battle or something. But Christopher said I was no lady. He said he thought I was the one who…who what?

Stop thinking about a delusion.

I study my drawing. To my relief, there's no sign of Christopher's form, angry face or even his piercing light eyes anywhere in the sketch.

Later, we pull up in William's car in front of my house. "So?" he asks.

"So wonderful," I say.

"That cathedral would make anyone a believer, don't you think? Imagine the poor medieval peasants, working with the swine and covered in muck, stepping into such a place. The awe they must have felt."

"Yeah. I guess so."

"But it's all just a big put-on, if you think about it. There's no proof. Just words. And everyone believes and just worships."

"I think you call that faith."

"What if it's all based on lies?" He scowls.

"You okay?"

His expression lightens. "Sure. Why wouldn't I be?"

"Thanks for taking me, William. I seriously needed this."

"That drawing you did was brilliant."

I shake my head.

"And you are so modest, too." He puts his hand to my face. "May I kiss you?" he asks, his voice husky. Before I can find my voice, he leans in and his lips touch mine. I close my eyes.

Is this for real?

The kiss is nice. But somehow it isn't *as* nice as the almost-kiss with a non-existent guy. Surprised, I open my eyes.

He says, "You make me want to be a better person somehow and I'm not sure..." He looks dead serious as he shifts his hand to my neck. His lips part and he leans in again.

I pull back. "I can't," I blurt out. "This is happening way too fast. I...I'm sorry." I escape from the car.

God, what's *wrong* with me?

Inside, my dad's by the front door, talking loudly on the hall phone. "You sound great, son. We're doing fine. How about you?"

I walk past him, ready to flee upstairs, when he rests his hand heavily on my shoulder. "Yeah," he says. "She's right here. Hold on."

I shake my head.

Dad covers the mouthpiece. "He called asking for you specifically."

"I'm really tired."

"It's okay, Shelly. Sounds like his new meds are working and he's feeling pretty good. So talk to your brother." He holds out the phone.

I set down my bag and take the phone. Dad whispers, "Talk."

So I smile and say, "Hey, Wayne. How's it going?"

"Hey, Michelle. It's better. Really better. I like it here. What about you?"

"Good. Nice here, too."

"I just wanted to ask you something."

I brace myself. In the past, Wayne has asked me if I ate all the cockroaches. Or if I could hear the Martians whispering on the line. "Go on," I say.

"Who's Christopher?"

12

"Today we are drawing still lifes, focusing on shading," Miss Turner says. "You'll notice the arrangements at the center of each table."

I pick up my charcoal stick and glance at an uninspiring cluster of plastic fruit in a wicker basket. A desk lamp is angled to shine on it. Guncha sighs and rolls her eyes.

Miss Turner says, "Roger, would you do me the honor of closing the blinds?"

Roger gets up fast and his chair falls back slamming to the ground. All the students seem to grow tense. Glowering, Roger pulls down the blinds, picks up his seat and sits.

"Thank you, dear," the teacher says. "Now I'll just shut off the main light. Find the best position at your table to really see the contrast between light and dark."

People shuffle chairs around and settle in. William scoots his chair close to mine. "There. That's better," he says.

I start to sketch and soon the composition takes shape.

"How do you do that?" William says. "Mine looks like I used my foot."

He's right. His grapes are little circles without depth, the bananas look like palm leaves and the basket is drawn like a circle as if it's seen from above.

"Could you help me? I don't think I could take another poor grade in this."

"Uh, sure. You just have to forget what you think it should look like and really see the way the shapes relate to each other. Try to draw exactly what is in front of you." In the corner of his page, I start to sketch some grapes. "See? Look at the way the shapes connect with each other. If you look closely enough, you'll see that none of them are perfect circles at all. That's what makes it so interesting."

"Those big eyes of yours see everything, don't they?"

"God, don't mention them," I mutter, suddenly feeling hideous.

"They're pretty." He stares at my sketch.

He's probably talking about the grapes but my pulse starts to race anyway. It picks up even more when William puts his face close to mine to see the exact same angle that I'm drawing. "Nice," he says in a low voice.

My eyes slide over to Guncha, who makes an "Aw" expression and places her hand over her heart.

There's a crash behind us. Roger stands by his table, panting, with fists clenched. The lamp lies on its side, bulb broken and the fruit arrangement has rolled across the table, some pieces bouncing to the floor.

"What on earth?" Miss Turner strides toward Roger with her high-heels click-clacking. Roger scowls at the students as if daring them to say anything. They seem to recoil from him.

He yanks his book bag from the back of his chair, pushes past Miss Turner and throws open the classroom door with such force it bangs against the wall. Then he's gone.

William starts to clap and soon the entire class is clapping and laughing. "First-rate Roger Mortley performance," William says. He gives me a knowing look.

At lunch, as I'm getting my food with Guncha and Justine, Constance comes up to me. "Michelle," she says, "why don't you sit at our table today? I need your help with something."

"Oh. Uh." I scour my mind for excuses and glance at Guncha and Justine, who look stunned.

Guncha says, "Could we also—"

Justine elbows her and says, "See you later, Michelle." She pushes Guncha away.

Resigned, I start to walk with Constance as she says, "Hope you don't mind sitting with me. It's just that I could use all my friends today, old and new."

I'm touched to hear her call me a friend.

She stops and takes a deep breath. "Sorry. I just need a minute before facing that lot." She nods at her table. "William and I have hit a bit of a bump in our relationship. Have you heard?"

I should tell her what happened with William. Now. Instead, I say, "You okay?"

"Oh," she says and seems almost surprised at my asking. She raises her nose slightly and says, "Of course I'm okay. Don't be silly. You know how boys are. William just needs to go slumming for a while so he can realize what he's missing."

Slumming. My cheeks burn as I nod.

When we get to the table, Constance and I sit across from William and Geoffrey. They're busy chatting with the other guys about some kid they pelted with bread rolls.

William notices me beside Constance, rubs his neck and shifts in his seat. I look down at my lunch.

"So, Michelle," Constance says in a sunny voice. "I've been emailing my cousin, the one in New Jersey, right? You won't believe our good fortune. She actually knows someone in your high school. Isn't that great?"

I feel a flash of alarm, then decide she's kidding. How could she find out anything about my high school when I didn't even give its real name?

"Speaking of good fortune," Constance says, "she's heard your mother is a fortune teller, isn't that right?"

My eyes snap to her. "How could you—"

"One good thing about being the Headmistress's daughter is that I can sneak a peak at your records. Funny that you got your school name wrong, wasn't it?"

I feel the tips of my ears start to burn.

"Your mother's a fortune teller?" William says. "Really?"

My entire face flames with embarrassment. It's as if my mother sits at the table among us and everyone is staring at her gaudy floppy hat and the huge hoop earrings that nearly touch her shoulders.

"Now what did my cousin say your mum calls herself?" Constance taps her chin with her finger. "Madam something or other?"

"Ooo, a madam?" Geoffrey says and cracks up.

William flings a soda cap at Geoffrey, whacking him on the forehead, and says, "Michelle, why didn't you tell me your mother told fortunes? That's rather cool."

"You know," Constance says, as she toys with her sandwich, "I once had my palm read. It was by some low-class smelly gypsy in Italy. You know, the sort who waits by the toilets to pick your pocket? Oh." She puts her hand to her mouth. "Michelle, I hope your mother isn't a gypsy."

"Uh, no."

For a moment, Constance's expression seems almost smug. My eyes narrow.

"So, Constance, what was your fortune?" Geoffrey asks, leaning over the table. "That you'd spend your entire life longing to be with me?" He grins and all the guys bang on the table and howl.

"Far from it," she says, once the noise dies down. "Apparently I will live a life full of privilege and get everything I want." Her eyes rest on William.

Another howl rises.

And I want to disappear.

Later, in history, Mr. Llywelyn talks about how the War of the Roses was a dispute over who was the real king of England. "Two families laid claim to the throne," he says. "One side represented King Henry, who had lost his mind. The other side fought for the

Duke of York to be king." He turns and jots a series of dates on the chalkboard.

Constance takes this opportunity to whisper to me, "Michelle, I just heard something rather upsetting. Did you go somewhere with William yesterday?"

"Ladies?" Mr. Llywelyn says. "No talking in class, thank you very much."

Constance is silent for a while but soon her lips are at my ear, whispering, "I understand if you did. William has a way about him. I just wish you had said something."

I swallow and whisper, "Nothing happened. Not really. You have to believe me. I never meant—"

"Miss De Freccio," Mr. Llywelyn says, "you are dismissed from class."

"But—" I begin.

He sets down his chalk and his bulldog face grows very serious. "Yes, sir."

I feel a hot wash of humiliation as I gather my books. Constance quickly turns away from me, but not before I catch the hint of a grin.

I leave the classroom. In a way I'm glad I got kicked out. Since history is the last class, I can now get a jumpstart on what I've been itching to do all day: get to the castle and get some answers.

13

Luckily when I get home Dad's not back from teaching yet, or I'd have to explain why I'm home so early. I change into my jeans, light-blue Chucks and a long-sleeved white Tee, and then head over to Mary's for her bike. It's another dazzlingly sunny day— which is weird because I thought it rained all the time in England.

"Hello, dear," Mary says. She's sitting on her back steps wearing a purply blue velour tracksuit, reminding me of the *Willy Wonka* girl who inflates like a giant blueberry. "Needing the bike again I see."

"Yeah. Thanks for letting me use it."

"Heading to the castle?"

"Actually, yeah."

"Where are your art things? I could use a bit of art for me sitting room, you know." She tilts her head. "Might be a nice way to repay my kindness. Meaning the bike and all."

"Oh. Okay, sure. Let me get some stuff."

Soon I'm pedaling toward the castle. Slung over my shoulder is my messenger bag loaded with a pad of thick Strathmore paper and a bunch of supplies. I coast downhill past some stone houses and a stretch of dense woods. And I don't know what to believe. I guess it's still possible this Christopher thing is a hoax. But if it is, it's the most elaborate hoax known to man.

Or maybe I *am* just delusional. Maybe everything was in my mind. But that doesn't explain the painting and the tomb… Still the mind can play cruel tricks. I think of that sketch of him about to strike with his sword and a shiver sweeps up my back.

The street intersects with Castle Road and I turn right, passing antique shops, coffee houses, bed and breakfasts, and gift shops. Then there's a visitor's lot where the tourist buses are parked in tight rows.

I wait at the next intersection for the traffic light to change, while I again consider a third possibility. A possibility I was convinced was impossible until Wayne asked, "Who's Christopher?" Even then, I was sure I was just hearing voices in my head and merely thinking it was Wayne. So I had my dad talk to Wayne and write down what he heard.

Dad jotted: "Who's Christopher? He's asking for you. He wears a cape. He's in my dreams." Then he stopped writing and said, "Wayne, son? You did take your meds today, didn't you?"

Now I pull the crumpled paper out of my jean pocket. To my intense relief, I find Dad's looping script still says the same thing.

The light changes and I shove the paper back into my pocket, push off the curb and ride across the street.

At the castle, I lock up Mary's bike and scan the jammed parking lot but don't see Roger's rusty truck. When I reach the admissions counter, there's James. I smile and say hi, and even mention Roger, but he just furrows his unibrow and says, "Fifteen pounds." I pay and notice this leaves me with just a few coins in my bag.

There's a lot going on today. Maybe it's the start of a special festival or something. Colorful tents line the grounds outside the castle walls. Reenactors run a blacksmith shop, do outdoor cooking over an open fire and demonstrate swordplay and archery. It's all pretty cool but it isn't *real*. It kind of reminds me of Gloucester Cathedral wowing the ignorant peasants. All smoke and mirrors and wishful thinking.

Everything suddenly feels so fake and ridiculous. God, what *am* I doing here? I'm about to leave but I remember the picture Mary wanted me to draw. And the fifteen pounds I'd just spent.

So I find a quiet spot up in an outlook tower along the ramparts. From here, the cars in the parking area look like toys and the tents and spectators are far below. Looking back toward the castle, there's a really nice view of the surrounding walls and towers. I settle onto a ledge. It's a bit windy and my hair keeps blowing into my eyes. So I wind my ringlets into a bun and stick a pencil through it to hold this in place. Pulling another pencil from my bag, I get down to business.

Soon I'm deeply involved in the drawing. Lost in it, you might say. Then I catch the smell of freshly cut grass mixed with hints of perspiration and cinnamon.

And I feel his warmth before I see him. "You have a sure hand," he says. He's sitting right beside me in the bright sunshine, his auburn hair tangling in the breeze. "But so do I." He raises a dagger to my throat.

14

"Who sent you?" he demands.

"N-nobody."

He presses the dagger against my throat. "Anyone who threatens the Earl is my own sworn enemy." He stands and nods toward my messenger bag. "Show me."

I hand it to him.

With his pale-green eyes fixed on me, he dumps the contents of my bag. "What weapon is this?" He holds up my sharpener.

I stick my pencil into the sharpener and turn it a few times. Pull it out and blow on the tip.

He squints. "What of this?"

I narrow my eyes, take my Chapstick from his fingers, pop off the top and coat my lips. "Really dangerous."

"This?" He holds up a tampon.

"God, enough." I dare to push away the dagger point, grab the tampon from his hand and start shoving things back into my bag. "You're nuts, you know that? Or I am. One of us is, that's for sure."

He looks amused and stows his dagger in the side of his boot.

I let out a sigh of relief.

He's saying, "You lay in wait, yet are unarmed. What manner of assassin are you?"

"Assassin? You've got problems. I get it. Boy, do I ever get it," I say, growing more angry by the moment. I scoop up my coins, my art supplies and, because I once sliced open my finger cutting a linoleum print, a tiny first aid kit. "Try taking your meds," I tell him, stuffing these things back into my bag. "Try not wearing that cape and boots all the time. While you're at it, why don't you take up a hobby, like going to Star Wars conventions as a Jedi knight?" I hang the bag over my shoulder and grab my drawing pad. "I'm leaving and if you follow me, I swear to God I'll scream and you'll be in prison faster than you can say Society of Creative Anachronism. Got that?"

He flashes a half smile. He's so attractive. He's so cocky. I grit my teeth and back away. I'm near the steps. I turn, about to run down, when I see over the wall something far below. My heart seizes up.

No tourists. No tents. No cars. *No parking lot.* Just grass, a water-filled moat and a deep forest in the distance. I drop my sketchpad, race to the other side of the rampart and look into the castle courtyard. No visitors waiting in line to get into the dungeon. No grass. Just dirt and some men dressed like Christopher in boots and leggings and tunics, talking with one another.

I stumble and sit back on the ledge. "Holy crap. Holy—" I'm hyperventilating. I put my head between my knees. The pencil holding my bun drops to the floor and my curls escape. I close my eyes. Concentrate on my breathing.

When I open my eyes, I see him through my tangle of hair, squatting next to me. "You are unwell," he says.

"Unwell?" I sit up and let out a certifiably whacked-out laugh. "You pull a knife on me and then everything…" I wipe sweat from my forehead. "Look, who are you? And don't you dare say Christopher Newman of Watley Manor, or my head will explode."

"That would be untidy." He grins as he sits next to me and pulls up a knee. "Well, I guess you could say I am a man newly arrived at the castle."

My head starts to throb, so I rub my temples.

"I do not pretend to be original or unusual," he says, glancing at my Chucks. "Like many a man here, I hope to curry the favor of my good lord the Earl of Blanchley to seal my fortune. I guard the Earl's life and interests as if they were my own. And nothing must deter me." He fixes a steely look on me.

"Huh. Okay, I'm not saying I believe any of this, but how old *are* you?"

"Already seventeen." He picks up my sketchpad and hands it to me. "And what of you? And do not tell me you are Michelle from the Isle of Jersey, because no one in this castle has heard of such a lass. And no one from Jersey would dress as you, in strange clothes ill-suited even for a man toiling in the field. So, what are you, a spy? A witch?"

"I'm nothing. Nobody. Just Michelle De Freccio from New Jersey, in the U.S." I stuff my sketchpad into my bag, put my bag on my shoulder and notice him shaking his head as if I'd answered the question wrong. "*So* nuts." I stand. Maybe I get up too fast, or maybe it's the shock of again seeing absolutely no parking lot whatsoever. Either way, my knees buckle and the floor rushes up to meet my face. Strong hands catch me before I hit. I blink and realize he has me in his arms, and is setting me onto the ledge.

"Rest a bit." He gently brushes my hair aside with his fingertips.

I stop his hand. "Then, you are telling me this is real? *You* are real?"

He twines his fingers with mine. "And so, apparently, are you." Christopher studies our hands for a minute, then his eyes flash with fury and his hand tightens on mine. "So that is your charm. That is how you plan to ruin me. I am no fool. While we spoke last time, the Earl was nearly strangled to death." He yanks me to my feet. "You are involved." Now he holds both of my hands in his grip. "You seek to distract me while another attempt is made. Who are you working for? King Henry's allies? Is Wallingford involved?"

"William? What does he—"

"Silence, strumpet. I know how to deal with the likes of you."

"Oh no you did not just call me that." I try to free my hands from his but I'm no match for his strength.

He pulls me to the spiral stairs and down after him so fast I can barely keep my feet from slipping on the narrow treads. My messenger bag bumps against my hip.

"Let go of me!" My voice echoes in the stone stairwell and sounds like it's coming out of a bullhorn. "Help, someone! Rape! HELP!"

Christopher stops and shouts, "Will you SHUT UP?"

I take in a deep breath and SCREAM.

He covers his ear with one hand and pulls me down the last few steps with the other. He drags me across the courtyard. I shout for him to let go. We near a hook-nosed man with a fur-rimmed cloak who strolls alongside a doughy old woman. Her liver-spotted bosom nearly bursts from her gown and her eyes are gray. Cat-like. *Constance-like.*

One step behind the woman is a plain-faced girl with a spray of freckles. Her blond hair is in an elegant up-do and she wears an elaborate green gown. She's probably no older than thirteen.

Christopher bows his head to them and the girl curtsies, but the woman and man merely raise their noses and walk on.

"Hey," I call to them, "how about a little help here?" No reaction. Is everyone deaf?

Christopher pulls me past the cluster of men I'd seen from above. They're in a huddle and one says in a loud voice, "I tell you all. There is word the Duke of York has returned and demands the crown." The others take in their breath.

"Newman," another man calls to Christopher, "come hear the latest tales. And the traveling magician has arrived." He waves to a man in a tattered gray tunic who makes a red ball disappear with a flick of his wrist.

"Perhaps later," Christopher says, turning toward them. "I am presently—"

I kick, catch him in back of the knee and he stumbles.

He regains his balance quickly and yanks me away with renewed fury.

"Help!" I shout over my shoulder. "He's crazy. He's got a knife."

The men don't even look up. "Damsel in distress," I screech, trying another tactic. No reaction at all.

"No one cares of the fate of a whore."

"A, a what? You jackass. How dare you." I kick again, missing him completely. "I can't believe I ever thought you were…"

"Thought I was what?" He gives me his cocky grin.

I bend over and bite his hand.

He growls, grabs both of my arms and pulls them behind me so hard my shoulders burn. "That is it," he says. "I am taking you far from here and that will be the end of your meddling. Be thankful I do not deal with you more harshly, though if you surface again, it will be your last act." He pushes me into a wide stable that stinks of rotted hay and manure. He shouts, "Thomas Haston, are you here?"

"Aye, master." A man emerges from one of the stalls. He's short and swarthy and the unfocused look in his eyes makes him seem a bit dim. "Just readying the horse for your afternoon ride, good sir."

"Good man. Make haste."

"Help me, Mr. Haston," I say, "please."

But Thomas Haston's vision remains barely focused on Christopher. "Yes, master." He bows his head. "I shall grab the reins."

He hurries toward us. Straight toward me. He must be completely blind, because he's going to walk right into me.

"Watch it," I say.

He doesn't walk into me. He walks *through* me. Like I'm a stream to be waded through. My skin feels itchy and a nasty saltiness fills my mouth. Christopher releases me and looks at me with horror. I look at my hands, expecting them to be see-through, but they're solid. "What the hell?" I say.

"What in hell," he says, his voice barely a whisper.

"Sorry. Be ready in a minute," the servant says, from right behind me.

Before I can step aside, he wades through me again, this time with reigns clutched in his sweaty fist.

A shiver runs through me, my flesh feels like it's been blistered with poison ivy, and my mouth like I've just gargled with ocean water. I scratch at my arms and spit into the hay, feeling sick. "Please tell me that isn't his sweat I'm tasting."

Christopher says, "What are you?"

Thomas Haston stops. "I am your loyal servant, sir."

Christopher steps closer to me, his eyes never leaving my face. "Leave me."

I think he's talking to me but Thomas says, "Aye, master. As soon as I finish with the horse."

"Forget that." He edges even closer to me.

"So you will not be riding after all, sir?"

"Leave, Thomas."

I hear the servant go. I feel the itch fade like a memory and the salt dissolve from my tongue.

Christopher takes both my hands, gingerly, as if he's afraid they'll burst into flames. "What are you? A sprite? A spirit? A phantom?"

"I'm a *freak*," I say. And burst into tears.

15

Tears stream. My nose runs.

Christopher looks heavenward. I must be disgusting.

"I'm sorry. I…I can't—" Now I'm crying even harder, hiccupping between gasps.

He squeezes my hands. "Stop this at once."

I try, but it's no use. I can't stop crying. I am the farthest thing from a normal person.

"Confound it," he says, looking annoyed. "Come here, then." He sets my messenger bag on the ground and pulls me to him, and I bury my face in his shoulder, my tears soaking the rough fabric of his cape. His arms surround me and I realize he's gently swaying me side to side and murmuring, "Shh, now. Shh."

Eventually, I grow calm, until I'm just hiccupping.

"Better?" he asks.

I shrug. "How can you be so calm? Don't you feel like you're losing your mind?"

"Now why would I feel like that?" His breath is warm against my hair.

"Oh, I don't know. Maybe because you see me and no one else does?"

"True. Perhaps you are a ghost?"

"But I'm not dead." I push away a bit and wipe my cheek. "You're all wet now." I touch the damp spot on his shoulder. I pick up my bag and loop the strap over my own shoulder.

"No matter," he's saying. "I'm quite used to this."

I look up and catch him smiling. "So," I say, "you always have freaky girls go hysterical all over you?"

"I have a sister," he explains.

"And I hear she is ripe for the picking," someone says.

"Wallingford," Christopher says with disdain. "Do not dare to speak of my sister."

I expect to see William. Instead there is a guy around my age with long black hair and a pointed nose.

Wallingford tosses his cape over his shoulder and toys with a pair of suede gloves. "She is rather too poor a crop for my taste. I am in the market for someone more, shall we say, worthy?" He steps nearer, raising his chin.

Christopher protectively pushes me behind his back. "She is far better than you will ever deserve."

"You are hiding something," Wallingford says with certainty. "What intrigue is this?" He circles Christopher and pauses facing me. His sky-blue eyes are just like William's. I hold my breath as he continues his circle and stops in front of Christopher. "The Earl's ward Elaine is far more to my liking than your poor sister. And my father is in quite good favor with the Earl."

"You mean," Christopher says, "he wheedles the Earl's wife, swaying the Countess about her wealthy cousin with his poisonous tongue and false flattery."

"He is a clever man," Wallingford says, with clear admiration. "So I warn you, do not set your sights upon the ward. You cannot win against me, I assure you. After all, only cream floats to the top."

"So does crap," I say.

Christopher looks confused. "Crap?"

"Yeah. You know," I say and lower my voice to whisper, "shit?"

Christopher laughs. "Yes. You are right. Let us go. This stable has become too foul for my nose." He walks toward a brown horse tied in the back stall and I follow.

"Talking with yourself?" Wallingford calls after him, while casually putting on his gloves. "Losing your mind, are you? Or are you showing solidarity with that insane pretender King Henry? Some would call that treason against our one true king the Duke of York."

Christopher concentrates on buckling the horse's reins.

"Poor move missing the Earl's meeting yesterday," Wallingford says. "He seemed quite displeased with you. Again. And you, once his assured favorite. And where were you when someone tried to strangle the Earl? Hm? Rather suspicious, is it not?"

I find myself thinking of Christopher's strong hands.

He tightens his fists. "A good man has already been brought to his death in that matter."

"A *good* man? Is that what you call an assassin? One wonders where your loyalties rest, Newman. One wonders entirely too much about you."

"I am *loyal*. And Craigston was a good man who will be missed. You yourself witnessed the Earl's grief at Craigston's conviction."

"Yes. Some said too much grief. As if his own son were being executed. Perhaps what they say is true and the Earl's careless wenching resulted in an heir after all." He chuckles.

"You are the disloyal one, Wallingford, to speak of the Earl so. The Earl was grieved because Craigston was an innocent. The case against him was weak. You know it was. Yet I helped apprehend him, as was my duty." His expression seems to darken. "That proves my loyalty." He swallows and looks at the ground.

"Hm." Wallingford casts a scornful look at Christopher. "Honestly, you will never rise from the muck of your past. Quite ambitious."

"What's he mean?" I ask.

Christopher clenches his jaw.

Wallingford chuckles to himself, spins on his boot heel and walks out.

"Hey," I call after him, "what muck?"

"He cannot hear you, remember?" Christopher tosses the reins over the horse's head.

The horse snorts and chomps. And it occurs to me it could easily bite my face. I haven't been this close to a horse since grade school when I was bucked off during a lesson. "But what was he talking about?" I ask.

"You are entirely too inquisitive." Christopher grabs me by the waist.

"Wait. What are you doing?"

He hoists me onto the horse. I land hard on its back, my bag slapping against my hip. "I need some fresh air," he says.

"No, wait." I look down at him from what feels like a dizzying height. "You don't understand. I don't do horses."

Christopher climbs up and wedges behind me. Our bodies are entirely too close. He reaches his arms around me and grabs the reins. "You do not 'do' horses," he says in my ear. "You ride them." He flicks the reins and, God help me, we're moving out of the stable and into the courtyard.

"Wait, I'm going to fall," I say, as the horse picks up speed and trots through the main gate. Guards with spears nod at Christopher as we pass. "The ground looks really hard. I can't stand blood. I'll faint again."

"Will you be quiet?"

"But no one can hear me."

"*I* can hear you." He grabs me tight around the waist with one arm, gives the horse a kick and we canter over the moat and onto a dusty road, away from the castle.

"You can't just kidnap me and dump me somewhere."

"Can I not?"

"No. Stop this thing. I don't feel safe."

"You are safe."

"You don't understand. I'm used to seatbelts and airbags and helmets and things like that."

"This is not war. Relax," he says, then pulls me in so close, it takes my breath away.

"Relax," I manage to say. "Sure." I start to catch onto the rhythm of the horse. Along the dirt road, tall grass lines the edges for about twenty feet, ending in trees. Two men on horseback approach, holding flags of red and blue. "What tidings, Newman?" one calls, his face flushed red and his hair orange.

"Greetings to you, Greenfeld. And to you, Plumson," Christopher says. Plumson, a tall man with white-blond hair grins and nods as they both trot past. A covered horse-pulled carriage approaches us and stops by our side.

Christopher pulls his horse to a halt and bows.

I look down over the edge of the horse. Even if Christopher didn't have me in his grip, how would I get down? Where could I possibly go?

From the carriage, a ring-covered hand pulls aside a thick green curtain and an attractive dark-haired man pokes his head out. His other hand squeezes the shoulder of the younger woman who sits beside him. "Ah, young Master Newman," he says.

"My Good Lordship, you look well."

"I would look better if you would care to come when you are summoned." He raises his chin.

"My sincere apologies, my Lord. Again, I did not receive notice of your summons." Christopher raises his chin too. "I will always be your most loyal servant."

"See that you are." The man smiles and his flash of white teeth makes him movie star gorgeous. "So, son, are you enjoying your stay at the castle? Everything to your liking thus far?"

"My Lord has been most hospitable. I have all the comforts."

"Yes, but still you are concerned about your family, are you not? Worry not, son," the man says in a kind voice. "All shall be well in the end. Come to me with any of your needs. Anything at all. Do you understand?"

"Yes. Thank you, my Lord."

The man studies Christopher for a moment and smiles again. He bangs on the side of the carriage and shouts, "Drive on!"

I squint against the dust cloud the carriage kicks up as it departs. "He seems nice. Who was that?"

"My good lord, the Earl of Blanchley."

"That wouldn't happen to be the *third* Earl of Blanchley?"

"Yes."

I think of the cursed spot and a weird shiver tickles my back as I realize that this must be the man murdered in the castle courtyard. Then I remember the Mating Chair and feel a bit creeped out. "The lady with him, was that his wife?"

"Certainly not. His wife the Countess is sour of look and foul of manner. You saw her in the courtyard with Wallingford's father."

Oh. Ew. "So was the Earl with his daughter, then?"

Christopher laughs. "No. The Earl has no children."

"But Wallingford said—"

"Listen not to gossip-mongers. The Earl has no children. The Countess and he wed when she was far beyond her birthing years."

"So why, exactly, did he marry her?"

"The usual reasons. She adored his fair appearance, he her fair title and sums of fortune." Christopher's grin fades. "I cannot understand. Thrice the Earl's summons was not delivered to me," he says between clenched teeth. "Thrice. By the blood, when I find out who…" He kicks the horse again and we ride on, not seeing any other people along the road. There's nothing but green grass and trees and blue sky forever. I try to think of another time when I've been anywhere without houses, cars, or signs in sight, and I draw a blank.

The road bends and turns down a hill. Here Christopher guides the horse off the path and we ride through the grasses and up another hill. He pulls the horse to a stop and jumps off.

"So, this is where you're dumping me?" I ask as he helps me down.

He gives me an odd look. "I am not dumping you."

"Oh." The view is sensational. The ground drops beyond the hill, spreading out into a quilt of wide lush fields, patched with varying shades of green and tan that fade into a haze in the distance as if their colors were mixed with more and more of the tint Payne's Gray. Clusters of trees are here and there. It would make an incredible painting. "Is your home near?" Is anything near, I wonder.

"No," he says with a sigh. He undoes his bear pin, removes his cape and spreads it on the grass and motions for me to sit. I hesitate, but set my messenger bag down and sit on the cape. He drops down beside me, fixes the pin onto his collar and leans back on his elbow, like it's the most natural thing in the world. "What of your home? Is it far?"

"Good question." I hug my knees. Our eyes lock for a while.

He says, "What *are* you? Will you tell me now?"

"Nothing special. Seriously."

"So you will not say, then?"

I shrug. "There's nothing to tell."

He rubs his chin. "Yet there is something, indeed. And you wield some power over me. I feel it."

I shake my head but I think there is something about *him*. Christopher has this rugged appeal that makes even William Wallingford ordinary in comparison. I can't seem to look away. It's as if I'm studying him for a portrait. I notice he tends to raise his chin. The very corners of his mouth curve up, making him seem slightly arrogant. And his eyes. Their light color gives them endless depth. Yet they seem so full of…of what?

Longing.

I glance away, surprised. "Do you have many friends here?"

"The two men guarding the Earl, Plumson and Greenfeld, are friends of sorts. Though it is difficult to make friends amid so much distrust."

"Because someone tried to kill the Earl?"

Christopher nods. We stare at each other again for a long while. I can't pull my eyes away from his. I feel as if he is very familiar to me. Like he is a very important part of my life. But that doesn't make any sense. None of this makes sense.

He's saying, "I know folk speak of the king's spies attempting to kill the Earl, but this does not seem to be so. You saw how the Earl rides about relatively unprotected. He is always thus when he goes a-wenching. If the king's spies wanted him dead, surely they would seize him in such a vulnerable situation. Not in the Earl's own fortified castle, when…" He frowns.

"What?"

"I should not speak so loosely in front of you."

"You still think that I—"

"I think the villain must be of the castle to have so easily approached the Earl in his own private room. While the killer was there, one of the Earl's lady visitors entered the chambers. So the killer was forced to flee."

"Did she see who it was?"

"She swore it was Craigston. Craigston swore his innocence right up to his execution." He studies his hands.

I again think about that sketch of him, about his hands raising that sword. Of that guy cowering beneath Christopher's blade. "You brought him to justice," I say.

He barely nods.

"And he was your friend."

"Yes." Christopher focuses on me again. "Yes, he was."

"I'm so sorry," I say.

He leans just a fraction closer to me and gives one of my spiral curls a small tug, grinning when it springs back into its coil. He draws his brows together. "Do you own any land, by any chance?"

"No."

"Do you have a noble title?"

Like Freak? "God, no."

"Wealth, perhaps?"

I laugh at this. "Why?"

"It would have simplified things." He runs his finger along the edge of my Chucks. "No matter what manner of being you are. I would not have cared…"

"I don't understand."

He takes my hand, gently for once, and touches his lips to it. Inwardly I melt. "Do you not?" he says.

My heart speeds up and I drop back onto his cape.

Christopher kisses inside my elbow, then leans over me and looks at me with those haunting eyes. He touches his lips to my neck. Rubs his cheek against mine. "Michelle," he says in an exhale. "Cannot you feel it?"

I nod as he kisses my cheek. I do feel it. An incredible closeness. His hair spills around my face. He smells of cinnamon, he smells of home. My whole being feels so powerfully drawn to him. Christopher runs his thumb over my lips. "I have never felt this way." He touches his nose to mine. "I would bind myself to you."

Bind away, I think, running my hands along his broad back.

"I would," he says, again. "If only you had but one of those three things." He leans toward my lips, as the words hit me hard.

I turn my face away. "Excuse me? What did you say?"

"I would bind myself—"

"The other part. The 'three things?'"

"Land, title, or money? How I dearly wish you had even a little. I have never felt this way about another, Michelle. It is a pity, truly."

He nibbles my neck and I have to force the fantasy out of my head. The one where I rip off his tunic and he tears at my shirt and we "bind" all over the field. "Stop," I say, my voice squeaking. I scramble away from him and clench my hands to keep them from pulling him to me. "I can't believe you're one of those guys. I can't believe I feel…"

"Feel what?"

Deep breath. "Doesn't matter." I stand on wobbly legs, feeling like such an idiot. "You're one of those guys. You don't care about me. You care about profit and status and crap like that."

"I have no choice."

I shake my head.

"If it were only me I had to think of, my choice would be my own and I would gladly choose you." He stands. "I would choose you," he repeats, this time with even more feeling. "But the fate of my mother and my sister is on my shoulders."

I shoot him a hateful look and walk away from him, down the hill.

"Wait." He catches up. "It is not my choice."

I keep on walking. He grabs my arm and spins me around. "I did not choose to feel this way for you." Now he searches my face, as if looking for answers. "But I do. And now that I do, I know not how to suppress it, yet I must."

"Wow, you really know how to sweet talk a girl, you know that?"

"And you really know how to aggravate a fellow." I start to turn away but he says, "My father died of the consumption last year." He focuses far into the distance. "My home is two-day ride from here. A small manor, yet we made a goodly living on rents from the tenants when my father was living." He touches the bear pin by his collar.

"Your father gave you that."

He sighs. "It was his." He sits in the grass. "After his death, it became my job to care for the family and run the estate."

I sit beside him.

He says, "Neighboring estates began to challenge our right to the manor. Said our noble title claims were falsified and we had no right to hold our land. Tenants ceased to pay rent. So I had to leave my sister and mother under the protection of a few faithful servants and seek security." His expression turns grim. "Security at all costs."

"You mean guards?"

"No." He rips out some grass and tosses it into the wind. "The Earl has been most kind to my mother. I must remain at the castle, because the Earl wills it. And I seek for him to elevate my family and secure my estate."

"And how exactly does that happen?"

"The surest way is for him to arrange a match. I must wed a wealthy woman with both title and land."

"Whoa." I stand. "Who's the strumpet now?"

He jumps to his feet. "I resent that. This is the surest way to secure my estate and protect my family. My sister, then, will be able to marry well and my mother be provided for despite the whims of the Earl."

"Okay, that's sick." I stride back toward the horse.

"Sick?" He strides alongside me. "What would be sick is to neglect my family. How can you be so childlike?"

I stop. "Childlike?"

"Do you not see the responsibility? I am the last remaining male Newman."

"But you're seventeen."

"Yes. My parents wed at fourteen. And my goal was so clear, until—"

"Until some nutty girl appeared in your life and messed with your head. And you wish I never showed up."

"No." He steps closer. "I do not wish that. I wish for other things."

I feel an overwhelming and completely emotional pull between us. It's like an invisible force. At once we are drawn together. His hands grip my waist. Our lips meet. Sweet and soft and warm. He pulls me closer. We wrap our arms around each other. Our kiss deepens.

"You using that?" a woman asks.

He's gone. My arms are empty.

The woman snaps her gum and studies her manicure.

I'm standing in the middle of the Washateria, next to an empty dryer. Around me machines hum, sudsy loads of wash swish behind glass doors. A man lights a cigarette and opens a magazine.

"No." I hug myself and my teeth chatter.

16

Thwap! A pile of mail shoved through our mail slot lands in the narrow foyer. I pick up the stack, which is soggy from the storm outside. There's a brochure from the town about community education classes and a crisp Wallingford Academy envelope addressed to my dad. I'm about to call him, when he bursts through the swinging door from the kitchen, saying, "Mail call?"

I hand him the pile. He rifles through it and I go into the little sitting room beside the hallway, and pace back and forth in front of the bay window.

Last night I hardly slept because I'd sat up in bed, searching the darkness for Christopher like some silly girl waiting for a caped superhero to come to the rescue. It *was* silly and ridiculous. God, I knew it. But I couldn't stop.

When waiting for him to appear got unbearable, I'd leapt to my feet and paced the small space beside my bed, trying to decide how to feel, what to do next. Just like I'm pacing now. *Get a grip.*

But it felt *real.* All of it. And Wayne knew about him.

Head throbbing from exhaustion, my mind goes over and over the same thoughts: What does it all mean? Am I psychic? And how, exactly, do I go back into Christopher's time?

My mother once explained her "sight" as being like an antenna tuned into frequencies that are there all the time but that other people can't hear. She was convinced Wayne was so sensitive and therefore attuned to too many different frequencies, and that's why they got all scrambled in his head.

If I were to follow this logic, then my "sight" isn't just audible, it's visual too. So maybe instead of an antenna, I'm like a satellite dish "channeling" stations from far away and long ago. Or maybe I'm more like a freaky psychic wireless connection. Instead of the Internet, I've got "Internalnet." Ha ha.

I pause and pull aside the lace curtain to peer at the wet gloom outside.

There's a problem with this psychic theory. Quite a few problems, actually. Like the fact that my mom isn't really psychic. She was wrong about so many things. When I was mercilessly teased back in New Jersey, Mom had predicted that soon the name De Freak-o wouldn't hurt me anymore. That didn't happen. She also predicted before she'd left that I'd take care of Wayne. I haven't. I've barely spoken with him. And the worst prediction of all: she said she'd always be there for me. She said this the day before she left.

And then there's Wayne. What sort of psychic frequency makes voices come from inanimate objects in his room, voices that speak gibberish mixed with threats of violence?

I'm nothing like Wayne or my mom. For one thing, I really really want to be normal.

I let go of the curtain and rub my aching forehead. So maybe this has nothing to do with anything psychic. Or with insanity. What if it's just about Christopher? And me? A guy and a girl with a deep connection. One so deep that it reaches across time. So we're like, what? Soul mates from different centuries? Yeah, right. How far from normal is that?

"Michelle?" Dad says, in his solemn "we have to talk" voice. Frowning at the paper in his hand, he walks into the sitting room and sits on the pea-green loveseat, which, like all the furniture, came with the house and looks like it went out of style about thirty years ago. "Seems you've been in some trouble at school." He waves a letter at me.

"Oh." I sit beside him.

"Oh is right. Kicked out of class? And now this is being counted against me during my probation. They can decide to toss me out at semester's end if I don't live up to their standards."

"What? Why should it count against you? It was my fault. Constance and I were—"

"The Headmistress's daughter? Great." He stares at the paper and his brows furrow. "Michelle, you've got to watch yourself. Your behavior can't embarrass the Academy. They're strict."

I nod. "I'm sorry, Dad."

"Okay. We'll say nothing more about this."

We sit quietly. Despite my best efforts, my mind whirls back to Christopher. I wish I could tell Dad about him. Ask how Wayne could possibly know about him. What if Wayne and I, simply by being brother and sister, somehow share part of the same mental wireless connection that links me to Christopher?

I bite my lip. "Dad, what if Wayne isn't really sick?"

He looks at the ground. "I don't think we should discuss this."

We never discuss this, or pretty much anything that deals with Wayne or my mom. Part of me wants to protect him like I always do and change the subject, but I say, "Well, Mom thought he was hearing real voices, didn't she?"

"Your mother heard what she wanted to hear."

I study my hands. "Did Wayne ever draw? Or did Mom? You know, pictures of their visions or whatever?" I fall silent and give him a sideways glance. His face looks pained. I want to kick myself for bringing any of this up.

"Soccer," he mumbles. "Your brother's thing was soccer. He was so good…" He stops himself and frowns, seeming more lost than ever.

"Dad, I'm so sorry. I didn't mean…"

"Just try to stay out of trouble." He sets the letter on the white Formica table and gives me a quivering smile. "It's okay. Everything's going to be okay, right?"

I nod and even force myself to smile back.

"What are your plans today?" He says this in a cheerful voice, as if dismissing all thoughts of my mom and Wayne.

I sigh and rest my head against his shoulder. "Could you drive me to the castle?"

"I can't. I have to run a ton of errands and go food shopping. Besides, you don't want to go in this weather. Save it for a better day. I'm sure you must have some homework to do. You'd better keep your grades up."

I nod. Probably a bad grade would be counted against my dad too. "It's just that I'm working on this drawing of the castle for Mary and…" The drawing. My messenger bag. I now realize I must have left them behind. But where, exactly? Or rather, *when,* exactly. And Mary's bike. I know exactly where that is—still locked in the castle lot, probably rusting away.

• • •

Not long after Dad drives off to the food store, headlights sweep the house and I hear the cough of an engine. I throw on my hoodie and dash into the teaming rain but Roger is already at the back of his truck, lifting out Mary's bike. He's dressed in torn jeans and a flimsy gray Tee, which, like his hair, is saturated and stuck to him.

"Why didn't you wear a raincoat?" I shout over the racket of his engine.

"It's just water," he shouts back. Rain courses over his face. He hands me the bike.

"Thanks so much for doing this." I wheel it to Mary's yard and set it against the side of her house under the overhang.

Roger is back in his truck. I rap on the window and he rolls it down. "You have to come in the house."

He pushes his wet bangs aside. "No, thanks."

"But I've got something for you." Now my hoodie is completely soaked. Raindrops drip from the tip of my nose.

He still seems hesitant. The shadows beneath his eyes look worse in the gloomy daylight.

"It's something vintage eighties," I say. Immediately he cuts the engine.

In the kitchen, puddles form around us, so I toss some kitchen towels onto the linoleum.

"Enjoying our lovely British weather?" he says, kicking off a pair of torn black sneakers and peeling off a pair of used-to-be-white socks.

I pull off my hoodie and drop it on the floor and kick off my soggy Chucks. "Be right back."

Upstairs I change before returning with my arms full of dry clothes and towels. There's an extremely awkward moment when I find Roger shirtless and standing over the kitchen sink, wringing out his gray tee. He's actually a really nice-looking guy, if somewhat pale.

"What?" he asks. "Aren't you used to having half-naked blokes in your kitchen?" He flexes a muscle.

"All the time." I hit him in the face with a bath towel.

"Oh, that's nice. I practically drown to rescue a bicycle, which, of course, some security arse thought I was stealing, even though I knew the lock's combination."

"Seriously?"

"And all just so you can beat me to within an inch of my life." He rubs his hair with the towel. "So why did you call me, anyway? Why not call Wallingford? His Porsche in the shop? He too busy terrorizing the less fortunate or shagging large-breasted girls?"

I grit my teeth and toss Roger a pair of my dad's sweats and an old blue long-sleeved Tee. Then I take a deep breath. "Look, I really do appreciate this. And to show my appreciation," I say and bend over to pick up a cardboard box, "I got you these." When I stand, he's unzipping his pants. "What the hell are you doing?"

"What? I'm changing."

"Bathroom is up the stairs."

"Have it your way." He pushes open the kitchen door while muttering something about "real appreciation."

I plug in the electric kettle and set out mugs and sugar and spoons on the island. I'm opening cabinets when Roger comes back in and dumps his wet things on top of his shoes. He sits on the stool that Mary usually occupies.

"I'm looking for something for us to snack on but all that's here is some kind of stomach medicine." I pull out a large wrapped tube that's labeled "Digestives" and set it on the counter in front of him.

Roger practically falls off the stool laughing.

"What?"

"Digestives. They're cookies, you silly arse. Oh, you got to love the Americans."

I cross my arms. "You know that vintage eighties stuff I told you about? It's all gone!"

He slams his fist on the counter and I step back, bracing myself. But Roger just laughs and says, "Touché, Michelle. Tou-bloody-che."

So I pour him his tea and give him the box containing Dad's tacky belt buckle collection. He rummages through it. "Oh, paradise. He's got Blondie, Irene Cara, the Cars. Thanks." He gives me a huge smile.

"I should thank you. You're the one making sure my dad never wears any of them again."

"Shame, that." Roger holds up a huge belt buckle that reads "Michael Jackson Thriller" in sparkly letters. "Your old man does know you are giving these away, doesn't he? Wouldn't want your skull bashed in." He sets the box on the floor.

"It's fine. But why the obsession with the eighties?"

"Actually, it's my business. See, I'm collecting everything I can from every source possible and cataloging the stuff. I figure if I hold onto it all for a few years, it'll become really valuable. Then I'll sell my collection on-line and make a fortune. You never can tell what rubbish will become a hot item someday. So, you holding out on me? Got any other treasures?"

"Well, there is this little rubber Smurf I have. It's holding a paint pallet and a brush."

Roger holds out his hand. "Give it over."

"No way. It has sentimental significance…" I remember sitting with my little watercolor paint box open by my knees, crouching on the kitchen floor and painting a crude flower on a large sheet of construction paper. My mother set the Smurf beside my paint box and touched my head. "Anyway," I say to Roger as I open the cookies and take one, "can I ask you something?"

"Right. Here it comes," he says in a nasty voice.

"Here comes what?"

"The part where you ask me what the hell is wrong with me."

I set down the cookie. "It is?"

"Course. Isn't it?"

"Actually, I…" I wish I could just blurt out what happened to me and not have it sound completely insane. Suddenly I'm again considering ghost theories. Is Christopher a ghost? Then why was I the one people were walking through? Maybe I'm like a Ghost of England Yet to Come. Was he in my time when I thought I saw him at the church? Was I in his time at the castle? Or were we just in each other's minds? "What do you think about going back in time?"

"Oh. Okay. Time travel. Um, why?"

"Um," I say, glancing away. "Just making polite conversation."

"Polite conversation? Not really my specialty, but okay. Time travel. Like in *Back to the Future*, right?"

I shrug.

"*Back to the Future*. Don't tell me you've never seen it." When I shake my head, he collapses as if shot. "God, De Freccio, you're killing me. It is THE classic eighties flick. Honestly, you are thoroughly and hopelessly uneducated."

"But what if you could do it? Time travel?"

He takes the mug and adds three heaping teaspoons of sugar. "Well, there are a few things I'd like to change, I admit." Roger spreads his fingers wide on the countertop. "A crap-load of things, actually." His expression is suddenly solemn. He takes a deep breath. "But I wouldn't. It's dangerous. You'd screw with the space time continuum."

"The what?"

"You really do have a lot to learn, don't you? Look, it means if you change something little in the past, like getting in the way of two people meeting, you royally screw up everything. People never get born. Twits get rich. If you see the movie, it'll all make sense. I only got it on video. You got a VHS player around this place? Then I could lend it to you."

I shake my head. "Maybe I could see it at your house."

"Nope. Never."

"But—"

He bangs the counter and stands. "I'm shoving off." He picks up the box of belt buckles, walks barefoot over to his pile of wet clothes and dumps the clothes and his shoes into the box.

"Wait." I follow him to the back door. "You going to the castle today?"

"I'm off this weekend."

"Oh. I was just thinking I'd like to go there and—"

"Yeah, I get it. And I'm just your free ticket in," he says, sounding annoyed.

"No, I didn't mean—"

"No one ever does. I'm keeping the belt buckles anyway. Got it?"

"Roger Mortley, you totally suck at this friend thing, you know that?"

"That's what they all tell me." He pulls off the shirt I gave him and tosses it to the ground. Bare-chested, he ducks his head and steps back into the storm.

17

Sunday. More rain. Can't stop thinking about Christopher and I'm starting to seriously feel like a fool.

Why didn't I listen to what he was telling me? He said he was seeking "security at all costs." He said he would marry someone else. So naturally I made out with him, right? And now he's gone. He's not even showing up in my dreams.

Suddenly I feel like I'm wearing that huge "KICK ME" sign on my back again. Only I, Michelle De Freccio, could manage to be played and then dumped by someone who isn't even from this century!

But whatever. It's not like he's going to step out of the Washateria and sneer at me, telling me what a joke I am, is it?

Before I know it, Dad's dropped me off at the Washateria with a week's worth of our laundry. Around me bored people sit in blue plastic chairs and watch their wash swish round and round. I load a machine, insert coins and hit the button. Then I move to the spot near the dryer where I'd kissed Christopher. And I stay there through the entire rinse cycle, thinking of him. Willing myself to him, or him to me.

People give me curious looks. But this is all perfectly normal, right? It's just some experiment, that's all.

My mom used to roll her eyes back in her head and moan just before she went into one of her weird trances. When I was really little, I used to sit quiet and awe-struck in the corner of her fortune-telling parlor, a small window-front rental in the center of town with a neon pink eye glowing over the door.

I used to believe in her.

I didn't even doubt her when she occasionally asked me to sit under the tiny table and rap it on cue. I was just so happy to be part of her "other-world experience." I loved it, even though it could get so hot, and the black velvet tablecloth made things way too dark, and it always smelled like feet. One day I collapsed in the darkness and was covered in sweat, trembling, barely able to breathe. Instead of knowing to rescue me, my "psychic" mother gave me a sharp kick when I failed to rap her table. It was like she kicked some sense into me and from then on I stopped believing.

Now, standing here in the Washateria, I don't roll my eyes back into my head or anything weird like that. I just continue thinking of Christopher.

Eventually I have to move our clothes into the dryer. And eventually, Dad comes to pick me up. I sit in the Clockwork Orange with the basket of folded clothes on my lap and stare at the rain streaking the side window, feeling ridiculous and wounded, and willing myself not to cry.

18

Several days have passed. I'm in art class trying to focus on sketching my fingertips but lately I can't seem to focus on anything. I remember how Christopher's fingers brushed my hair aside and how I twined my fingers into his. My heart starts a staccato beat because in my drawing I find another set of fingers starting to form and—

William's knee rubs against mine. My charcoal skids across the page like a needle scratching a vinyl record.

"Someone's wound tight today," he says.

I stare wide-eyed at the page.

"Michelle?"

I exhale and blink. "Right." I pick up my kneaded eraser and remove the mistake. I try again to picture Christopher's hand and start sketching my own hand but nothing extraordinary appears.

William sets down his charcoal and turns to me. "What are you doing after school today?"

"Actually, I want to pick up some art supplies."

"I can take you, okay?"

Now Guncha, who sits on my left, hits my knee with hers. When I look at her, she raises her eyebrows and mouths, "Say yes."

"That's okay, William. I'll manage." I say this even though my dad's already told me he can't take me. He's starting this new Thai cooking class that Mary pushed him into joining at the community school. And I'm really itching to get a linoleum block. I want to start on the print I'd thought about the very first time I'd seen the castle. I could sit outside the castle walls working on it, and I won't have to worry about money to get in. And, well, if Christopher shows up again, who cares?

My pulse starts to race. Who am I kidding?

"Let me take you," William says.

"The store's in another town. What did Miss Turner say? Cheltenham?"

"No problem."

"Big problem. Constance." Something tells me I'd be wise stay out of her crosshairs.

"What does she have to do with this? Honestly, Michelle, I'm just giving you a lift to the store. Aren't you being a little over-dramatic?"

I tap my charcoal on the page. Maybe he's right. And I could really use the ride.

"You can clear it with Constance, if you must," he says.

Or not. "Do you think you could drop me off at the castle afterwards?"

He smiles.

At teatime, Guncha drags me over to the school's library, saying we have to start on our term papers for History. The library is a wing of the Academic Building encased in glass but filled with old bookcases and antique desks.

"Do you have a topic yet?" I ask.

"I'm calling it 'Romancing Power: Women in the Middle Ages.' But who cares?" She pulls me into a back corner. "So spill. I want to hear everything."

I set my book bag onto a table. "What do you mean?"

"Aren't you going to Cheltenham after school with William?"

"It's not like that."

"Well, somebody better tell *him* that. What's going on with you two?"

"Nothing. Really." I feel an uncomfortable flush rise from my neck. I wander over to a lit glass case. Inside are brittle and brown pages covered in handwriting that is barely legible. What words are clear are mostly unfamiliar. Sort of a blend between French and English.

"That's the Wallingford Papers," Guncha says. Together we lean over the case, our breaths fogging the glass. "There's a bunch of books written about them, with translations and all."

"A bunch of books? All about these few pages?"

"There are a lot more pages, all of them letters between Wallingford family members. The library just displays these because they talk about how Percival Wallingford captured that Earl's assassins."

That nasty pointy-nosed Wallingford definitely looked like a Percival. "So Percival Wallingford actually saved the day."

"Not exactly. He just single-handedly captured the two killers, was rewarded and became stinking rich and powerful. Big deal, right? We had to study all about it last year." She rolls her eyes.

"So the translations have all the details about the Earl's murder." I think about the Earl and the way he smiled at Christopher. "That's kind of sad."

"Sad?" Guncha gives me a curious look.

"I mean good. Because I was thinking of doing my term paper on that topic. This info would be really helpful."

"You won't find too many details. This is just a short summary. Nothing was ever written about the murder when it actually happened. Our instructor last year harped on it, calling it a history mystery. He thought he was rather clever." She shakes her head. "See, the papers stopped just before the murder. A few years later, the letters started up again with these pages." She taps on the glass, then sighs. "Well, if you don't have any exciting news about your love life, I guess I might as well get to work."

I give the pages one more glimpse, then hit myself on the forehead. How could I be so stupid? I hurry over to the computer and type "Christopher Newman of Watley Manor" into the search page, but it doesn't find any matches.

Instead I enter: "Christopher Newman" and "Blanchford" and a pamphlet of burial monuments at St. Paul's appears on the screen. I quickly press delete.

When I type "Wallingford Papers," the screen fills with book titles like *The Papers in Depth, Chronicle of a Great Family* and *Spies, Traitors and Heroes*.

I start a new search for "Earl of Blanchley." Several books with the words "Debauchery" and "Murder" in their titles pop up. I click on *Murder in the Dark* and read the synopsis about how the popular Earl, slaughtered in the castle courtyard on March 1st, 1461, was a victim of prominent courtiers who had turned against him. No mention of the king's spies. At least not in the synopsis. The book's entry ends with SEE ALSO: *Tourism, Ghost, Legends, Curses*.

They should also have added SEE ALSO: *Nasty Sex with Anyone in a Chair*.

"Look at this." Guncha drops an open book in front of me and points to a passage. "I was looking up relationships and it says here that in the Middle Ages, all two people have to do is say they are married to each other and they just are, even if there's no priest or anyone watching." She shuts the book. "Isn't that romantic?"

"Guncha, you think everything is romantic."

"Even trips to art stores."

• • •

After school, I hurry home and change, which takes longer than I'd planned because I'm kind of hoping to look really nice. I try not to think about why. I finally settle on a pair of black jeans and flats, and a deep red long-sleeved top with a scoop neck. When I look in the mirror, my hair looks almost tame, with long waves that end in spirals. There's more color in my face and sparkle in my brown eyes, but otherwise I'm the same as I've always been.

I dump my books out of my school bag and take my linoleum cutting tools, some pencils and an eraser from my desk drawer. I spot my little artist Smurf stuffed in a corner of the drawer and set it on top of my desk.

I tighten my lips, toss the Smurf back into the drawer and search for my little first aid kit. Then I remember the kit is not exactly in this century right now. Well, I'll just have to be extra-careful when I cut my print.

The doorbell rings and I take one last look at the mirror, wondering if the scoop neck is a little too low. Hm. At the last second, I throw on a dark blue zipped hoodie and pull up the zipper.

Despite the hoodie, William claims I look fantastic. I give him a skeptical look. We sail smoothly down the High Street, sealed off from all traffic sounds in his sleek car.

"I saw some of the Wallingford Papers in the library today," I say, trying to sound casual. After all, there's nothing weird about two friends driving to a store, right?

"Ah, the great Wallingford Papers." He raps on his steering wheel. "I wish those damned things never existed."

"Why?"

"People expect things from you when you're a Wallingford. You have to act a certain way. Dress a certain way. I'm sick of it."

"Isn't it kind of nice being admired and liked by everybody? I mean, it sure beats the alternative."

"What alternative?"

"You know, being the one everyone picks on, or the one nobody sits with."

"I guess. But those chaps are their own worst enemies. Take Mortley. If he weren't always going into these mad rages, perhaps he'd have a chance. And his family…"

"What about his family?"

"Let's just say he comes from bad stock."

"Huh. You talk about him like he's a breed of cattle," I say, my voice sharp.

"I didn't mean it that way. I just meant he's a product of his environment."

"Just like you are a product of yours," I point out. "The best." I expect him to puff up at this and extol the glories of the Wallingford's but instead his expression darkens.

"Yes. Just like me, I'm afraid." He suddenly looks miserable.

"Oh." I feel like I should apologize for some reason.

"Forgive me," he says, beating me to the punch. "I'm a bit out of sorts today. I'm truly glad we get to spend some time together." He puts his hand on my knee.

I stare at his hand with a weird mix of emotion. "Uh, what are we doing here, exactly?"

"Getting to know each other better? So, how does this fortune-telling thing work? Do you think your mother could be persuaded to tell my fortune? I wouldn't mind seeing a bit of what's coming up ahead."

"Actually, she's not with us." I push his hand off my knee.

"Oh." He gives me a pained look. "Michelle, I didn't know. I'm so sorry."

"No, it's okay. She's not dead. She's just not here. She's away." Then I lie, "She's working."

"Ah, rather like my own mother. Always off doing charity work in lands far away. So, do you have any of her abilities? ESP or anything like that?"

"No." My cheeks burn.

"Are you sure? You seem rather intuitive to me." He gives my knee a squeeze.

I push his hand away again. "I can't do this to Constance. It… it just doesn't feel right."

"Why? You think that Constance is your friend?" He laughs. "Constance doesn't *have* friends. She has ambitions and she uses people to get what she wants. Take me. I was merely a way for Constance to feel more important."

I shake my head. "You're pretty full of yourself."

He raises his chin. "It's not like that. Constance never cared for me. Not really. She was just in love with my family name."

I remember Constance pointing out to me that her boyfriend was a Wallingford. It was one of the first things out of her mouth.

"I just wish you would believe me."

"Huh. I think I do, actually."

"Good. That's good." He touches my cheek.

My mind flashes to Christopher. I can't help it. "William, can I level with you? I think you're great and all, but maybe I don't feel quite the same way about you as you do about me. Maybe it has nothing to do with Constance."

"Ah." He frowns but otherwise doesn't react. He just merges his car into a heavily traveled roundabout, then smoothly maneuvers onto a turn-off and continues down a two-lane highway.

"I've pissed you off."

"No. It's okay. I told you I like a challenge. And I meant it." His gorgeous blue eyes flick to me. "It's high time I actually *earned* something."

"We're *friends*."

"For now."

I cross my arms, feeling almost angry. How can he be so sure of himself?

"Wallingfords are used to winning," he says.

19

Block prints take planning. The areas that you carve away will be white, what is left on the block will be inked black. Once you cut a piece away, there's no changing that.

I'm sitting cross-legged by the edge of the grassy moat between the partly full parking lot and the outer castle wall. And I'm sketching the crenellated walls onto the linoleum block, trying to work out a system of light and dark for the image.

There's about an hour and a half until my dad is supposed to pick me up. The afternoon sun is bright, casting wonderful shadows along the jutting towers. But nothing seems black and white anymore. William was a perfect gentleman today, opening my car door, patiently waiting for me to pick out the block and a few other supplies, then driving me without complaints to the castle lot. He was really sweet.

And now that I'm finally at the castle, it feels like Christopher really is part of the past. A distant dream as old as the pitted rocks in the towering walls. Why be a part of that? Why not live for now? Don't I have a choice?

I would choose you.

I can almost hear his voice in my ear and I pause, expecting to smell cinnamon, but there is only the faint whiff of exhaust from a car idling in the lot.

Stupid.

I should choose normal.

Suddenly I'm tired of looking at the castle. I put the block back into my bag. Try to think of normal things like homework and what's for dinner and if Roger is working today. I didn't notice his truck.

I lie back on the grass and watch a fluffy cloud move across the sky. What if normal is over-rated? I close my eyes and murmur, "Would I choose you?" In my mind I picture him close to me and I feel a pull in the pit of my stomach.

At once my stomach starts to throb. I realize it's actually the ground throbbing. And when I sit up, I face a moat full of sloshing brown water. Behind me, horse hooves pound the ground, echoing the pounding of my heart. I turn to see not the parking lot but a wide swath of green and about a dozen men on horseback riding hard for the castle. They near and race past me, but one of the men pulls his horse to a rearing halt, turns and rides back to my side.

His thighs and arms are strapped into armor that reminds me of goalie pads, only metallic and not as bulky. His face and hands are blackened with dirt, and his hair's matted with sweat beneath a bowl-like helmet. But it's him. He smiles and my heart feels like it stops completely. Then we both laugh like it's all a tremendous joke. He reaches down a filthy hand. Without question, I sling my bag over my shoulder, grab him, set my foot on top of his and let him swing me in front of him onto the horse. He reaches his arms around me, looks over my shoulder and pulls the reins.

I inhale deeply, expecting cinnamon. "Phew, you stink," I say.

"How do you expect me to smell after battle?"

"Battle?" I quickly turn my head, accidentally head-butting him in the face.

He winces, then feels his nose as if searching for broken carti-lage. "Seems I need a helmet with a visor."

"God, I'm sorry." I face forward. "But you mean real battle? Like people stabbing each other?"

"With blood and death and the carrion crows circling. What other type of battle is there?"

"Video games. Sports. Contests. Things like that. Christopher, you could have been killed."

"But I was not. Besides, if I can survive you, I can survive anything."

"Ha ha ha."

"There is someplace I must take you. That is, if you can survive my foul odor a bit longer." He turns the horse away from the castle.

"You don't smell *so* bad. It's just that you usually smell better. Spicier."

"The cinnamon oil. My mother's home remedy to resist the pox."

"Pox?" I turn again. He pulls away in time to avoid being head-butted. I face forward. He chuckles in my ear, but I'm thinking about all the vaccines he's never had, and there's nothing funny about that.

We gallop off, following the moat, then veer off to the right through endless fields. It's not long before we arrive at a cluster of dense trees and bushes. Christopher dismounts and helps me down from the horse. We're face to face and I'm overwhelmed by the attraction between us. And I suddenly don't care about anything else. Not his need for a wealthy wife. Not the strangeness of it all. I lean toward him…

But he quickly lets go of my waist and I feel my cheeks sting. He looks away and busies himself with tying the horse to a bough beside a small winding stream. The horse immediately starts lapping water.

He drops his helmet to the ground and unbuckles the armor from his arms and legs, setting it beside his helmet. I notice a dent on the piece from his arm. "You were hit?"

"It was nothing. See?" He pulls up the sleeve of his navy blue tunic and the white linen shirt beneath it, revealing a nasty purple bruise across his bicep. "My opponents did not fare as well. Much flesh was torn."

I feel the blood drain from my face.

He takes in my expression and laughs. He pulls the tunic off over his head, tosses it to the ground and rolls up the sleeves of his long loose shirt. While he kneels by the stream and splashes water over his hair and neck and under his arms, I pace back and forth trying to shake off the image of carnage he's painted in my mind. Feeling warm, I take off my hoodie and stuff it into my bag. "Were you gone a long time?" I ask.

"Riding off and on for a few days and—" He glances up at me in my scoop-necked shirt and for a moment seems completely distracted. But he looks at the stream, clears his throat and says, "We battled for one day." He busies himself scrubbing his hands and face.

Right. He obviously doesn't feel the same way that I do. Of *course* he doesn't. I don't care. I *don't*. "Tell me about the fight."

He drinks a few handfuls of water, then sits back. "First you must tell me, do you support the House of York and the true and rightful king? Or are you with the so-called King Henry, that addlepated idiot who is not sane enough to know his own name?"

"You shouldn't call him an idiot. He's sick. Like your father was sick."

"He is nothing like my father," he says, indignant.

"I mean King Henry is mentally ill. It's a sickness. It's pretty sad."

Christopher snorts, which seriously annoys me.

"Lots of people are mentally ill, Christopher. Lots of good people." The tremble in my voice makes him look up. "If there was a cure, maybe he would get better and have this really great life."

"Michelle, I happen to know for a fact that physicians have bled the king and attempted to drive out the demons that possess him, and to no avail."

"That's not science. It doesn't fix anything. You know, some day in the future they'll come up with all sorts of medicines and treatments that will—"

"You think too much." He stacks his armor in a neat pile.

"And you don't think enough. You are so, so..."

I'm about to say "medieval" when Christopher says, "So concerned about getting through every day alive." He holds up the dented piece of armor to punctuate his point, then throws it clattering to the ground. "So, am I to take it that you are a supporter of King Henry, then?"

"Honestly, I don't know about kings or crowns. We haven't even studied this part in history yet. I only know that I don't want any harm to come to you."

He nods. "Yes, I have guessed as much. And that is why you bring me luck." He takes something shiny hanging from a chain around his neck and kisses it.

"Whoa. Is that one of the coins from the bag I left behind?"

"It brought us victory. How else can you explain it? Henry's allies outnumbered us two to one. Yet an entire wing shifted sides at the critical point to fight for our side. I call that wondrous luck, indeed."

"But it's just a coin."

"And you are just a girl, right?" He laughs and douses his head with another handful of water.

My throat tightens up. "You know, I think I'd better go." Of course it would help if I knew HOW to go.

"No!" Christopher stands. Diamonds of water sparkle from the tips of his hair. "Please." He reaches for me and I think he is going to take my hand, but instead he pulls back. "Come, follow me." He jumps the stream.

"Why? What's the point?"

"Do you not recognize this place?"

"Should I?" He doesn't answer, so I jump the stream too and we weave through dense growth, parting bushes as we go and unsticking briars that cling to my sleeve. A thorn snags his black leggings, leaving a hole at the knee. Christopher pushes back a heavy bough and the greenery opens to a sunny grove. A cracked mosaic floor split by roots and partially covered with leaves paves the ground.

Part of a stone column protrudes from a corner and another column lays on its side, broken into sections.

"What is this?"

"Ruins of a Roman villa." His eyes linger on me and I feel drawn yet again. My heart picks up the pace, but he just says, "It must have been part of a grand estate once, hundreds upon hundreds of years ago when they ruled Britain."

I realize this must be the Old Roman Grounds, the tract of land that in the future is doomed to be replaced by blacktop and stores.

"I discovered this several weeks after we last met," he says, "and have come back here almost daily, since then."

"But it's only been days since I last saw you."

"*Weeks.* It was August then."

"And now?"

He raises a brow. "Late October, of course."

"Oh. Of course." I step over a log and onto the mosaic. It's made up of tiny colored tiles depicting the head of a woman with swirling dark hair and light surprised eyes.

"It is you, is it not?"

I study the mosaic more closely. The face is of an older woman. If I didn't know better, I'd think it was my mother.

"You see? I well understand," Christopher says. "How else could you possibly be invisible to all but me? How could you disappear from my very… If you are from the ancient gods, lingering here from a time before Christianity, then everything makes sense."

"You think I'm some Roman goddess? From New Jersey?" I burst out laughing and he awkwardly rubs his neck. "Sorry. I'm not laughing at you. It's more I'm laughing at me. I am *so* not a goddess. If you only knew how ungoddesslike I am, you'd be laughing too."

He furrows his brows. "But I thought…"

I blink. "Christopher, that means you came here every day just to see—"

"To see the Italian design and craftsmanship," he says quickly. "I thought to perhaps gain some skill for future construction at my own estate."

"And that's why you came?"

"What other reason is there?" He doesn't meet my eye.

"No other reason," I say quietly, feeling the truth in his words.

"Come, there is much more. Walk carefully. There are weak spots on the ground."

We climb over the column and avoid a bit of caved-in floor. "See beneath?" He points to a stack of bricks in the hole. "There is a space under some of the floors and these rows of bricks are blackened. I believe they put fires under the floors to warm the house."

"Sounds dangerous."

"But clever, given the winters, true? I am thinking of trying something similar in my own home. There is one thing I have not been able to figure out. Right over here." He disappears around an evergreen.

I circle partway around the evergreen and find him beside a long but narrow stone slab with ten circles cut into it. The slab leans sideways like a seesaw. He's rubbing his chin.

"I bet it's the bathroom!"

"It does not look like a bath." He stands very close behind me.

"Not that kind of bathroom." I turn to him. We both take a step away from each other. "What do you Brits call it? A W.C.?"

He shakes his head.

"What's W.C. stand for again?" I say. "Water closet? Toilet? Latrine? You know, men use it standing up, while women…"

"A guarderobe?" He looks at the holes. "So many?"

"Gross." We both crack up. After this, we both seem to relax. He tells me about his own manor house. How he'd ride by his father's side visiting their tenants for news and to offer assistance in any way possible.

"You know, he could have sent me off to a nobleman's house when I was a lad to learn the ways of the world, but he kept me by his side. Taught me. I hope to be such a father to my own children someday."

"I bet you'll be a wonderful dad." An image of him holding a little boy's hand while carrying a little girl on his shoulders springs into my mind.

He looks wistful as if he, too, can see this image. "My father believed we were set on this earth to make each day better than the last. He felt no man is truly greater than another. That we are all equal."

"All equal?" Sort of the exact opposite from the Wallingford Academy's "the best win" motto. "Do you believe that too?"

"I used to." He gives me a bitter smile. "Being equal with others is, I am afraid, just a wonderful dream. For we are none of us equal, none of us truly free to live our lives as we see fit. We can change nothing."

"But couldn't we? Isn't believing in a dream the first step to making it true?"

He narrows his eyes at me.

"What is it?" I ask.

"Just something worth thinking on." He walks ahead. "This, I think, was the outer wall of the estate. Note its thickness."

All that's left of the foundation wall is a wide row of tumbled-down stones, which, aside from a narrow opening, is almost completely covered with vines and shrubs. Remarkably, right beside this stands a tall pillar with snakes of vines coiling up its length. There is the beginning of an arch curving precariously from its top.

Christopher gestures beyond the wall. "There must have once been a vast orchard, because look." A line of bent and twisted fruit trees can be clearly seen between the vines and scrub, and beyond the trees the stream ends in a pond. "Come. I will help you over this pile of rocks." He offers me his hand.

I look up at the arch. "Is it safe?"

"I do this all the time. There is no other way in."

"Okay then." I scramble up and step over the uneven stones. Some tilt or slide as I walk on them. I hear Christopher move behind me, along with the sound of shifting stones. I step slowly, balancing myself with my arms held out. Gritty powder falls onto me. And then I hear something that makes my stomach sink. Shifting stone, from *above*. I whip around to Christopher.

The arch drops like a guillotine, heading straight for him.

20

Massive stones plummet. Instinctively I grab Christopher's arms and pull, leaning backward with all my weight. I free fall and he flies toward me. Everything hits at once with an angry crash. The arch onto the foundation wall. Me onto the ground. Christopher onto me.

Dust whooshes around us and Christopher shields my face with his arm. After all the noise, silence, except for Christopher coughing and me groaning because of a stone poking into my ass.

"My god," Christopher says. His chest presses against me as he coughs again. Suddenly he pushes off of me. "Are you hurt?"

"Just my, well…" I shift. Okay, my ass really hurts, but there's no way I'm telling him that. "I'm fine."

He dusts himself off and helps me up. I sway my hips from side to side to assess the damage. I'll probably have one hell of a bruise down there.

Huge and deadly jagged stones now rest on the foundation ruins. For a moment, it's as if I can't breathe.

"You saved my life." He kisses the coin and gives me a reverent look. "Again."

"Stop that." I breathe deeply, trying to calm myself. "Not a goddess. Remember?"

"Then you are my guardian angel."

I shake my head. "I'm no angel. Think it'll be safe to go back this way?" I nod toward the pile of rubble.

"Safer than ever. But you saved my life. If you had not moved so swiftly, surely I would—"

"It's okay," I say with a tremble in my voice. He leads me to the pond and we sit on a patch of moss. Across the water I notice a white stone sculpture of a dancing nymph. Its finely carved figure and billowing toga glisten in the sunshine. "Oh my God. That's so beautiful." I pull out the linoleum block and erase the castle, then sketch the nymph. Her tilted head, joyous laugh and swirling toga.

"What manner of canvas is this?"

"It's a linoleum block." I draw dark areas of bushes to contrast with the nymph's luminescence, while I explain how I'll carve off areas that I don't want printed, and how I'll roll ink over the whole thing and print it onto paper.

"Like a wood cutting."

"Exactly." I even take out one of my cutting tools and cut away some of the white toga area to demonstrate.

We sit silently while I carve, listening to the chatter of the stream. "This is the way I pictured it," Christopher says after a while. "Being here with you."

"You pictured us here?"

His mouth becomes a tight line. "My apologies. I do not want to make the same mistake again."

"Mistake. Right." I feel stung and I'm suddenly hyper-aware of my too-curly hair, my too-large eyes.

"I am famished. I am going to get us some fruit from the grove. But if I do, I have to know you will still be here when I get back. Promise me you will not vanish?"

I nod. "Sure. I'll try."

"I shall be fast. I swear."

I shift to find a more comfortable position and carve some more, but the dancing nymph seems to mock me with her joy.

So he and I are just friends. No big deal, right?

I set aside the block and cutter, and hug my knees as if it would hold in the sadness welling up inside me.

He returns with his arms full of apples and one in his mouth. He kneels and sets them down and snatches the bitten one from his mouth. "I am glad you remain. I swear I am heartily sorry for my behavior last time we met. It was ill-mannered of me."

I pick up an apple. "Like you said, a big mistake. That's all."

"It will not happen again."

"Right. Of course not. That would be ridiculous, improper, heinous. It's not like this is a normal relationship anyway, right?" I'm babbling. I try to sound casual, when I say, "So, how is your wife-shopping coming along?"

He sighs deeply.

"Come on. Tell." I sound like Guncha, anxious for gossip, but I dread his answer.

Christopher regards me for a moment. "Since you insist. The Earl talks of his ward, Elaine. His wife, the Countess is very particular about the person Elaine shall wed, since this is her own dear cousin and her family line means all to her. I have not spent much time with the ward, but the Earl feels she is very well favored and witty and comely."

"Comely." I grit my teeth.

"Well, you have seen her. The girl in the courtyard last time you were here."

"Her?" I picture the girl's slight figure and plain freckled face. "But she's so young."

"And so rich. Wallingford salivates at the very mention of her estate."

"Oh? And what do *you* do?" I say with an edge to my voice.

His expression becomes grim.

We both take a bite of apple and chew.

"I have a bit of a confession, actually," he says. "I was quite furious with you."

"No kidding. You did pull a knife on me. You have quite a temper, you know that?"

He grins, "Do I?"

"Well, I don't see it now, but you do."

"I suppose, after so much battle, the fight is out of me for the moment." He glances at the nymph. "I became most angered with you *after* you left."

"Why? What did I do?"

"It is what you did not do. Did not say you were going. Did not come back. It was a foul loss. But I came to understand. I had no right to behave so toward you. I insulted your honor." He takes a final bite and chucks the core into the pond.

"I suppose my anger was not for you alone," he says, his eyes returning to me. "My father went so suddenly. It was just over a year ago. He did not even let on he was ill. I thought we had many years for him to train me and show me the ways of stewardship and to finally talk one man to another about my life and future, but—" He glances away.

"But then he was gone." I touch his sleeve. "My mother left me. About a year ago."

"I am heartily sorry." Christopher sets his hand on mine. It's warm and comforting. We sit like this for a while. "When your parent dies, you grow old. Do you not find it so?"

"She's not…" I pull away my hand. "Yeah. I find it so."

"It is nice to have someone to talk to."

"It *is* nice," I say and mean it.

"It has been hard to form bonds at the castle. There has been naught but mistrust, especially after the latest attempt on the Earl's life."

"Really?" I fidget, feeling somehow guilty for knowing that the Earl's going to be killed in March.

"It was an attempted poisoning. Fortunately, the Earl noticed at once that the flavor of his brew was off."

"Wow." I stare at the nymph's reflection dancing in the pond. "So you think it was an inside job again?"

"If you mean do I think that the perpetrator was within the castle, I would say yes. And he has access to the kitchens as well."

"So who could get into the kitchens?"

"That area is not as secure as it should be. Why only last evening, I went in there and found—"

"So you can go into the kitchens, where the food is prepared?"

"Well, yes."

"What about the Earl's private rooms. Could you get into there, like the strangler did?" I raise an eyebrow.

"Well, yes. I suppose. Wait." He flashes me an angry look. "What are you implying?"

"Don't be so touchy," I say. "I was just wondering out loud."

"You really are most…" Christopher stares at me for a long moment. His eyes drop away. "Sorry," he murmurs. "I do not want to offend."

"Hey, about last time: I didn't try to leave you, you know. It just sort of happened. You were just gone. And you weren't in my dreams or drawings like you had been."

"I was angry and hurt and worked to push you out of my mind, yet I kept coming here."

"To see the architecture," I offer.

He nods. "But once, I had a brief vision of your hand in mine."

"Once your hand started to appear in my drawing."

He holds up his hand. "Is that how it works? You conjure me in your drawings? Is that your magic?"

"Not magic. I don't know how it works, exactly. I guess when I'm in or near the castle, somehow I can meet you in your time. And the drawings seem to open some sort of window between us. You might say I subscribe to the 'Internalnet.'" I laugh.

"What is that?"

"It's this thing I made up. You know, a play on words?" Realizing just how much I would have to explain to him about wireless connections and computers and even electricity to make my stupid pun even slightly comprehensible, I quickly give up.

He picks up another apple and takes a huge bite.

"Look," I say, "all I know is we're connected somehow. Our lives intersect, even though you're from the past."

He starts to choke and I hit him on the back. "What do you mean, the past?" he asks.

"The past. Like the ancient Romans are to you? I guess you're like that to me."

His mouth twitches at the corners. "I am like the ancient Romans?" He looks behind him at a fragment of ruined wall and bursts into laughter.

"It's not funny, Christopher. I'm serious."

He shakes his head and continues laughing.

I lift the coin hanging from his neck. "Didn't you see the date on this?" I flip it over and read, "Two thousand and eight. That's three years ago."

His laughter stops as he takes the coin and squints at it. "That is a *date?* I do not believe it."

"What? You think the Roman Goddess story is more believable?"

"I have heard of goddesses. Of unexplained powers and mysteries. But this…" He stands, hands on his hips, and stares into the water. "You want me to believe you live nearly six hundred years into the future?" He turns to me and I shrug. He squints at the fragment of Roman wall, studying it in silence. Finally he says, "Then I am long dead and departed."

"Don't."

"So if I am, indeed, as dead as these Romans, then why do you worry so over each battle I am in? Or of the pox? If my bones are rotted away and—"

"Please." I stand, my hip stiff and sore. "Let's not talk about any of this. Suffice it to say that I live and that you live in this same general area, give or take a few centuries. And I don't know why or how, but we have some bond." I remember him whispering, *I would bind myself to you.* I shake off the thought.

"But this is too incredible." He rubs his forehead. "The battle must have taken a toll on me. Perhaps I was hit on the head and my mind has become weak and addled. And now I am a crazed moronic idiot like King Henry."

"Mentally ill. He's mentally ill," I say in an exasperated voice.

Christopher gives me a perplexed look. "None of this is real."

I watch him pace for several minutes, shaking his head. Then he stops in front of me, rubbing the coin between his fingers. He stares at me for a long while before saying, "Michelle, can you truly be from the future?"

I nod.

He paces some more. "You had said you had not studied my time as yet. This means you *can* study this time? In histories, in records left by scribes?"

"Yeah. Of course."

He stops in front of me again, kisses the coin, then grabs my arms. My breath catches at his touch.

"Michelle, do you realize the meaning of this? It is fated. You truly *have* been sent to help me. You can warn me of battles and outcomes, of the Duke of York's enemies. It will mean victory for him and for *me*." There's a glint in his eyes. He smiles, squeezes my arms and lets go. "This way I will live a long and prosperous life by aiding my Lord the Earl. Do you see? He will surely reward me and I will provide for my family's well-being and prosperity."

"Oh. Great." I focus on putting the linoleum block and carving tool into my book bag and my throat feels choked as I say, "I'm sure I'll help you get an incredibly rich wife. Security at all cost, right?" I hang the bag on my shoulder and try very hard to smile back. "I'm really happy for you, Christopher."

His smile fades.

"Guess I'd better run on home somehow and get to work on that, then." I glance around as if expecting a shiny door to the future.

Christopher touches my wrist. "Stay. I would have you stay."

"Then I can't do your research for you, can I?" I try not to sound bitter. "Besides, what would I do here? Be your imaginary play-mate? Whisper dating tips to you while you serenade some rich chick with the lute?"

He grins. "The lute?"

I hate that my eyes are welling up. I manage to blink away the tears.

He grows serious. "Michelle." His eyes are locked on mine and I see reflected in them the feelings that haunt me. Longing, desire, loneliness. But I remind myself I am wrong. Obviously I am only hearing what I want to hear. Seeing what I want to see.

I force a smile, determined to be as classy as William was when I told him I didn't feel that way about him.

"I would have you stay," he says. "But if you can change my fortune first, then stay with me always, it would be best. Can you not see?" He takes my hand and kisses it tenderly.

I pull away. "I already said I'd help, so just stop. I'm not some fool."

His expression turns icy. "My actions offend." He bows his head stiffly. "Forgive me."

"Yeah. Whatever. My dad will be wondering where I am. I'd better go."

"I will ride you back to the castle at once."

"Great. At least the place will be right."

In an angry silence, we return to the horse. Christopher tosses his blue tunic over the saddle and hangs the armor and helmet from hooks on the saddle's edge. He puts his hands on my waist to lift me but pauses, his brows furrowed. "Michelle, my father's sudden death has taught me time is fleeting."

I feel Christopher's hands tighten at my waist.

He swallows. "I realize you do not feel so of me, yet I must avow my heart to you. If we can secure my noble title and wealth through deeds for the Earl, then I will not have need of a wealthy wife." He takes a deep breath. "And then I could lay my very life down to give you my protection and love, no matter what obstacles rest between us. Your indifference is to my heart a very spear. If I had even the slightest hope you would one day suffer to have me…"

For a moment I'm speechless. "So, you don't find me repulsive?"

"I find you bewitching and lovely." He lifts one of my curls between his fingertips and kisses it.

I feel almost dizzy. "But what if we *can't* secure this noble title?"
He studies my face as if memorizing every feature. "We shall."
"But I'm invisible here."
"Not to me. Could you love me?"
I bite my lip.
"You do not hate me, at least?"
I fervently shake my head.

He pulls me toward him and touches his lips against mine. My arms cling to his back. I hold on like I've never held on to anything in my life. We kiss tenderly, then hungrily.

At once I'm standing alone in a parking lot next to the Township Museum of Roman Artifacts. "You *can't* be serious," I shout and kick an overstuffed metal trashcan.

21

The Township Museum of Roman Artifacts may have a grand name but it's in a crappy cinderblock building with fluorescent orange carpet. Glass cases hold small remnants of the villa that Christopher and I had just explored. Most of it is unrecognizable. Tiny shards of stone claiming to be pottery. Pebbles labeled as beads from jewelry.

Some of the displays, though, take my breath away. The image of an eye and hair from that Roman goddess mosaic. A piece of curved stone I swear fell from the arch. And in the rear of the museum with a spotlight on it, the left half of the dancing nymph sculpture. The nymph's facial features are melted off from time and weather. The stone is now gray and pockmarked with chips and black spots, but it's still beautiful.

"I'm sorry, but we have to close now," says the woman who has been silently watching me for the past thirty minutes. She holds a key ring. "We will be open again tomorrow."

"Right. Thanks. And thanks for letting me use the phone."

"Sure."

I pull a few leftover pounds from my pocket and slide them into the slot of a plastic box beneath a sign that reads: Save the Roman Grounds. Donate Today!

"Thank you so much!" the woman says with real gratitude.

"I wish I could give more. What will happen to all this, if, you know…"

She shrugs. "Don't know. It will relocate, I suppose. What I really worry about are the treasures that remain in those woods."

"There's more?"

"I'm sure there is. This was a limited excavation done years ago. If we could do another dig with more advanced equipment, why there's no telling what we'd find."

I step out into the lot as the door locks behind me. It's getting dark now and chilly, and I rub my arms as I wait for my dad to get me. A breeze swooshes through the trees of the Roman Grounds, making them seem wild and alive.

• • •

"Well, of course I'm aggravated," Dad says, dropping the keys by the hall phone. "I waited for you for over twenty minutes at the castle. It was all closed up and abandoned. What was I supposed to think?"

"Not that I'd been dragged off by a murderer, or…" I trudge up the stairs, my backside really sore. I was prepared to disappear into my room, but maybe a hot bath is a better idea.

"Just a minute, young lady. I'm not done."

I spin around. "Look, I'm really sorry I made you worry. I called from the museum and left a message, didn't I? If we had cell phones, none of this would have happened."

"If you were at the castle like you were supposed to be, then I wouldn't have almost had a coronary worrying about you. And what were you doing by that museum?"

"This, okay?" I pull out the linoleum block of the Roman nymph sculpture.

"Oh." The anger seems to drain from him and now he seems just tired and sad. "Listen, I just worry. If anything happened to you, I don't know if I could…"

I picture my dad, all alone, tears streaming down his cheeks like when my mom left. I step closer. "I'm so sorry I worried you."

"And you've been kind of strange lately. Moody, acting up in class. I was afraid…" He draws his brows together. "I'll get cell phones as soon as I have a free moment, okay?"

I nod and there's an awkward pause.

"Want some dinner?" It's his cheerful "pretend everything is fine" voice. "There's some extra Thai food from the cooking class."

"Sure. Let me just put this stuff up in my room."

The phone rings. As he answers, I continue upstairs but freeze when he says, "Flo? Is that you?"

Mom. I run back down and hold my breath.

"Oh. Sorry, Guncha." Dad's voice trembles. "Yes, she's right here." He hands me the phone and wanders away.

I stand there trying to collect myself.

The night my mom had left, my dad spoke in that same trembling voice. He had said, "Flo, don't do this." I had peered at them from around a corner. "I have to," she said. He begged her to at least tell him where she was going. For how long. Why. But she just picked up her rose-covered bag and said, "I'm sorry. Some day you'll understand." She turned to me as if she knew I was watching all along, and then she was gone.

"Hello? Anyone there?" Guncha asks.

I take a deep breath. "Hey, Guncha. What's up?"

"You tell me. How is William? Things progressing?"

"Progressing, but not with William." I bite my lip. Why'd I say that?

"What? With who? Tell me everything."

Down the hall from behind the closed kitchen door, I hear the jangle of silverware being pulled from a drawer. "We can talk tomorrow."

"Don't you dare make me wait till then. *Who?*"

I hesitate but finally can't contain myself. "Would you believe, Christopher?" I immediately cover my smile with my hand.

She shrieks so loud I have to pull the phone from my ear. "You are kidding! What happened?"

I open my mouth, longing to share everything. Longing to have a close girlfriend. But I say, "Yeah, I'm kidding. It's just a joke. Nothing happened with anyone." The phone grows heavy in my hand. "Bye," I say and disconnect.

That night I sit in bed poring over my history textbook. But it's all general stuff about kings and politics, with a mere chapter on Christopher's time period. There's basic information about the struggle of power between the king and the Duke of York. No mention of Christopher, or even the Earl, so I shut the book and slide it onto my night table. What I really need are details about the Earl's murder. If Christopher could stop that, he'd be set.

I close the light and remember that kiss, wishing it could have lasted a little longer. But the pattern is unmistakable: kiss Christopher and immediately get kicked out of his time. It's as if whatever connection we have to each other is scrambled when our lips meet, forcing my "Internalnet" suddenly offline.

At last I fall asleep. In my dreams Christopher and I hold hands and walk. The sun is bright and warm, and his arm feels warmer as he slips it around my waist.

The next morning in math class, the teacher fills the blackboard with symbols. I start doodling. Christopher's eyes first, then his confident smile. His hair. Soon he's looking back at me and I smile at him, hoping he somehow sees me too.

At teatime I head straight for the library and get right to work. I key Christopher's name into the computer catalog, just because I can, even though I know that only the burial pamphlet from the church will appear. Except it doesn't. Weird. Anyway, I scan the stacks for the most relevant books. A bunch of them are checked out but I'm able to take out six good ones, the maximum the library allows. The pile includes a translation of the Wallingford Papers, some other books about the papers and two about the Earl's murder. It's a start.

•••

After the school day is over, my book bag is loaded with the library books and a slew of homework. I also need to study for a test in math. No sneaking off to see Christopher today.

On the way home I decide to stop by St. Paul's churchyard to see his grave. It's a creepy thing to do, but since I thought I saw him here before, maybe he'll show up. I swing through the rickety wooden gateway and make my way through the graveyard and around to the back of the church.

But his grave is not where I'd remembered it. Another monument shaped like an obelisk is there instead. Convinced I've come to the wrong corner of the church, I start looking around at the other graves. At the carvings of knights and ladies and at cracked stones. He's not anywhere. How's this possible? Then I remember the library search and how the burial pamphlet didn't come up under Christopher's name.

Stunned, I start walking home. Somehow, something has changed.

22

I rush through my homework, then spend the rest of the night in bed reading the library books, looking for ways to help Christopher.

My dad peeks into my room before he goes to sleep. "I'm glad to see you're taking your studies so seriously. That means a lot to me, kiddo."

I feel my face flush as I smile at him and turn back to the book in my lap.

I wade through reams of useless information and feel more and more frustrated. Even the Wallingford Papers translation isn't much help because nothing was written from mid-1460 through 1461. But I do learn something stunning: The two murderers were Plumson and Greenfeld, Christopher's friends. Not good.

I start to seriously worry and pull out my sketch pad for some reassurance. I try to draw him. My lines form a cartoonish face that looks nothing like him at all.

• • •

Two days go by without Christopher appearing anywhere.

On Friday morning I somehow manage to focus on taking notes in math, but my doodles in the margins remain lifeless sketches. What if his so-called friends the murderers did something to him? I rub my eyes, pushing away these thoughts.

In art class, I start an oil painting, roughing out the image of a castle turret with charcoal. I lay in color, hoping Christopher will appear somewhere in the shadows, but my strokes reveal nothing.

Instead of taking tea in the cafeteria with the others, I hurry to the library. One boy with thick glasses pores over a textbook and bites a nail. Otherwise the area is empty. I sit, flip open the sketch-pad I'd swiped from art and touch the charcoal to the paper.

And I think of Christopher. I try to push away the growing panic inside me and center my thoughts on remembering the hair hanging over his forehead and how it felt to have his haunting eyes look into mine. I stare at the blank page and pretend I'm staring right at him.

Where are you? I need you. With a jerk, my hand starts to move and the charcoal scritches against the page. Cross-hatching fills the paper with dark shadows. At the very center is a lighter area and I see his eyes. The charcoal dances lightly across the paper shaping his nose, his smile. After I trace the edge of his chin, the charcoal drops from my fingers and rolls away.

"Hi," I whisper, moving my fingers to almost touch Christopher's face. "I was so afraid I'd never see you again. I—" My throat feels too choked to continue.

"Hello, gorgeous," a guy says from behind me. I whip around to find William looking over my shoulder. "Who are you talking to?" He gives me an odd look.

Immediately I flip the pad over. "Nobody."

"Look, I know Constance has a way of twisting the truth to suit herself, but I have to ask. She told me you and Mortley are, shall we say, involved. Are you?"

"Constance said that?"

"Yes. Constance. Your *friend.* She seemed rather delighted, actually. Said someone spotted him shirtless, coming out of your house. Are you and Mortley anything more than friends?"

I stand. "No. Of course not."

"Of course not." He rubs his eyes. "I thought so, though how you can be friends with him is a bit beyond me. Okay, that's it. I'm trusting you and I'm never listening to Constance again. Enough said on that matter, okay?"

"Uh, sure." I shift my drawing pad in my hands.

"Something wrong? You seem rather distracted."

"Distracted? Oh, it's just…" I look around the library. "It's my term paper. Yeah. I can't seem to find enough research."

"What's the subject?"

"Subject? Er. The Earl's murder? Well, see ya."

"Wait." He suddenly seems nervous and glances around. "I might be able to help with your research. There's something I could show you."

"Great. Thanks. Could you excuse me?" I take my book bag and drawing pad, and almost run to the ladies room. When I flip the pad over, Christopher's face is gone, replaced with a smear.

• • •

Seven more days pass.

There's no sign of Christopher.

Not in my drawings. Not in my dreams.

23

I'm walking through the hall to History in a semi-trance when William snags my arm. He says, "Can I speak with you?"

I blink and focus on him. "Sure."

"I haven't really seen you for a while. How about we go to the chip shop right after school? I'll buy."

"Yeah, okay," I say and move toward my classroom.

His hand stops me. "After that, there's something I need to show you at my house. For your term paper."

I remember that library of books at his house and perk up. "Sounds great. What—"

Before I can finish my sentence, he nods and quickly walks away.

In History, Mr. Llywelyn gets my attention when he says, "Now we are going to look at the personal life of Englishmen from this time period." I take notes about the black plague killing half of England's population. Entire families were wiped out.

My hand shoots up.

"Yes, Miss De Freccio."

"Was this around the year fourteen sixty?"

"Ah, one of the two missing years of the Wallingford Papers. The hardship continued through fourteen sixty, certainly. Actually that was a year of great conflict and battle."

I feel someone's stare, and sure enough, Constance's cat-like eyes are trained on me. She smiles.

Mr. Llywelyn continues, "King Henry was insane and the Duke of York was rallying his troops to take over. We'll be discussing this later in the term. Now the monarchy had grown unstable—"

My hand flies up again and I blurt out, "So there were lots of battles? Lots of people killed that year? Plague too?"

He tents his fingers. "Plague came and went throughout that period. Certainly the life expectancy was short at that time anyway, and much battle and intrigue helped to further decrease the population, especially when you factor in the beheading of many traitors whose skulls were then set on a pike outside castle walls for all to see."

At once I picture Plumson and Greenfeld's heads, open-mouthed and bloody. Did Christopher suspect his friends were the traitors?

Now I see Christopher's head on a pike. It is lifeless yet horror-stricken and so real.

I can't feel my feet. I try to breathe deeply but think I'm going to be seriously sick. I grab my books and bag and stumble out of the class. Behind me Geoffrey shouts, "She's pulling a Roger Mortley!"

I stumble down the stairs and push open the school's front door. I take in great breaths of cool misty air and convince myself the vision I just had of Christopher wasn't real. It was just a thought. An imagining.

The sky is mottled gray and a mist covers my face and forms pearl-like drops on the sleeves of my black Academy blazer. I hug my books to my chest, feeling queasy.

What if Christopher gets the plague or if, right at this moment, he's fighting a battle he won't win? What if Plumson and Greenfeld harm him?

That can't be right. He wouldn't be doing *anything* now. Whatever happened, happened a long time ago. Maybe there's nothing I can do to change history. But if that's true, why did his grave disappear?

And why has he been gone for so long?

I nibble on my thumb. Roger had said something about a space-time thing in that movie. What if I somehow hurt Christopher just by seeing him?

Among the sleek and the expensive cars in the front lot, I find Roger's junker. He's still in class, like everyone else, so I lean against the truck and wait.

About a half hour later, students pour out of the Academic Center ready to head home. My hair is damp and frizzed from the mist and my woolen blazer smells like a musky dog.

Roger arrives at his truck. "What?" he says in a weary voice.

"*Back to the Future.* I think I have to see it, like, today."

He gives me a lopsided grin. "Let me get this straight. You're experiencing a Michael J. Fox emergency?"

I shrug.

"Michael J. Fox. You don't know who that is? Jesus, Michelle, what the bloody hell is wrong with you?"

"Can I see the movie today? At your house?"

He shakes his head.

"But—"

"Let it go, De Freccio. You are not coming to my house and that's final." He climbs behind the wheel and slams the door.

"Michelle?" It's William, at the other end of the lot. Crap. I forgot all about going to the chip shop with him today.

Roger starts up his truck. There's an odd moment when I think about pretending I was just here waiting for William. It passes, and I race over to the passenger side of the truck and jump in.

"What the hell?" Roger says. "Get out."

William strides toward the truck, his usually serene and beautiful face reddening.

Roger catches sight of this and a smile spreads on his face. "On the other hand, this could be a bit of fun." He revs the truck and swerves out of the parking spot, then zooms toward William, purposefully hitting a puddle that sloshes brown water all over William's charcoal slacks.

As we peel out of the lot, I look in the cracked side mirror to see William shaking his fist, screaming with fury.

I sink into the seat.

"Thanks, De Freccio. That's the most fun I've had all week."

"He's going to make your life a living hell, Roger. You know that, don't you?"

"Par for the course." He steers the truck down the High Street and pulls into a spot in front of the butcher shop. "Get out."

"But what about the movie?"

"You've had your fun pissing off your boy; now the game's over."

"This isn't about William."

"Bollocks it ain't."

"Seriously, Roger. I just need to see that movie. It's important."

Roger taps the steering wheel. "Important, eh? You and your lot have no idea what is or isn't important. Everything is so damned easy for you, isn't it?"

"What is your problem?"

"Oh, here it comes."

"You think you know me but you don't. I know what it's like to be the loser of the bunch." I raise my voice. "The one everybody loves to torment and mock. And believe it or not, I know damned well what's important in this world because nothing has EVER been easy for me. I'm outta here." I throw open the door and swing out my leg, when Roger's hand closes on my arm.

"Hey," he says. "I thought you wanted to see the movie."

I blink a few times.

He says, "It might be okay. So long as my old man's out." He nods.

After a moment, I nod too.

24

"Want more?" Roger asks, nudging me with a bowl of buttery popcorn.

"Huh? Oh, yeah. Thanks." I'd been so lost in the movie, I'd almost forgotten that I was at Roger's house on a ripped couch in front of an ancient TV. Cardboard is taped over a broken window-pane, leaving us in a murky darkness. It's like I'm trapped in an old sepia photo—one that's coated with dust and reeks of cigarettes.

I grab a handful of popcorn and pass the bowl to his sister Violet, who sits on the other side of me. Violet is nine and has the same straw-colored hair as Roger, only it's a little longer. Her too-short pants and T-shirt make her seem like she's taller than she really is.

When I first came in the door, Violet looked really surprised. Roger gave her a hug and whispered something in her ear, and she nodded, seeming to relax. Violet then slipped her little hand in mine and we were instant friends.

Now Violet takes some popcorn, sets the bowl on the floor and snuggles against me. I drape my arm around her shoulder and smile at Roger. He rests his arm behind me along the top of the couch. This feels like the most natural thing in the world. Like we're a cozy little family.

We continue to watch but I fill with dread when Doc in the movie warns Marty about meddling in the past. About how it

could have catastrophic consequences. The music becomes ominous and Marty's family picture starts to disappear.

"Whoa. What's happening?"

"Space time continuum," Roger says. "He messed with the past
and if his parents don't get together, then he won't ever be born."

Now Marty's hand becomes invisible and soon it will be like he
never existed. Is this why Christopher's tomb vanished? "Oh my
God. No."

Roger touches my back. "Relax. It's just a movie."

Suddenly Roger's hand becomes tense and I hear a rattle at the
front door.

"*Shit!*" Roger jumps to his feet and shuts off the set.

"Wait. You can't stop it now," I say.

I hear a growling voice in the front hall.

Violet instantly has a doe-in-the-headlights look.

"What the hell kind of greeting? What the hell!" a man's gravelly
voice shouts.

Roger grabs Violet's shoulders. "Get her out," he says to her
and races out of the room. "Hey, Dad. Back so soon? Dinner's
almost—oof."

It sounds like the air is knocked out of Roger. I go to help him
but Violet grabs my arm with surprising strength. "No," she whispers intently. "You'll make things worse. Just *go*." She pulls open
the window and I barely have time to grab my blazer from the
couch when she practically shoves me out into a trash-strewn alley.

"Is someone here?" the dad shouts.

"No, I swear," Roger says, fear in his voice. There's a crash.

"Violet?" I whisper, my voice trembling.

She shakes her head and shuts the window.

Even with the window closed, I can hear their father shouting,
things crashing. I stand there, unable to move. Unable to stop the
intense pounding of my heart and jittery weakness in my legs.

Unable to do anything to help them.

I soon realize where I am: in an alley on the wrong side of Castle
Road, with the sun going down and no way home. I don't even

have a cell, because my dad just got it and it's still charging at home. My school bag is in Roger's house. Normally I'd just knock on the door and ask for my bag and a lift home, but there is absolutely nothing normal about this.

So I emerge from the alley onto the street crowded with row houses in various stages of decay. A breeze whistles by, stirs the edge of my pleated skirt and sends a white plastic bag skittering along the cracked sidewalk. In the distance off to the left is the edge of a castle turret.

Hugging my school blazer tight, I start walking in that direction, telling myself once I get to the castle, I'll be able to figure out the way. I quickly reach the corner of Roger's street and turn left onto a winding road crowded with rotting row-homes. Shadows crawl across the sidewalk as the sun sinks lower and I quicken my pace. As the road twists, I see a cluster of guys ahead of me. They're hanging on a doorstep, laughing and talking loudly.

One of them spots me and shouts something, and before I know it, I'm surrounded by about eight guys in torn shirts and jeans, and extra-large sneakers. They tug at my blazer. "Oi, here's a posh one," a freckled one says. "Give us the high society treatment, love," shouts another.

"Leave me alone!" I say in a strong voice as I start to walk forward. I'm almost past them, when a cold hand grabs my wrist and pulls me back.

"Leaving so soon?" someone with horrible breath says. "Think you're too good for us blokes?" He clamps both of my wrists now. I scream and kick and try to free myself. They laugh. Hands grab at my waist. A hand goes under my skirt.

I thrash and give the guy holding me a hard kick between the legs. He lets go and falls back on his buddies. I dash away. Race as hard as I can, my legs pumping faster than my heart. But somebody is right by my side wheezing. Someone else shouts, "Get her, Bobby!"

I don't dare look behind me. I'm guessing the castle is a block away. If I can only make it there. Someone lobs a wooden plank at my legs and I trip. My knees and hands hit pavement with scorching pain. The one named Bobby, a short muscular guy, throws me on my back, and with a flash of silver he holds a knife at my neck. We stare at each other, panting. The others surround us again.

"Get her into an alley," another says.

"Don't," I manage to gasp. "Please."

As rough hands drag me off the sidewalk, I shriek "Christopher!"

They laugh. "Calling your posh boyfriend?" Bobby says. "Guess he can have you when we're through."

I close my eyes and hear a scream. It's not me.

My eyes fly open. Bobby cradles his arm. Blood seeps through his fingers. "Who did that?" He looks around wildly.

I back away and another guy tries to grab at me. He shrieks as his thumb is sliced off, seemingly by nothing. It lands bloody beside me. I catch a glimpse of a rusty truck in the street before I close my eyes and curl up in a ball. Tears streak my face.

There's more terrified screaming, then I hear them run away.

"Michelle. Michelle?" someone says and touches me. I whimper. "It is okay. I came. They will not hurt you now." I feel the hand rub my arm and he says, "Shh now. Shh."

I dare to open my eyes and there is Christopher kneeling beside me, a blood-smeared sword in his right hand. He drops the sword and gathers me into his arms.

25

Christopher leans his head against mine. "You are safe now."

I can't respond. My hands throb. My knees burn with pain. My entire body is trembling. I realize we are no longer in the alley between two row homes but on a strip of dirt between two rough wooden shacks. It's dusk and inside a shack I see the smoky orange light from a fire.

Christopher looks over my shoulder. "Thomas, search for them."

"For who, Master?" The servant studies him with unfocused eyes.

"The men who attacked this lady."

"What lady?"

"Do as I say!" he shouts. Thomas bows and runs off.

"You are cold as stone. Take my cloak." He unpins his cape and drapes the heavy brown material around my shoulders. When he takes my hand, I wince, so he turns both of my hands palm up. They are deeply slashed and bleeding from my fall. He grabs his sword and stands. "They will die for this, I swear it."

"Don't go," I say in a very small voice.

His jaw becomes tight, then his hand relaxes on the hilt. "No. No, of course not." He wipes the blood off his sword in a patch of weeds and slides the weapon into a scabbard hanging from his leather belt. He takes my elbows and gently helps me to my feet, cursing between clenched teeth when he notices my knees. Hot blood oozes down my shins to my black knee socks. His brows furrow and he pulls the cloak tight in front of me.

"No sign of the ruffians, Sir," Thomas says.

"Bring my horse closer." He lifts me into his arms. "We must return."

Thomas looks right through me. "But, Sir, what of the Earl's mission? Wallingford said—"

"Mission be hanged. Lady Michelle is wounded."

"But, Sir? Where is the lady?"

"Here." When he hoists me onto the horse's back, I feel weak and light-headed. "We must get her to the castle at once. *That* is our mission." Christopher climbs behind me onto the horse. "Do not look at me so. I am in my right mind. Ride quickly. She is losing much blood…"

I feel like I'm falling backward into a dark black hole.

• • •

A ripping pain in my knees makes me groan.

I smell cinnamon oil and I open my eyes to see the drawing I'd worked on for Mary. It hangs on a rough stone wall. I'm on a small bed in a tiny chamber lit by a fireplace.

"Sorry. I am being as gentle as I can," Christopher says. He sits beside me, wringing out a cloth into a small wooden bowl.

"It's you. Not a dream."

He smiles, then becomes serious and looks away. "Your wounds need care but certainly are not life-threatening. One on your left knee is a bit bad but I bound it tight and it should mend."

"I thought I wouldn't see you again."

He stands and says in a cool voice, "When you feel well enough, you may leave. Your things are over there." He nods to a corner where my shoes and socks are set and where my blazer hangs from a peg in the wall. "Farewell." He bows.

I sit up. "Farewell? Are you kidding me?"

"I am no fool." He turns away.

"Then why are you acting like this?"

"I saw you in a vision. Perhaps you were conjuring me through a drawing. I saw him standing too near you. Saw his eyes looking over your shoulder. Did you think I would never discover the truth?" He turns back to me. The anger in his face hits me like a slap.

"Who? I don't know what you're talking about."

"Wallingford," he shouts. "What do you take me for? I admit I believed your words. You knew just what to say to me, how to manipulate my emotions. Then you vanish again, leaving me bereft, with naught but a few tokens." He tears my drawing off the wall. "You and he must have had a great laugh. I trusted you, let myself give in to my feelings, and what do I see? A vision of Wallingford and you."

"No, Christopher, you've got it all wrong."

"Then when I felt you threatened, I had to come to you. I let myself be pulled to your side, abandoning the mission the Earl sent me on. Only caring for you. Not caring what the consequences would be to my future. All only to find this." He points at my blazer.

"My uniform? Sure, it's kind of ugly, but—"

"You wear Wallingford's crest."

I laugh. "For *school*."

"Dare not mock me." His eyes are bright with fury. "Wallingford is the one trying to deter me from wedding the ward. And I suspect Wallingford is the one who sees to it I miss most of my missions. And you, you are Wallingford's minion. His whore."

"No. You've got it all wrong. Everything."

"Why should I let your words work their poison again?"

"Because you have to trust me. That is my school uniform. I go to Wallingford Academy. I'm sorry, okay? I can't help it if the Wallingfords are big mucky-mucks in the future." My voice becomes choked. "I can't help it."

He sinks into the chair and fingers the coin around his neck.

With a steadier voice, I explain, "The eyes you saw belong to William Wallingford, Wallingford's great-great-great something or other." I reach out my hand, which is bandaged with a thick rough cloth. "He looked over my shoulder when I drew you. And he means nothing to me. You do believe me, don't you?"

He silently digests all this for a few moments. Finally he sighs. "And tonight I have yelled at you. Again. Forgive me." He swallows hard and gently takes my hand. "But why were you out there showing your legs?" His voice grows stern. "And unescorted in such an unsavory sector? What did you expect to happen?"

"It's not like that in the future. Girls wear short skirts. They walk by themselves."

"And men freely attack them. You must be more sensible."

I smile. "You're sexy when you're all overprotective. You know that?"

"This is not an amusing matter. I must know that you will be careful or I shall lose my sanity." He shakes his head. "When I felt your fear and then found those men attacking you something snapped inside of me. I felt I *would* go mad if I could not save you."

"And you did save me. You cut them, sent them screaming." I shudder. "How?"

"I do not know. Somehow your danger brought me to you."

"I wasn't meant to be there on that road. It was all an accident." I fall back onto the downy pillow. "I was at my friend's house. I'm pretty sure his dad hits him. A lot."

"Him?"

"Chill out. We're *friends*. And I couldn't help him."

"Worry not and rest." Christopher smoothes my hair and pulls a quilt over my legs. "All is well."

"But is it? Christopher, what does it mean if someone is not buried in a churchyard?"

He brushes his hair off his forehead. "Well, it could mean that the person is damned to hell and therefore unfit for holy ground."

"Damned? What do you mean?"

"A sinner, a suicide, a criminal."

"Or it could mean the person never died. Couldn't it?" I wish that this could somehow be the reason for his missing tomb.

He laughs. "Yes, one would hope that that would prevent a burial."

I rub my eyes and try to make sense of everything. "Okay. Tell me what's changed since I last saw you. Better yet, tell me what's changed *because* I saw you."

He leans back in his chair. "Well, I suppose I have been quite a bit more cheerful of late."

This makes me smile.

"Humming. Joking about. *Not* playing the lute, however. My temperament has actually put me in rather good standing with the Earl. He considers me quite good company and I have accompanied him on several hunts.

"Wallingford was actually quite livid with jealousy. It seems he has not been able to plead his case with the Earl for a wealthy match with his ward or any other female. Yet I have the Earl's ear for afternoons at a time and now it seems I have no need for a wife whatsoever." He runs his finger along my jaw. "I confess the Earl finds Wallingford a gloomy and detestable fellow."

"Not good."

"On the contrary. This is all quite good."

"Not if Wallingford thinks he's got to bring you down in order for him to shine. You don't want to make any enemies."

"Wallingford is no threat. He is a spineless, witless, sniveling cuttlefish. But his father…" His expression darkens.

"What about his father?"

"He is a sour, power-hungry man indeed. One I would not turn my back to."

The image of the hook-nosed man with a fur-edged cloak walking with the Countess springs to mind.

Christopher is saying, "With a father like that, I actually feel a bit sorry for Percival."

"Right. Just don't feel too sorry." I throw back the blanket. "Could you get me my stuff?"

Christopher hands me my shoes and knee socks and blazer.

"Just remember, Wallingfords aren't used to losing." I finish tying my shoes and put on my blazer. And when I stand, the room spins.

"Steady, there." He grabs my arm and helps me back onto the bed. "Rest now. Your wounds need time to heal and I need time with you." He rubs his thumb on my cheek.

I groan. "We don't have time. Can't you see? You have to ride out on that mission for the Earl. The one you didn't go on because of me, right? What was the mission, anyway?"

"To visit the Earl's estate and see to the safety of his ward Elaine who is currently residing there. There have been threats against all Yorkists. But do not worry. Wallingford discovered my delay and has sent Greenfeld in my stead to fulfill the Earl's request."

"Greenfeld. Huh. Won't the Earl be angry with you not going? I don't want anything to change, especially because of me."

"Perhaps the Earl will be angered, but he cannot doubt my loyalty."

"You sure about that?"

"I will talk with him."

"Good. And watch out for that plumb-guy and Greenfeld too."

"Plumson and Greenfeld? Whatever for?"

How much will I mess things up in history by telling Christopher about them? Or about the Earl being murdered in March? "Just mind your own business and stay away from them. They'll only get you into trouble."

"They are harmless and honest fellows. What can you mean?"

I could tell him what I know. Christopher could save the Earl's life. He'd be a hero and be rewarded big time. But that movie...

I bite my lip. Before I start really screwing with destiny, shouldn't I think things through? Get as many facts about the murder as I can? The books I've read weren't much help, but maybe William does have some info I can use. Anyways, March is months away. I've got some time to figure it all out. "Just trust me, those guys are really bad news. Actually, maybe you should hang out with Percival Wallingford once in a while."

"You jest."

"Maybe he can be okay." Especially considering how he ends up a hero. "Look, I've got to check out some things that might help us. I definitely need more information." I grab his tunic with my fingertips and pull him close to kiss him.

He grabs my shoulders and pushes me away. "Wait. Each time we kiss you disappear."

"I know. But I have to go so I can help you. And I'll be back." I tease him with my lips barely touching his.

"Not fair," he whispers. Our lips meet and I passionately kiss him. I press myself against him and he is right there with me, one hand tangled in my hair, the other slipping my shirt off my shoulder.

Until he's not there.

26

"Oi, what are you doing here?" James says. "The castle's closed." He stands at the door leading from the castle chambers back into the courtyard. "Trying to nick something, are you?"

"Uh, no. It's just me, Michelle. Roger's friend. Remember?"

"Come out into the light." He steps aside and I follow him into the courtyard, my hands and knees seriously burning with pain.

"I just got a little lost." I wonder how late it really is. Except for the lights mounted above the main gateway, the courtyard is shrouded in darkness.

"And I'm supposed to believe that? The castle closed over a half hour ago." He crosses his arms and I notice an "Assistant Manager in Training" nametag pinned to his Blanchley Castle T-shirt. "I have to report you."

"But I didn't touch anything. I just got misdirected. I fell and…" I look down at the blood soaking through the cloths tied to my hands, feel the hot blood drip down my shins. For a moment my head whirls.

"Jesus. You aren't going to sue now are you? You Americans love to sue."

"I'm not going to sue. Just let me go."

"And risk my job? It's bad enough this damned Ghost Tour isn't staffed yet." He pulls out a cell and slides it open.

"Listen. What if I sign up to work for the Ghost Tour?"

He puts his cell in his pocket. "I'm listening."

• • •

I shiver in the dark and empty parking lot beside the castle. Finally I hear Roger's bomb of a truck approaching. He pulls up beside me and I climb in. "Let's get out of here," I say.

"Not so fast." Roger kills the engine, turns on the overhead light and gives me a weird look.

"What?"

He pokes my shoulder.

"Can we go now?" I say. "My dad must be freaking out."

"*I'm* freaking out." He runs his fingers through his hair. "And so is your dad, for that matter. When I called, he asked me all these questions about when I last saw you and he was seriously worried."

"What did you say?"

"Not the truth, I'll tell you that." He stares out the front window. "Then William Wallingford calls and harasses me. Says he knows I did something to you and that he'll sic the police or his goons on me."

"Roger, I'm sorry. What did you say?"

"Who cares what I said? De Freccio, I spent the last two hours driving the streets, torturing myself over what might have happened to you, whether I should bring in the cops and kicking myself for putting you in danger in the first place. And thinking… I don't know what the hell I was thinking."

"It wasn't your fault."

"Bollocks it wasn't. Everything is always my fault. I'm Roger Mortley, remember?"

"Roger, it's okay." I touch his arm.

He grabs my wrist and looks at the bloodstained bandage. "Bloody hell." He looks at my other hand and my knees with the blood seeping through the cloths. He covers his eyes. "Christ."

"It's okay. I'm okay now."

He pinches the bridge of his nose and takes deep breaths. "Thought I'd imagined it."

"Imagined what?"

"Doesn't matter." Roger starts the truck and pulls onto the castle's drive leading out. "Nothing matters anymore, eh?" He flicks off the overhead light and we drive past the massive dark castle wall to the main road.

"Some things matter a lot. Like your sister. And what's happening with your dad. That's not right, we should tell—"

"We tell no one." He makes a sharp right. "Got that? You didn't see anything. I didn't see anything. And I've got it all under control."

"Right. Look at us. Two people with things completely under control."

"I can handle it. I've got a job and a plan and money socked away, and when I'm eighteen I'll take Violet and we'll never have to deal with that sorry bastard again. You blab like some do-gooder and all you'll get us is a series of beatings and Violet taken away to some home without me to watch over her."

"That's why you don't sleep?"

"Shut up, De Freccio. Don't talk about things you don't understand."

"What about your mother?"

He's silent for a while, then says, "You'd asked me if I could go back in time and change something, what it would be, remember? That would be it. I'd notice my mom's illness and make her see the doctor in time. My dad, he took it hard." He looks haunted.

"I'm so sorry, Roger."

I start thinking about hauntings. Legends. Curses. The lore of the past. Maybe it holds some truths I can use. "Hey, can you tell me about the castle ghosts now?"

"Ghosts?" He snorts but seems very distracted, looking in the rear and side mirror over and over again, until he quickly pulls over onto the side of a dark winding road and turns off the motor again. We sit silently, listening to the tick of his engine. "Look, I know it's going to sound like I do drugs or something. But I don't, got that?" He turns to me but his face is cast in shadow.

"Yeah, I got that."

"I got away as soon as I could get Violet over to Mrs. Sawyer's next door. Then I drove after you. I saw those guys in the alley." He swallows.

"Oh." I hug myself and feel fear creep over me again.

"And you. I was about to honk my horn and jump out to give you a chance, when… I don't know."

"You saw something." I turn on the overhead light.

He squints against the brightness. "Nothing." He moves his hand toward his key.

"Don't you know by now you can tell me anything?"

Roger sits back and gives me a sideways look. "Okay, then. A flash of a sword. Not a knife. A *sword*. A guy in a cape. And you disappearing." He levels his gaze at me.

"Yup."

"Yup?"

"Yup. That's what happened. I need to hear every castle ghost story you know."

"Ghost stories? God, De Freccio, I thought *I* was nuts. Tell me where you went."

"Into the past?"

"The past? Back in time? Like Huey Lewis and the News sings? Like Michael J. Frikken-Fox? You're crapping me."

"Remember that guy Christopher I asked you about? The one in the drawing I did? The one in the painting at the castle? Well…"

"Well, what? He's the one in the cape I saw? He's real? You actually expect me to believe he's real?"

"Why not?"

"Look, if you don't want to tell me the truth, just say so, okay?" He reaches up and clicks off the light, restarts the engine and pulls back onto the road.

"Fine. Whatever." I yawn and my head sinks against the window. "The ghost stories?"

He shakes his head, looking annoyed, but soon he starts talking about how the Bloody Chapel is so named because there's supposed to be bloodstains on the floor tiles, only he's never seen them and there's no story behind it. And he says that during past Ghost Tour nights, people claimed to hear moaning from the dungeon. "And you already know about the cursed spot," he says, "right where the Earl was found with a dagger in his back."

Christopher keeps a dagger in his boot. But I bet everyone had one of those back then. I say, "I read there were two killers: Plumson and Greenfeld."

"Yeah, Plumson. My noble ancestor."

"You're kidding."

"I told you, nothing but blame here. Everything is my fault, or my family's. We're low-lifes, yeah?"

"You are not a low—"

"Save it. And then there's the story about the ghost hanging from the rafters. A suicide that supposedly appears every once in a rare while. I'd love to see that one."

I sit up. Suicide? Christopher said that was one of the reasons someone wouldn't be buried in a churchyard.

I notice we're almost at my house. I also notice William's car parked out front.

"Uh oh," Roger says, seeing the car too. He stops just past Mary's house. "Think I'd best bugger off."

"Thank you, Roger. I think you're wonderful, you know that?"

"Yeah, right, like bad cheese left out until—"

I kiss his cheek and that shuts him up fast. I get out of the truck. Before I close my door, he says, "Don't forget your book sack. It's in the back. So, what are you going to tell them?"

"Oh, I'll just say I was kidnapped by a very attractive ghost. I'm sure they'll totally understand."

"Yeah. You're screwed."

27

As soon as I reach my driveway, Mary trots to me. She grabs my arm and crows, "Oh, thank the heavenly gods." Her white tracksuit glows in the streetlight.

"I'm fine."

"You are not fine. You're bleeding, child." She takes my book bag. "Donald? Donald! Come quickly."

My dad rushes down the drive, cell phone in his hand. "Michelle." He hugs me, scrunching my face into his chest. "I was so worried. Yes, she's arrived, Officer."

I look up and see he's talking into the phone.

"I will. Yes, thank you." He slides the phone shut and kisses my head. "Oh, my little Sea-Shelly," he says with a tremble in his voice.

I swallow hard.

"Who did this to you?" It's William, who stands just behind my dad. He glares at my knees.

"Oh, well, I fell."

"Mortley."

"It wasn't him, William."

"I saw his truck just now," he says in a sharp voice. "I don't know why you're covering for him and I don't care. The guy's a danger and he's going to be sorry." He pulls his car keys from the pocket of his leather jacket.

"He's a good guy and he's the one who found me and brought me home, okay?"

My dad holds me at shoulder length. "Where were you? What happened? You seem so preoccupied lately. Is there something you need to tell me?" His forehead is lined with worry.

"Never mind that, Donald. Mind her legs. And just look at her hands. They're bleeding!" Mary wrings her own hands. "We need to take her to hospital."

I'm convinced Mary's just being dramatic until my dad peeks under the dingy cloth on my left knee and I make the mistake of peeking too and nearly pass out. William's stern look softens and he lifts me in his arms. "Right. We'll take my car."

"Not your car. I'll bleed all over your fancy seats." I again picture what my knee looks like and almost swoon.

"You'll be okay." William kisses my head and gently places me in the back seat. Dad slides in next to me and William takes the wheel and starts the engine. Mary slides into the front passenger seat and the car sinks to the left.

"Mary," my dad says, "why don't you stay home? This could take a while."

"Nonsense." She turns back to me. "Don't worry, little lamb. You'll soon be mended."

British hospitals aren't much different from American hospitals, except everything seems to be white: the walls, the sheets, the uniforms, the floors, which seems impractical for hiding blood stains like the ones that drip from my legs as we wait for a doctor.

Mary and William stay in the waiting area, while my dad and I are led back to a room with a bed. The doctor has a black beard and moustache and wears a turban on his head and a stethoscope around his neck. "How did this happen?" he asks while unwinding the cloth from my hands.

"I fell."

He glances at my dad.

"I wasn't there," my dad says.

"The wound is starting to look infected. No wonder, with this unclean cloth." He swabs and bandages my hands, then turns his attention to my knees, cutting away the layers of the fabric and throwing it in the trash. Some is stuck with blood to my knee and he gives it a quick pull. I see stars...

After, back in the waiting room, I sit between Mary and William while Dad answers some questions at the front desk.

"So? How's our little patient?" Mary pats my cheek. The seat beside her is filled with empty candy wrappers.

"Okay. Tired."

"What did the doctor do?" William asks.

"Gauze on my hands. A tetanus shot in the arm. A butterfly bandage on my right knee and five stitches on the left."

William whistles and wraps his arm around my shoulders.

"Oopsie!" Mary says. "I just remembered something I have to tell your father." She winks and stands.

"You poor thing." William rubs my arm.

"Ouch," I pull back. "Tetanus shot, remember?"

"Sorry. Quick, before they come back. Tell me what really happened. What did Mortley do?"

"I told you. He didn't do anything. Like I told my dad, I went to the castle to sign up for that job and found out it was really late and started to run home but I fell, and Roger drove by—"

"Roger did this to you. Why don't you admit it? Are you afraid of him? I'll protect you, you know. I'll tear that moron apart and make him sorrier than he ever thought he could be."

"That's sweet in a way. But you're wrong about Roger. Everyone's wrong about him. You complain that everyone expects you to be perfect because you're a Wallingford. Well maybe everyone expects Roger to be this jerk because they've labeled him, too."

William frowns. "You saw him in art class. This kid's completely out of his head."

"Why? Did you ever wonder why?" I stand slowly on my stiff knees. "If you want people to see you as more than just a Wallingford, then maybe you should see more in them."

William stands. "Looks like your dad's ready to go now," he says in a cool voice as he pulls the keys from his pocket.

On the way back, I doze until William stops at our house and lets us all out.

My dad shakes his hand. "Thanks, son."

"My pleasure, sir."

"Bye!" Mary titters and waves, and yanks my dad away, leaving me and William by the curb.

"Thanks again," I say. "I didn't mean to sound harsh back there, really. You're always so nice to me and I feel like I'm so horrible to you. You don't deserve that. You're great."

"Not as great as Roger Mortley, though."

"Come on. Don't be like that. Listen, this weekend maybe you could help me with my term paper on the Earl's—"

"I'm busy this weekend." He ducks back into the car and zooms off.

When I get into the house, Mary says, "So? You and William? What is happening?"

I'm so exhausted, I can barely explain that we're just friends. I think that after tonight, we'll probably not even be that. Mary leaves and I trudge up to my room, kick off my shoes and drop into bed.

"No P.J.'s?" Dad asks. He's hovering by my door.

"Too tired." I close my eyes.

"Your new cell's down in the kitchen, fully charged. Bring it with you tomorrow and from now on."

"'Kay."

I feel my bed shift and know that he's now sitting at the foot. "Shell, you got anything else you want to tell me? Anything at all? If something is wrong, if you're afraid something is happening to you, if you feel yourself losing control in any way…"

"G'night, Dad." I snuggle my face against the pillow. I'm almost lost in my dreams where I see Christopher's hand reach out to me. I smile and murmur, "Love you."

"Love you, too," Dad says.

28

It's Monday. I wander down the school hallway, my knees and hands still throbbing with pain, and my mind in a sleep-deprived funk. I've spent too many late nights drawing Christopher's image over and over again, and skimming through history books packed with too much general information. Even books that were supposed to be about the Earl's murder had barely any facts about that and devoted most of their pages to things like the customs of the day and what people wore.

William walks past me with some friends. I hurry to his side. "Hey, got a sec?"

He closes his eyes for a long moment, before giving me an icy glare. "Not really."

"Ugh. What happened to your knees?" Geoffrey says to me. "You look like hell."

"Mortley's going to regret that, eh?" another guy says and he and Geoffrey high-five.

"What do you mean?" I ask.

"Forget it," William says, then leads me by the elbow back toward the stairwell. "Look, what do you want?"

"Well, I've been having trouble with my term paper. You know, about the Earl's murder? So I thought that you—"

"That I *what?*" He looks almost fearful. "Don't answer that." His eyes dart about.

"But you'd said that you had some info at your house. I just wondered when you could show it to me."

William's icy glare returns and he laughs. "You're really crazy, aren't you?"

I step back, stung.

"I can't believe I've been trying to impress you. You're just like everyone else. You use people and only care about yourself."

"William, please. I'm sorry you're angry with me. I really am. I never meant to hurt you."

His look thaws a little.

"So, could you help?"

He drops his gaze. "I don't have anything for you." He walks away.

• • •

"So it's off between you and William?" Guncha asks.

"It was never on."

I'm sitting beside her and Justine is in the seat across from me. We all hold up our mugs of tea. I take a sip, hoping the warm liquid will somehow soothe my throbbing head. I need to start sleeping more and drawing less. But sketching Christopher is irresistible. Charcoal drawings of him riding a horse, or striding through a castle corridor, or donning armor. Sometimes his eyes look in my direction. Sometimes he must see.

I have my back to William's table but I know he's there. And so is Constance. It's Thursday and William has barely spoken to me for days. He's been acting weird ever since I'd asked him for info about the Earl's murders.

Guncha sets down her mug. "Maybe you and William can work things out. True love wins, you know."

True love wins. I can't help but sigh.

"Leave her be, Guncha," Justine is saying.

"But it just seems a shame, you know? Chances like this don't come that often. Or ever. Look at this place. It's a boy wasteland."

Tiny Peter Nunnly looks up from his Suduko puzzle to give her a nasty look.

"No offense," Guncha tells him. "But you know what I mean."

He considers this, nods and goes back to his puzzle.

I stare at my tea and wonder what my life would be like if Christopher and I had never met. Would I feel more attracted to William? Or would I still feel that there's something missing between us and that William is somehow lacking? Then again, maybe I'm the one who's lacking. Maybe I *am* losing it after all.

Justine gasps.

I turn and gasp too. It's Roger. His bottom lip is purple, swollen and there's a cut on the side of it. His right eye is swollen shut and the surrounding skin is crimson.

"God, Roger. No." I jump to my feet. "You have to report him. You *have* to."

Roger barely forms a crooked smile with his misshapen mouth. "I already did." He nods behind him toward the door, where the Headmistress herself guides William out of the room.

• • •

William's not in art class when I arrive. He's probably suspended, which is fine with me. Roger's already at his table in the back, hard at work on his project. I set my book bag on my chair, walk over to him and peer over his shoulder. He's hunched over a large sheet of Bristol board doing a pen and ink pointillism of a large Smurf.

"Looks pretty good," I say.

He lifts up his pen and glances back, his partly swollen right eye in a semi-permanent wink. "I figure," he says and winces, touching his split lip, "sales ad someday. For my business."

"Smurfs and the eighties. Right."

"So why don't you give me that artist Smurf of yours like the friend you claim to be?"

"Give it up." I lean closer. "Look, what really happened with William?"

"Think I'm lying? Kiss off, De Freccio." He turns his back to me.

I try to squat next to him but the stitches in my knee stop me. "Just tell me what happened."

Geoffrey says, "Your asshole buddy here became a rat-faced bastard. That's what happened." He chucks his blazer on the table.

"Go to hell," Roger says.

Miss Turner claps her hands sharply. "Everyone get to work on your independent studies now."

I'm surprised to find William now at his seat, setting out a pot of India ink beside a piece of parchment.

"Great," I mutter and head to my spot next to him. Guncha sits on the other side of the table sculpting a small mound of clay. I lift my canvas onto an easel and study my roughed out image of the castle tower. I put on a blue apron and it aggravates me to no end that it has the Wallingford crest embroidered on its pocket. I give William a nasty glare.

"What's your problem?" William asks.

"My problem is—" I bite my tongue. I refuse to talk with this jerk. Of course he's off the hook. Constance Hunter must have worked some of her magic with her Headmistress mother, or Mr. Wallingford probably demanded every charge dropped and it simply was. Must be nice to be so privileged.

William uncorks his inkbottle. "I didn't do anything to Mortley. Though I wish I did."

"Why would Roger lie?"

"Ask yourself that one. And by the way, it's really touching to know how much you believe in me." He mumbles, "Don't know why I ever bothered…"

I glance at the calligraphy project he's working on. It starts off with, "Wallingford Lies. Herein rests the truth as," and it stops abruptly.

Well, he would know about lies, wouldn't he?

I twist my hair up into a bun and stick a thin paintbrush in it to hold it in place. I squish out blobs of color onto the palate. The warm, oily smell of the paint is comforting and familiar.

Okay, deep breath.

My brush swirls into the powdery Prussian Blue and dabs into the zinc white and the blood-red crimson, and in the center of the palette I form a pool of rich smoky blue. Will it look right for the moat? I dab the color onto the stark canvas and step back, studying its tone.

Instead of getting lost in the picture, I'm hyper-aware of William sitting beside me. How could this guy, who was so sweet to me when I was hurt last week, be the same person who did that to Roger? Then he wonders what my problem is. Of all the nasty, self-centered, evil…

I grip the brush tightly.

Forget him. I obviously didn't know him at all. I think of all the cruel things William and his buddies did to kids—tripping them, throwing them into ponds. And how he always thought he was above everyone else. The nice, kind part of him that I kept seeing was probably just some act. That's what's missing from William. He lacks real character.

Just paint and relax, I tell myself. I touch my brush to the canvas and it yields just a bit, as I press color on in flowing strokes. I spin my brush and an image of flowing water forms with darker eddies and flecks of dancing light.

My mind circles back to William. Really, he's just a bully. And bullies are cowards. Maybe it's genetic. In the books about the Wallingford Papers, you could tell Percival was a total coward. In the translated excerpts, whenever Percival would make a suggestion to his father, he'd follow it up with several written lines of apology for daring to do such a thing.

While I've been lost in thought, my brush has dappled the water with shadows, but I realize the shadows aren't random. I pull back my brush and notice something hidden within the depths of the moat. It's as if I've zoomed into a battle scene.

I drop my brush on the palette and grip the edges of the canvas. It's covered with a succession of images. In each, Christopher wears a helmet. His hand wields his sword. His arm is sometimes raised, sometimes pulled back. His teeth are clenched. The muscles in his neck are tensed. In the final image he's collapsed to the ground, his head tipped back, his mouth open.

"No. No!"

Silence surrounds me. Everyone gives me weird looks. William's eyebrows are raised.

"What's wrong?" Guncha asks as she comes toward me.

I grab a rag and, with a shaky hand, scrub the canvas until all that is left is a muddy swirl.

29

I rush toward home after school. Clutched in my hand is a small book called *The Cotswolds at War: Battles in the Mid-Country*.

I never bothered with this book before because it didn't have any info about the Earl. But I've decided a March murder is too far into Christopher's future. I need to help him *now*. The pages spell out all the battles in this area during the War of the Roses. After quickly flipping through it, I've already learned that on December 30th, 1460, King Henry's forces lay in wait for an ambush at Wakefield.

I try to tell myself everything will be fine. And think of what Christopher will do with all the information these pages hold. How not only the Earl but maybe even the Duke of York himself will shower Christopher with riches and protection. He'll be able to provide for his family. And to be with me.

And we'll be seriously messing with history. People will die that shouldn't. People will live that shouldn't. Who knows what ripples of change will flow from that into the present.

But he's fallen.

I stumble and try to steady myself by holding onto a low stone wall. I realize I'm in front of St. Paul's cemetery and for a moment I feel completely lost.

I throw open the rickety gate to the churchyard and make my way to the back of the cemetery where Christopher's grand tomb once stood. The obelisk is still in its place. It's covered with green lichens and it seems so solid. It almost makes me wonder if Christopher's tomb was ever really here at all. Time suddenly feels so jumbled and uncertain.

I should run to his side, give him this book, but...

I sink onto the grass and page through the book. There were a lot of battles during 1460, but what month would Christopher be in now? It was so cold the last time I was there. Was it November? December? His time goes so fast.

That image of him, lifeless, fills my mind.

But it wasn't real. It was a painting. Just a painting. Everything will be okay.

I deep breathe. Try to focus on something else, anything else. My vision rests on a small yellow slab of stone beside the obelisk.

My God.

I run my fingers over the stone's etched words. The feel of them adds truth to what they say: Here lieth C. Newman in the reign of our King Henry VI.

The year of death is etched in Roman numerals in the stone. The first letters are illegible. The last ones, "LX," are all too clear. Sixty. Fourteen sixty.

I jump to my feet. Hurry through the cemetery and trip over a broken gravestone. When I hit the sidewalk, I flat out run as fast as my torn-up knees will allow.

In my room, I yank on warm jeans, a black tee and a gray woolen sweater, and throw a thick black hoodie into my book bag. It could be deep winter there by now. Nearing the end of fourteen sixty. I *can't* be too late.

I slide my new cell into my pocket and grab the library book. I know I'm messing with history. I'm messing with the space-time continuum.

And I don't care.

30

"Here's your visitor's badge, Miss De Freccio," a woman sitting at the castle admissions counter says. She hands me a sticker and I put it on my sweater. "Let me just ring up Personnel and let them know you're on your way." She picks up a phone and I ease away from the counter and get lost in a crowd of tourists.

So far so good. Mary's bike was available. And, thanks to a little lie about needing to fill out paperwork for my Ghost Tour job, I'm now on the castle grounds.

Entering the castle under the dark archway, my mind focuses on Christopher. His light eyes. The warmth of his hand. And there he is at the other end of the gateway, silhouetted from the sun in the courtyard. His cape flutters in the gentle breeze.

"Michelle?"

It's not Christopher. It's Teddy the lute player. "Personnel is waiting for you. I'll take you."

"I can find it on my own."

"I've been asked to take you myself." He turns on his heel.

"Oh. Great." I follow him across the courtyard and he holds open a small wooden door.

We enter into a modern office space with desks and computers. At the main desk a woman says, "Miss De Freccio? Why don't you have a seat? James will see you shortly."

James? Maybe he was already promoted. I sink onto a plush wingback chair. Set down my book bag. Crack my knuckles. Think about Christopher's gravestone. I stand. "Sorry, but is there a bathroom near?"

"You mean a toilet?"

I nod and she points with her pen down the hall to the left. "Thanks." I hoist my bag onto my shoulder and head for the hall, hoping for a doorway out, or at least a large window.

"But you could make me look like a ghoul," someone says. "Like a victim of some of the instruments of torture. That'd be brilliant."

I freeze.

"Sorry, Roger, you know I'm new at this. I can't just bend the rules for you. Consider this a vacation, eh?" James stands at the door to an office and practically pushes Roger away with a beefy hand.

Roger's back is to me. He crushes his feathered cap in his hand. "James, please. You don't understand. I need the money."

"Sorry." James steps back and slams his office door.

"Damn it!" Roger throws down his cap and strides past me, his face now marred with a new slash down his left cheek.

I pick up his cap and rush after him.

"Miss De Freccio?" the receptionist calls.

Roger throws open the wooden door with his usual fury and storms into the courtyard. A schoolboy raises his camera and says, "Say cheese!"

Roger growls and steps toward him, and fear fills the boy's face.

I clap my hands. "Wow, the Tortured Courtier makes another appearance. Kid, you're lucky you got to see him. Take your picture fast." I hand Roger his cap and whisper, "Smile. You don't want to lose your job permanently, do you?"

Roger plasters the cap on his head and forces a hideous smile. The boy takes his shot and runs away.

"My God, Roger. He's actually *knifed* you," I say, my stomach churning. The raw cut runs from his cheekbone nearly to his jaw. "William should be in jail for this. And you should see a doctor."

"I should see a shrink for hanging out with the likes of you. This is all your fault. You had to come to my house. You had to mess everything up. Now I can't even make money for me and Violet to…" He puts his hands on his hips and blinks.

"I never knew William would be like this. I'm so sorry." I put my hand on his arm.

He jerks it away. "Sorry? Lot of good that will do me now, eh?"

"Roger, please. Don't be mad at me. You're my friend. From the looks of things, you're my only friend."

"You and me, we don't need friends. Remember that and go straight to hell." He marches past me and past a bunch of boys.

One points and says, "See? That's the Tortured Courtier."

"Oh kiss my arse," Roger shouts as he leaves the courtyard.

Suddenly people are looking at me. After all, I was the one talking with that crazy cursing maniac. Head down, I cross the courtyard toward the door on the opposite side.

My fists clench as I'm seized with wild anger. I wish William was here right now. I'd slash his perfect face with a linoleum cutter and laugh as the blood flowed over his strong chin and onto his neatly ironed shirt. Then in my head I hear a man's bitter voice: *"How would I profit…"*

A young man says, *"Unhand the Earl!"*

The bitter voice says, *"Take death."*

A deep voice speaks. *"I will haunt you."*

I stagger forward as a fierce pain stabs at my back and my breath escapes in a desperate gasp.

The pain dissolves, along with the wild anger. I realize I've just walked through the cursed spot where the Earl was killed.

Trembling, I glance frantically around the courtyard. No one is around who could have said such things. My heart flutters with panic.

I'm hearing things. I'm losing it.

With my hands still shaking, I pull open the huge wooden door and disappear into the dark castle hallway, trying to forget the voices, trying to forget Roger. All that matters is Christopher.

31

After weaving through halls lit by electric torches hung on the walls, I find myself in the sitting room with the Persian carpets. The Earl's Mating Chair is back and several elderly ladies ogle it with a mixture of delight and disgust.

Christopher's painting is gone. Nothing's on the wall over the chair. Not even a nail for it to have hung from. It's like it never existed.

Never existed.

I tear down the corridor and up a narrow flight of stairs, thinking: please come to me. *Please.*

I notice a smell. Not cinnamon but smoke. The torches aren't electric but real torches, burning and sputtering. I see the small alcove where I had first found Christopher, but his seat is empty. And I feel very alone.

I turn a corner. A door flies open and I jump. Christopher's servant Thomas comes barreling out, his arms full of torn, stained cloths. He closes the door and speeds past me.

I take a deep breath and open the door. The flickering fire in the small stone hearth casts a shadowy light. Christopher is in his bed asleep. I close the door and press my back against it. My eyes fill with grateful tears. I'm not too late.

He is bare-chested, a sheet covering him just below his arms. His one arm is flung over his head and his chin is turned toward the fire. The coin he took from me hangs on a chain around his neck, a silvery orb resting in the hollow of his throat. I quietly set my bag beside the door, peel off my sweater and crouch beside the bed, wincing from my sore knees. But what do sore knees matter? He's here and he's real and he's safe and he's even more beautiful than I'd remembered. I'm glad he's asleep so I can look closely at him without embarrassment. The pout of his lips. The curl of his dark lashes. His flexed bicep. I long to touch him but can't bear to wake him.

I'll draw him.

I tiptoe back to my bag, rummage for my sketchbook, but all I find is the book and my jacket. Damn.

Suddenly I remember my messenger bag with my art supplies. They must be here somewhere. I scan the shadowy room, barren except for a high-backed wooden chair, a rough side-table covered with stacked cloths and a bowl of water, and a wooden chest at the foot of the bed.

I open the chest and feel a whoosh of affection as I find the green tunic he wore the first time I'd met him. There's also a bundle of letters tied with a ribbon, probably from his mother, a brush, some woolen stockings and a thick long brown cloak. And my sketchpad. I take it out along with my pencils, which I find at the bottom of the chest. There I also find a large leather purse.

I bite my lip. Of course it's none of my business what's in the purse. I sneak a glance at Christopher, who hasn't moved.

I'm sure he would show me the contents if I asked. I untie the leather strap and open the top. Inside I find his treasures. The bear brooch and what appears to be a deed of some sort. The writing is impossible for me to read, just like the Wallingford Papers were, but it has a large red waxy seal on the bottom and I can make out the words "Earl of Blanchley."

At the very bottom of the pouch I pull out my Chapstick and my little first aid kit. *He loves me.* My entire body floods with warmth. I carefully replace these things in the chest and close it.

I pull the heavy chair to his bedside and start sketching, capturing the highlights and shadows cast by the dancing firelight.

Now joining the warmth in me is a weight that presses against my throat and my ribs. A gentle ache. Is this what being in love feels like?

My pencil draws every line of his face, the curve of his mouth, the familiar way his strong chin juts out slightly, the line between his brows.

I lift my pencil and look at him more closely. His breathing seems ragged. His brow furrowed. I now notice his color is pale. There's a sheen of sweat on his brow.

"Christopher?" I drop the pad and touch his brow, pulling back quickly as if burned by its scorching heat. "Oh, God." I rest my ear to his chest and listen to the reassuring lub-dub of his heart, and when I sit up, the sheet slips, revealing a lumpy cloth tied across his ribs.

It's soaked with blood.

32

"Christopher?" I shake him. He doesn't wake up. "No. You can't do this. I can't be too late." With a trembling hand I pull my cell phone from my pocket, sliding it open. It doesn't even light up. I shove it back into my pocket.

Tears fill my eyes and I gasp. "Stop it," I tell myself sternly. "Pull it together. I just have to save him. That's all." God, why didn't I ever enroll in a first aid course?

First aid! My kit. I toss open the trunk and rummage through it, pulling open the purse and taking out the impossibly tiny first aid kit. I hurry back to his side. "Okay, modern science to the rescue." I open the kit and inside are three Band-Aids, a Midol pill, a small foil tube of antibacterial cream and one alcohol wipe. That's it. I sink onto the chair.

"Okay. I can make this work. Don't worry, Christopher. I've got this totally under control." If he can hear me, I desperately hope he doesn't notice the terrified tremble in my voice.

I stand. "It's way too hot in here. You're way too hot, and not in a good way." I notice the shuttered window and pull at the latch, till the shutter swings open and cold air blasts into the room. "Right. That's better."

It's a clear, moonlit night. From the window I see the snow crusting the land below. So it is winter. But is it still 1460, the year etched on that tombstone?

I turn back to him and my heart takes a nosedive. His hair lays damp around his face.

"Are you overdressed?" I peek under the sheet and feel my own feverish blush rise. "Okay, definitely NOT overdressed." Pulling the chair close, I pick up a cloth from the side table, dip it into the cold water and blot his forehead and neck. "I could never be a nurse. I don't mind taking care of people but I can't stand the sight of…"

I swallow hard and dip the cloth in the water again, squeezing it out. I run the cloth along his arms and across his broad chest. "I wish you'd wake up. Just blink your eyes or something. *Please.*"

No reaction.

I set the cloth into the bowl, take a very deep breath and peel the sheet back away from his wound. I slowly unknot the cloth tied there and, squinting, pull back the cloth. My breath catches. It's a long bulging slash, oozing blood and… I cover my mouth and swallow again as my stomach knots. I can't bear to think of what is oozing out of that slash.

I grit my teeth and force myself to really look at his wound. I was so afraid it was his guts bulging there, but now I see it's actually leaves and mashed brown stuff that's been packed into it. "What's all this crap in it? No wonder you have a fever." I move my fingers close to the wound, but can't bring myself to take any of the junk out.

"I…I'll just see if anyone is around to help, okay?" I smooth back his damp hair and kiss his clammy brow. "Don't go anywhere."

Pulling open the door, I hear voices down the hall. It's a gray-haired gentleman, along with Percival Wallingford and his father who again wears that mangy fur-edged cloak.

"But we must apply leeches immediately," the older man says. "If we bleed him, there is still hope."

"No leeches!" I shout.

"No leeches," Percival says and purses his lips. His father nods at Percival with approval.

Yeah, Percival.

"But sirs," the gray-haired man says, "the Earl commanded the best care for Newman."

"The Earl, in his absence, put Newman's care in my charge and my son's charge, good man," Baldwin Wallingford replies in a condescending voice. "I cannot believe the way the Earl dotes, especially after what happened."

"Father, you know Newman had nothing to do with Greenfeld's death. I was the one who sent Greenfeld in Newman's stead. I know the ambush on him was random."

"Silence," Baldwin hisses, giving Percival a murderous stare.

Percival flushes.

So Greenfeld is dead... That's one less person to murder the Earl, then.

"The Earl left us in charge," Baldwin says to the gray-haired man. "And I say let nature take its course."

The man shakes his head. "If I did not know better, I would say you would see this man dead."

"I assure you this could not be further from the truth. My son happens to hold Newman in some regard and so Newman is dealt with differently." Baldwin pulls something from his cloak and presses it into the man's hand. "And you would be wise to say nothing more on this."

The man hesitates, then nods and as he passes me, I see his hand holds three gold coins.

"What the hell was that?" I march to the Wallingfords.

Baldwin pats Percival's back. "All will be well. Follow my instructions to the very letter."

"Sirs!" Christopher's servant rushes toward the Wallingfords. "I brought more cloths as asked. Is the leechmaster in there now?"

Baldwin raises his shaggy brows at Percival. "I must go at once to attend to matters at home. I trust you can handle this?" He claps his son on the back, turns on his heel and goes.

Percival clears his throat. "Thomas, I am afraid the leechmaster had to leave quite suddenly."

"Leave? That surly bastard. My master will not last the night without a sound bloodletting. But with your aid, sir, we can see to his care. Order a fresh poultice for the wound. Scare up some leeches."

"Uh, I am afraid I am rather busy, Thomas. I have my orders. The Earl has charged me with running the workings of the castle in his absence. Being sure it is well guarded."

"But, sir—"

"Remember your place, servant. Do not question me."

"Yes, *sir*," Thomas says, clear hatred in his voice. As Percival goes down the stairs, Thomas mutters, "You fetid lump of horse manure."

I suddenly like Thomas *very* much.

Following him into Christopher's room, I'm touched by how he pats Christopher's cheek and says, "There, now, good young master. All's well. Thomas will see to it."

He scowls at the open window. "You need the sweats." He pulls the window shut.

"No, Thomas," I say. "He's too warm." I push the window open.

"Must have not latched it." He shuts it again and closes the latch.

I turn open the latch and open the window. "This is better. Trust me."

Thomas looks wild as he backs against the wall. "W-what is this? Ghosts? D-demons?" He waves his hands. "Go away! God curse you and send you back to hell!"

I cross my arms. "Great."

Christopher moans and I sit by his side in the chair and touch his hot cheek. "You're burning up. Thomas, we have to save him. Do you hear me?"

"Shoo!" He kicks at the air.

"This is *serious*." I pick up my sketchpad and wave it at him. "Yo. Over here."

He starts chanting something in what I guess is Latin.

"Well this is just frikken great." I set the drawing pad at the foot of the bed and sit back.

Thomas jumps. "W-what is this?" He takes a few cautious steps toward the pad.

"You see it? You do, don't you. Yes!" I pick up the pad.

"W-where did it go? Oh heavenly angels protect me and my master."

I scrawl: It's me, Michelle. Christopher's friend. I need your help to save him.

I set the pad down on the bed and no sooner do I let go of it, than he jumps again. He shakes his head. "Devil's work."

"No, it isn't. Read it."

He picks it up and frowns.

"You can't read, can you? Fantastic." I try to snatch it from his hands, but my hands rake through the pad as if it were a mere hologram. "Okay, so I can't take it from you then. Put the pad down."

He keeps staring at the pad.

"Put. It. Down," I shout.

He sighs and finally does.

I flip the page and glance at Christopher. My heart feels strangled. I bite my lip and sketch a goofy Valentine's Day heart complete with an arrow slicing through it. In the middle I print out "CHRISTOPHER," hoping Thomas knows his master's name at least.

Thomas looks thoughtful. "Lady Michelle? My master's spirit friend? You really exist?"

"Yes!" I draw a big smiley face.

"Be praised. I had thought his mind had twisted."

I flip the page. We need to think of what to do. Clean the wound. We need sterile cloths, clean water. I sketch a kettle filled with steaming water, then a pitcher and a glass of water so we can keep him hydrated. But what we really need is a miracle.

Thomas studies my drawings and mutters, "A boiling pot. A bottle of mead. Yes Milady. At once."

"Water. A bottle of water," I say, but he's already left the room.

I sit by Christopher. "We'll get you better. I swear."

But his breath is shallow and ragged.

33

"We'll build our own Roman villa with a wonderful wing for your mother and sister," I say and sponge sweat off Christopher. "Can you hear me?"

No reaction. Christopher's natural rugged color turns a waxy yellow. He's fading. Why is Thomas taking so long to return?

"And we'll put a mosaic of both of us on the floor of the main room. And we'll try that heating idea and have an orchard where I'll feed you apples, and you can strum on the…" Filled with emotion, I can barely whisper "lute." I kiss the tip of his nose.

The door opens and Thomas orders two men to carry a heavy kettle to the fireplace. The men hoist the kettle on top of the logs and dust off their hands.

"Now be gone both of you," he says and shuts the door behind them. "Oh, he looks bad, Milady." He sets a tray with a mug and pitchers on the bedside table. The first pitcher is filled with red and pungent mead. The second, water.

I pour water into the mug and open Christopher's mouth, dribble a little bit into it, but it just leaks out the sides. "Okay. Maybe we'll try this later. We have to clean this injury, Thomas, and fast."

I could try to communicate this with a drawing, but…

Wincing, I tug at one of the leaves stuck in Christopher's wound and fling it to the floor. The room spins.

Thomas squints at the wound. I tug at another leaf but it seems to be stuck. Bile rises in my throat. I pull a little harder and it comes free, along with some of the brown stuff, which spills onto the sheet beside him. I sweep it to the ground. Fresh blood drips down Christopher's side.

"But, Miss, that is the poultice. It is a fine one of the best herbs and nuts and berries. We cannot get a fresh one and without the leeches this is our only sure hope."

"No, Thomas. If there's one thing I know, it's that we have to clean this thing out. We have to." I pluck out another leaf and throw it. Christopher's breathing is wheezy now, his chest rises and falls rapidly.

Thomas puts his coarse hands in front of the wound. "I will not let you do this. You will kill him."

I know I can reach right through his hands to Christopher but I don't know if I can handle touching that stuff much longer. I grab the pad and draw a huge heart and set it on the floor.

Thomas clenches his hands. "I love him too," he says hoarsely. He furrows his brows for a long moment, then pulls up his sleeves and fearlessly scoops out the horrid poultice, placing it on a square of linen set on the floor. Poor Christopher writhes but his eyes remain closed. I whisper to him and press the cool cloth to his neck.

"There, done." Thomas wipes the gore off his hands and throws the rag with disgust into the corner.

"Now we have to really clean it, right?" I toss some of the cloths from the table into the now-boiling kettle. I have no idea how long to boil them. After a minute I use a poker beside the fire, fish them out and hang them, steaming, on the back of the chair.

"Use these, Thomas."

He just stares at the cloths. So I grab one and blow on it till it cools a little and start wiping Christopher's torso. When the cloth gets too filthy, I grab another. Now I dab at the edges of his wound. Thomas puts more cloths into the hot water and hangs them along the chair back.

I wipe and dab and the blood comes fresh, but I can't see any more of that poultice junk. So I clean my hands and rip open the alcohol wipe, swabbing the ragged edges of the wound. No reaction from Christopher. I squeeze antibacterial cream into the wound. It's not much but there's enough for a clear line of gel to run the length of the cut. The oozing blood quickly hides it.

"Right. Now we have to stop the bleeding. Apply pressure." I look at the gaping wound. "I don't know what to do. What should I do?" I turn to Thomas, who is mumbling a prayer. Then I look back to the tiny kit. Three Band-Aids.

I dry the area around the wound, pull the skin closed with my fingers and put Band-Aids crosswise to hold the edges together. When I let go, the edges start to separate. Blood soaks the Band-Aids.

"God. More cloths." It's as if Thomas hears me because soon I have a wad of sterilized cloths over the wound, holding the Band-Aids in place, and two more wrapped around his torso, pulled tight to apply pressure.

I clean my hands, then Thomas takes out the bloodied cloths for cleaning.

I drip water into Christopher's mouth. He seems to swallow some. The only thing left in my kit is the Midol pill. That's like, what? Aspirin and some other stuff for period cramps, I guess. It couldn't hurt, could it? I break it up into the cup and swish it till it dissolves, and then drizzle some of this liquid into his mouth. "We'll ride your horse over the grassy fields," I tell him. "And I promise I won't head-butt you at all. And you know what? We'll even find a way to kiss without it sending me back. Won't that be amazing?" I lean close. Touch my cheek to his. And I whisper in his ear, "Live."

Thomas returns with a tall stack of fresh-torn fabric. "Miss, the night is half gone and I confess I did not expect him to last." He stokes the fire and tosses some cloth into the kettle. "Last he has." His voice has become husky. "Your ways are good."

Thomas fishes out the material and hangs them onto the chair back. Exhausted he sinks against the wall. "Always a sensible lad, full of purpose. From the day he could walk, always seemed to be heading toward something. I just knew it could not all end here. He is destined for grandness, I tell you. He was always looking out for others, too. When his sister was born, she was a weak one. I never seen a boy so full of worry and care. Often seen him giving her his extra bit of food or sweet. Always." He rubs his eyes and yawns. "He never would hurt a friend. That whole story about him setting up Greenfeld's death is rubbish. You and I, we know why he did not ride out that day. He was tending your wounds, right? You know what I thinks? I thinks me master was the one meant to die in that ambush. A set up, it was."

"Why would anyone want to kill him?" Percival is competing for the ward's hand. Having Christopher gone would only help him. But then again, Percival just defended Christopher as innocent in Greenfeld's death. Hm.

"But I been always looking out for me master." He yawns again. "Do not you worry, Milady. I swear I will always be by his side."

• • •

Westron wind, when will thou blow?
The small rain down can rain.
Christ, that my love were in my arms,
And I in my bed again

The singing is deep and sweet and warm. I smile in my sleep as an arm tightens around my shoulders. I nuzzle into him. It's a wonderful dream.

"Sing it again," I mumble.

"What," he whispers, "without a lute?"

I blink awake. Morning sun fills the room. I'm lying beside him in his bed and his light-green eyes are half-open, his face weary with exhaustion and pain, but he manages a faint smile and says, "So, you love me?"

I bite my lip and at once I'm filled with warmth and a weight in my chest, and it's far warmer and heavier than last night. I nod and bury my head on his shoulder, wetting his skin with my tears.

"Hush, do not cry. I will heal fine."

"It's just…" I sniffle.

He kisses my hair. "I know."

I force a smile and I suddenly know something with a certainty. "That's it. I'm not going anywhere. Being normal is overrated. You got that?"

"Overrated. Right. Wait. You can stay? So do you bring news from your time that will help me, then?" His expression brightens.

Warning bells clang in my head. I sit up. "What do you mean?"

"News of the future. We need to work our advantage." He reaches for my hand.

I pull away. "And without that news, I'm not welcome to stay?"

"What do you mean, not—" Christopher moves to reach for me but winces and falls back onto his pillow. He closes his eyes. "Who did this to you?" he whispers. "Who made it so hard for you to accept my complete devotion unto you?" He slowly opens his eyes.

I study my hands.

"I only want our life together to be peaceful and joyful. I want the same for my mother and my sister. These are dangerous times. Or perhaps you had not noticed." He waves at his wound.

"I might have." I sigh and move closer. "What happened?"

"We were riding hard against a brigade flying King Henry's colors. Our numbers were good, yet they fought with a zeal I had not yet seen. I was unhorsed and rose to my feet. A tall bear of a man ran toward me, growling and swinging his sword at me over and over, yet I managed to parry his blows."

In my mind, the succession of images I'd painted of him battling becomes animated and gritty.

"Yet the man persisted. It was clear he intended to wear me out. Then…"

"Then he struck you?"

Christopher blinks. "Not him. The blow came from behind. I fell. Percival Wallingford dragged me from the field."

"So he was the one who cut you? That slimy disgusting—"

"He was the one who saved me. If not for good old Percival, that monster of a man would have driven his sword point home. You were right. He is not all bad. We have spoken from time to time and not all discussions were full of hate and bravado."

"Huh." I touch his face. "Listen, I *have* brought you something. Just wait until you see this." I stand to get the book. But my bag is gone.

And so, I notice, is Thomas.

34

"Easy now. You women of the future are exceedingly dramatic. The book shall turn up." Christopher takes my hand and touches the bandage on my palm. "Why has it not healed? Is it diseased?"

"It's only been like a week in my time and it's healing fine. And I'm not just being dramatic. You don't understand. This book holds all this information about what will happen. In the wrong hands, it could be disastrous. At least according to Hollywood."

"I do not know of this Hollywood person, but I do know Thomas cannot read. You can ask him about the book yourself when he returns. I sent him off to fetch some food. I am ravenous." Christopher shifts and groans.

"Don't move. Just stay still, okay?"

He nods.

"Having an appetite is a good sign." I touch his brow with my wrist. "Your fever's down too. I'd better check your wound again."

"First hand me a cup of mead, would you? I am parched."

"A cup of water, I think."

"Mead," he says in a firm voice.

"Fine." I pour him a mug and he struggles to sit up, clenching his teeth. I hand him the cup and he downs it. "Another." He hands the mug back to me.

I fill it again and he downs that one and asks for a third.

"This time you get water."

"Michelle," he warns.

I glare at him and he breaks into a smile. "You are quite the old mother hen."

"Oh thanks," I say sarcastically. I offer him the mug but his lids have drooped. His breathing is heavy and he's nearly asleep.

"Do not go," he whispers.

"Shh. I won't. I told you. You can rest."

He's fast asleep now. I set the mug on the table and marvel at how his skin is again its natural healthy tone. I gently untie the cloth that binds his bandages and tenderly lift off the bundle of sterile fabric that's directly over the wound. It catches a bit in the dried blood, but the wound seems so much more manageable now without fresh oozing blood. Noticing a few more sterilized cloths hanging on the chair, I soak one in the now cool kettle water and swab off the brown dried blood around the edges. The Band-Aids are still holding the cut fairly closed.

"Not bad, all things considered," I whisper. He continues to sleep comfortably, as I place a smaller wad of clean dry fabric over the wound and again tie the top binding across it. Noticing the top sheet has been replaced with a clean one, I pull it up to his chest. "Good work, Thomas." My vision shifts again to where the book used to be.

I spend some time looking out the window at how the faint sun glitters like tiny blue diamonds on the snow. And I try to imagine myself here, forever. Would I continue to be invisible? Of course being invisible has some advantages. No one stares at you like you're some freak, for one thing. Invisible or not, Christopher and I could have a life together. It has to all work out, it has to be fated. Why else would we be brought together? *True love wins.*

I nod to myself and trace small circles in the soft snow dusting the window's ledge. In some ways it seems so beautiful and peaceful here. Yet in other ways…

I return to Christopher's side, mesmerized by the steady rise and fall of his chest and the way his good luck coin rises and falls too.

"Sup's made, good master," Thomas bellows, coming in.

"Shh. He's sleeping."

"Mm, not anymore." Christopher rubs his eyes. "And he cannot hear you, remember? Hand the food over, good man."

"Aye, Master." Thomas seems almost giddy as he gives Christopher a wooden platter with a large hunk of meat pierced by a dagger. Beside the meat is a hunk of dark bread.

"Ask him about the book," I say.

Christopher picks up the dagger and bites into the meat. With a full mouth he mumbles, "Lady Michelle wants to know why you stole from her?"

"I didn't say that."

"Me, steal?" Thomas looks struck. "That is the second time I have been accused of such a thing today. I have done nothing of the sort, I swear to that."

"I believe you, my good man. See?" Christopher wipes his chin. "He swears."

"Why, I have done nothing but follow her orders, if that is all right with you, Master. And, thanks to her, you are all right, or almost so." He smiles. "Is she here now?"

Christopher takes another bite and nods.

"Ask about the book," I insist. "It's important."

"And can you see her, Master?"

"Ask him now. Please!"

"Oh, yes. I see and *hear* her. She is asking about her book. Did you take it?"

"I did *not*. Tell her that."

"I can hear you," I say.

"She can hear you," Christopher says.

"She can hear me?" Thomas says.

I sigh.

Thomas speaks to the wall on the opposite side of the room, saying, "I did not take it, my lady."

"She is here, beside me, on the bed."

"Oh." He turns, looking awkward. "Perhaps I should leave now."

"Yes, she is quite unladylike right now."

"Stop that. I am not!"

"Pardon then, sir." Thomas looks to the ground and backs away. "I will leave you then."

"Christopher, tell him the *truth*."

"You are spoiling my fun. Besides, Thomas knows all of my secrets."

I glare.

"Very well. Stay, Thomas. I am only trifling with you. Michelle is nothing, if not a complete lady."

"And a life saver," Thomas says.

"Yes," Christopher whispers and gives me a warm look.

"And I couldn't have done it without Thomas."

"She says I owe my life to you as well. Along with Wallingford, of course."

"Wallingford," Thomas and I both say with disgust.

"Listen, my good man." Christopher sets the bare dagger on the platter. "The lady said there was a book and now it is gone. Know you anything?"

"I do, in fact, Master. Percival Wallingford came to your bedside and must have thought me asleep, because he tore back your bed sheet in a most ungentle manner."

"Because he wanted you to die," I say. "That's why he sent away the physician. He gave him money to go."

"Perhaps he was paying for his services. The man rescued me from the field, Michelle."

"Master, I am sorry to say he did not seem at all pleased to find you mending. He said, 'This complicates matters,' and he reaches for your wound. And up jumps I, like so." Thomas hops, his hands out like he's a Ninja. "And he screeches like the pig he is, begging your pardon for speaking so of my better."

"Better. Ha!" I snort. "And I can't believe I slept through all this."

"And he falls onto the floor. I am truly in a right fury now. So I says, 'Ye best be leaving my master alone.' And he stands holding the bag he fell on."

"My book bag!"

"And he makes like he will throw it. So I grab it, see, and he pulls at it and a most marvelous book falls to the floor."

I hold my breath, almost afraid to hear what happens next.

"And I say, 'Leave, sir.' And he grabs the volume and says, 'What is this, traitorous writing? A spy document?' And I say it is none of his business and pull it from his hand, toss it into this chest and sit on the chest, daring him to move me. He says he will have my head." There is a hint of fear in his voice now. "But he leaves. And here it is." Thomas pulls my book from the chest.

"Thomas!" I leap from the bed. "I *love* you." I hug him, or try to, since my arms go right through him. My skin again prickles with itching and my mouth fills with a salty, bitter taste, but it quickly fades.

"I thought you loved *me*," Christopher says laughing, then wincing. He gently touches his side. "Hand me the book, Thomas."

Thomas squints at the cover. "Have a care, young Master. This text is too finely wrought." He turns a few pages. "I fear it is dark magic. Surely only the devil could craft such a thing. The pages be as thin as a spirit. And such regular letters. Surely no monk's hand formed these."

"Now Thomas, have you not heard tell of the new printing press?" Christopher says.

"Aye. More devilry if it be true." Thomas hands the book to Christopher, who gives it to me.

I sit on the edge of the bed again, smiling brightly. "This is the answer to all your problems. Now we'll know what's going to happen, which means no more wounds for you. And you can advise the Earl. And," I say and swallow, "I can stay."

"I have dreamed of this," he says and seems unable to say more.

I open the Cotswold battle book. "Okay, Christopher, what day is it?"

He laughs. "Why it is the best day of my life! The third of December, fourteen sixty."

"The fourth, Master." Thomas yawns. "You lost a day."

"And you lost a night's sleep, my friend. Go rest. I am in good hands now." Christopher winks at me as Thomas bows and leaves.

I look at the table of contents, thumb to the section on winter fourteen sixty and start reading aloud. "This was a critical time in the war. The king's allies were in the north, gathering forces and the Duke was poised to make several serious mistakes." I pause. What if sharing this book is a serious mistake?

Christopher shifts and grits his teeth at the pain. "Go on."

Glancing at his wound, I nod. I run my finger over the text to where I left off. "The Duke, misreading his opponent, brought his forces for the Christmastime to the castle of..." Suddenly the page looks different. More white space. Less words.

"The castle of?" Christopher prompts.

I try to focus on the words. "...for the Christmastime to the castle of Sandall, but..." Something seems to move across the paper. My skin crawls, as I slide my eyes downward. I watch with horror as the letters at the bottom of the page disappear one by one.

I flip the page. Letters disappear from the bottom here, too. The white of the paper grows, eating away at the words. Frantic, I flip back to the page I was just reading. Completely blank. "Oh God."

"What is wrong?" Christopher tries to sit up.

I flip ahead a few pages. Two paragraphs are left. I quickly read, "Henry's forces had been gathering throughout the area for some time and the land was heavily for—" The rest of that word is gone, as is the rest of the writing on that page.

"Why did you stop?" Christopher says and peers at the book. He draws in his breath as the words I'd just read vanish like a fabric unwound by a pulled thread.

I skip to later in the book but something eats away at the words even faster now.

"Read," Christopher says. "Quickly."

"The King's forces..." The page is now blank.

I whip through the book. White space crawls up the pages, consuming every character, leaving nothing.

The only page I can find with any writing is close to the end. It reads, *"and so the Duke unknowingly went to"*

Its few letters are consumed from both the start and the end of the phrase, until it only says "unknowingly."

This is nibbled down to "know," "now," and finally "no," until this, too, is gone.

I stare at the emptiness for a moment and slam the book shut.

"Dark magic," Christopher says, his expression grim. "Show me the book."

I hand it to him and pace back and forth. God, I was foolish to mess with history. The book suddenly does feel like dark, dark magic. And so does the information I still remember about the upcoming battle on December 30th. About the king's forces ambushing…where was it? Wakefield.

Christopher pages through the blank book and suddenly seems weary. His eyes close. I wait a few moments, then take the book from his hands, setting it on the floor.

I decide to draw Christopher now and pick up the sketchpad, turning to a fresh page.

Sitting here, sketching the curve of his jaw and the lock of hair on his forehead, still feels so right. Even with the book useless, I feel everything is going to work out. Maybe it's because, after all these years, I've finally found where I truly belong. And I do have some information. I can stay.

In my drawing, Christopher's face is captured beautifully. I surround his chest with folds of the sheet, shading them with cross-hatching. But something appears in the shadows.

It's a face of sheer terror.

And it belongs to my father.

35

Christopher grabs my arm. "You are not going, Michelle. You cannot."

"I don't *want* to go. Especially with you so vulnerable."

"Vulnerable?" He reaches his right arm over his head and, teeth gritted, pulls his sword from beneath his pillow, holding it high.

"Wounded, then," I say. He sets his sword at his side and I notice a quarter-sized dot of fresh blood soaks the cloth. "See that? You can't stretch so much. You've got to let this heal."

"I can defend myself if need be. And still I say you are not going back there. I am not allowing you to face whatever danger is there without me. Besides, your father can surely handle himself."

"He can't. He needs me. He's always needed me. And it won't be that dangerous. It won't involve swords, I promise you that."

"He is a man. He does not need you."

"You need me," I point out.

Christopher's eyes darken. "That is a different sort of need. Your life is here now. You said so yourself."

"I know. And it is. But it's there too. My father, my brother, my friends. Well, maybe no friends."

"You never mentioned your brother." He tucks a lock of hair behind my ear. "Is he younger to you?"

"No. A few years older."

"Then he can care for your father. And you need not worry."

"He can't. He's…" I look around the room, searching for the right words. "He's smart and kind, but he's not well, in his head, you know? Like King Henry?"

"He is mentally ill?" Christopher says carefully.

"Yeah. But then again, who am I to judge about sanity?"

He reaches toward me. Tangles his fingers in my curls and holds my face between his hands. "I know only one important truth: you and I are connected. We belong to one another. And I say you cannot go."

"But what if this were your mother in the drawing?"

His eyes narrow. "Get my clothes. I am going with you."

For a wild moment I imagine that this is possible. That I won't have to deal with the past, only the future. "But how?"

"I have been there before. We shall have to discover how." He leans forward. "Now hand me my tunic and my hose, but not the black ones. They have not been mended since they were torn at the Roman villa."

More blood has soaked onto his bandage.

I stand. "God, Christopher. Lie back. You're ripping open your cut."

"If you will not get them, I shall do so myself." He pulls the sheet off his lap and swings his bare legs onto the floor. I barely have a chance to register that he's sitting completely glorious and naked in front of me, when he hunches over. His hair hangs over his face but it's obvious how much pain he's in.

"You're hurting yourself."

"No," he says, breathless. "Nonsense." He starts to stand.

I touch his shoulder. "I'll get you your things but you have to lie down."

"Knew you would see it my way," he whispers, sinks back onto his pillow and pulls the sheet across his lap.

I whisper, "Stubborn obstinate pig-headed guy." I open the chest and toss him a pair of footless gray leggings and a dark blue tunic.

"No. The green one." The blue tunic comes flying back toward me. "I need a shirt as well. Would not want to look shoddy in front of your father."

"If he can even see you." I toss him the green one and a loose white shirt, and fold up the blue tunic. I tidy up the rest of the clothes in the chest and close the lid. I find Christopher now wears his stockings, but breathes deeply from the effort of putting them on. "Take it easy," I say.

"Take it easy," he mimics, swiping his bangs from his eyes. "I am no babe in need of coddling."

He looks so petulant and adorable, I laugh and swoop in for a kiss, stopping just a breath from his lips. We both linger there, our lips parted. I feel the heat of his breath and I fall back onto the chair, my heart pounding. "So unfair."

His nostrils flare. "Unjust."

"I…I wonder what else we can't do."

"I wonder as well." He looks at me like a lion about to pounce on his prey.

I touch my throat, feeling my pulse pounding there. "Too bad you're injured."

"I am not *that* injured," he says in a husky voice.

"Aren't you? Then—"

"Shh." He holds up his hand and his attention shifts to the door. A man shouts something a distance away. Christopher seems puzzled. "It cannot be. Not so soon."

"What?"

Christopher's hand closes on the hilt of his sword. With effort, he stands and pads barefoot to the door.

"What's happening?" I ask, following.

"You may be safer in your own time. At least for a while."

"Why? What is it?"

I hear people race down the hallway. The knob starts to turn but Christopher throws the lock. "Brother?" a man says. Someone pounds on the door. "You are called."

"In a moment," Christopher says.

"As planned, then," he says. Another man says a gruff, "Right, then," and their footsteps fade.

Christopher turns and leans back against the door, sighing.

"What was all that? What's planned?"

"It is complicated." He combs his hair out of his face with his fingers, suddenly looking weary.

"Is this about what happened to Greenfeld? Thomas told me."

He looks down. "Poor fellow. A good fellow, too."

"Do you think you were the one meant to be ambushed? Is someone out to kill you?" I grip his arm.

He pats my hand. "I think something foul is happening and the Earl trusts me little after Greenfeld's death, but this does not matter. All will be well as long as *you* trust me. Do you?"

"I trust you with my life," I say, stunned by this simple truth.

"Then you must go. Kiss me."

"No. I'm not leaving you here. If it's dangerous for me, it's dangerous for you. We'll figure out a way for you come back with me first. And you've got to rest."

"We have no time. I must go at once."

"Tell me what's going on."

"I cannot. You do not understand."

"Help me to understand."

His grip tightens and he pulls me closer. "Trust me and kiss me, Michelle. I do not want you to leave, but you cannot be here now. No one is to be privy to…you must go."

"But why?"

"Trust me and kiss me," he says, his voice gentle and sad. "I will try to find my way back to you as soon as I can. Please."

"Fine. But I should tell you first, on December thirtieth there is a battle at this place. It's called Wakef—"

"Brother!" a stern voice shouts just outside the door, startling us both.

Christopher pulls me towards him. Kisses me hard. I'm lost in his passion.

36

Christopher is gone. Gone is his furniture. The library book. The sketch I drew of him. Why didn't I take that with me? I stand for a long while in his now-musty bedroom filled with too-ornate, too-fragile antique furniture. I wait and try to concentrate, but I don't return to his time.

Finally I push my way out of his door, leaving him too far behind me, but alive. Alive but in danger. And I didn't give him any information that could help. I'm useless. The steps leading down to the main floor are suddenly clogged with kids in blue school uniforms, clutching notebooks and pencils, and I have to push my way against the rising tide to get down.

I jog through the castle's main parlor. Still no portrait of Christopher on the wall. What does this mean? I make it out into the courtyard and pause just before the cursed spot. If I walked through it, what would I hear?

A shiver shoots through me, starting at my hip. It takes me a while to realize it's actually my cell phone vibrating. Too late, I pull it out. The screen reads "86 missed calls." Whoa.

I flip it open to a long listing of messages. Scroll through them. Many of the calls are from my dad. And there is a bunch I don't recognize, which is interesting since my dad is the only one who even has my new number.

Now I'm really shivering. This time it's from the chilled air and I realize my sweater and hoodie are back with Christopher.

I hit some buttons on the cell and listen to the last message.

"Shelly?" It's my father. The fear and sorrow in his voice make my heart speed up, especially when I realize I've been missing all night. But he doesn't sound furious, like I'd expect. Is he ill? Or did something happen to Wayne? My heart races.

"Where are you? Where—" he says. His voice seems to catch. Now someone is talking to him in the background and my dad says, "No. Nothing." Then a chipper automated British voice says, "End of message."

I have to get home but there's something I *must* do first.

I find Mary's bike lying on the ground, grab it and ride hard. I barely stop for traffic. Cars honk. Someone shouts, "Barmy bitch!" I don't stop until I reach the churchyard. Pushing open the squeaky gate, I drop the bike just inside the wall and run, weaving around headstones and effigies and praying stone angels, until I arrive at the obelisk that still stands where Christopher's grand tomb once rested. I turn to the right and find Christopher's latest headstone gone.

I touch the grass where he once was buried. The sun glitters on the dew droplets as crystalline and lovely as it had shone on the snow by the castle. He's not dead in 1460. That's what I have to believe this means.

I race back to the bike.

Somehow without even being aware of it, I've ridden to my house. Cars fill the drive, including William's.

I push open the door. Mary is whispering with William, who looks unusually disheveled. One tail of his button down shirt sticks out over his charcoal slacks. To my surprise, I find Mr. Wallingford sitting on the couch, proper as always in a pinstriped suit, and beside him is the Headmistress. I take a few steps into the lobby and finally see my dad by the front window. His hair stands up, he's barefoot and he's wearing a ratty T-shirt and a pair of plaid P.J.

pants. He's talking with a policeman, who's scribbling notes onto a pad.

"Dad?"

The room falls quiet. At once there is an explosion of activity. Mary rushes toward me and grabs me in a hug. Mr. Wallingford and the Headmistress rise to their feet and eye me. William rubs his head and looks at the ground. My dad collapses onto the couch and buries his face in his hands.

I manage to shake off Mary, run to my dad and crouch in front of him. "Dad, what's wrong?" I hold his bony hand and his long fingers close around mine.

"Oh, Shelly." He looks at me through red-rimmed eyes.

"What happened?"

"Guess my services are no longer required," the officer says. He flips his pad closed and stows his pen in his pocket. "Now it's up to Health Services. Unless you need me to assist you with…"

"No," Dad says.

"I'll show you out then, shall I?" Mary says.

Mr. Wallingford says into his cell, "Thank you. I've got it." He jots down something and disconnects. "Here you go, Donald." He hands the paper to my dad.

"Thank you," Dad murmurs. "I appreciate it."

"Not to worry," Mr. Wallingford says. "He's an old chum. Call him anytime and the school will foot the bill. It will all be quite hush-hush."

"Certainly," the Headmistress says with a disapproving sniff. "And I insist you take today off. Oh, and I'm afraid I must also give you this." She pulls a cream-colored envelope from her blazer and sets it on the coffee table. "Another warning, I'm afraid. Walking out of a class." Her steely gray eyes dart to me. "Perhaps once you get things, ahem, sorted out, you can return on Monday. Good day, Mr. De Freccio."

She and Mr. Wallingford head toward the door and Mr. Wallingford says, "Come along, William."

"Actually, Father, I was thinking of taking the day off myself, seeing as I didn't sleep." William stretches.

"That is no reason to miss classes."

"It is." William raises his chin with defiance.

His father glares at him and William nervously looks away. "Good day, all," Mr. Wallingford says. "And De Freccio, I'm terribly sorry." He casts a dark look at me and he and the Headmistress go.

I squeeze Dad's hand. "Tell me."

Dad opens his mouth and closes it.

"It's okay, Donald," Mary says, standing by the couch. "She's back now. And we'll soon get her the help she needs."

"I suppose we could call the doctor," Dad says, gazing at the slip of paper Mr. Wallingford had given him.

"You're ill?" I ask.

"Michelle." His brows furrow. "*You're* ill."

"What?"

"It's okay, dear." Mary grabs me by the shoulders and sets me in a chair by the window. "It's not your fault. How about a lovely cup of tea?" She turns to my dad. "She can still have tea, can't she? I won't make it too hot."

"What's wrong with everybody?"

By the door I notice rolls and rolls of my drawings in the corner on the floor. I stand. "What are these doing down here? They're my personal things."

"Not when you start wandering around all night," Dad says.

"I wasn't wandering. And what does that have to do with my drawings?"

"You were gone all night. You've been injured. Disoriented. Acting out in class. Saying odd things. Obsessed with that castle. And you are obviously obsessed with other things as well." He waves at the admittedly huge pile of drawings. I glance again at them. Frantic charcoal sketches of Christopher in his armor, Christopher swinging a sword, Christopher with his cape swirling around him. The jagged lines cut deep into the paper.

"Dad, I can explain." Well, sort of.

"It's Wayne all over again, Michelle."

My eyes dart around the room. "Can we talk about this later?"

"Mental illness is nothing to be ashamed of," Mary says, her voice overly kind.

I step back and whisper, "Everyone knows about Wayne? Dad, how could you?" My lip trembles.

He rubs his forehead. "I had to tell someone. Don't you understand? I was *alone*."

"You had no right." I cross my arms tight and tears sting my eyes. I notice William edging toward the door, so I start talking fast. "I'm an artist. So I draw pictures from my imagination. Is that a crime? So I'm a little different. Is that mental illness now?"

Dad gives me a hollow look. "Why are you always at the castle?"

"I'm drawing it. Doing studies. And I got a job with the Ghost Tour there too, if you must know."

Dad looks at his hands, which are clenched in his lap. "Where were you last night?"

"I was with a friend. He needed me. He was in trouble."

Dad shakes his head and looks away.

"It's true. His name is Christopher Newman," I say. Now the only person looking at me is William. I wisely decide to not talk about the whole in-the-past thing. Even Dad, who was married to Madame Florabunda, Psychic Extraordinaire, will probably not believe me. "Christopher lives near the castle. And he was in trouble. It was a matter of life or death. And if I could have called, Dad, I would have. The phone didn't work there. I swear to God. You believe me, don't you?"

The room remains silent. The tension is palpable.

"Goodbye, Mr. De Freccio." William promptly leaves the house and slams the door.

"I'll just see about that tea," Mary says in a cheery voice. She disappears through the swinging kitchen door.

I sit beside my dad and he remains silent. "I'm sorry," I whisper.

He shakes his head. "I thought I'd lost you forever. I can't live like this, Michelle. You are seeing that doctor. I need you to."

My throat feels like it's closing. Images of straitjackets and injections fill my brain. "I'm not crazy. I'm, well, I'm a teenager."

Dad's hand closes on mine.

My phone buzzes in my pocket. Surprised, I answer it. "Hello?"

"I believe you, even if you don't believe me," a voice says.

I stand. "Who is this?"

"And I do have something for you to see. Of course, you probably already know that. Call me as soon as you can get away."

"William?" I whisper.

"Yeah."

Stunned, I slide the phone shut.

"Was that that Christopher guy?" Dad tries to sound stern, but it comes out only as exhausted.

"Wrong number." I slip my phone into my pocket and sink onto the couch. He wraps his arm around me, but his other hand grips the paper with the doctor's phone number.

37

I knock at the grand front door again. William finally opens it, blinking. He's in a white Tee and a pair of gray boxers and his hair is messy.

"Sorry I woke you."

He steps back. "Come in. It's perfect. We're the only ones here."

I hesitate, then follow him across the lobby with its gleaming marble floor. We enter a vast kitchen, which is larger than the entire bottom floor of my house. The ceilings are an impossible height and everything is white, including the pots hanging over a center island.

"It's so…clean."

"Because no one ever uses it." He opens a cabinet and pulls out a box of cereal. "Want some?"

"No."

He digs his hand into the box, pulls out a fistful of corn flakes and chews on the cereal. I shift from foot to foot, hyper-aware of time ticking away. How long can I continue to do the stuff I've been doing and not be bound on a gurney in some mental ward? How long do I really have to help Christopher? "So, why am I here?"

"It's in my room. Come on." He walks into the main lobby and climbs the wide sweeping staircase with the carved banister.

I pause at the foot of the stairs. "Huh. Give me one good reason why I should follow you to your bedroom."

"Oh, come on, Michelle. I'm trying to be the nice guy here, but you aren't making it easy."

"Nice? First you beat up Roger. But obviously that wasn't enough, so you knifed his face, and—"

"Do you seriously think I did?"

"It is hard to believe," I admit.

"Wait. You said his face was *knifed?*"

"Don't act so surprised," I say but he's already racing upstairs.

I run up after him, my feet sinking into the plush maroon carpet that covers the treads. At the top, I pause on the landing when I hear him talking to someone in angry tones. I follow the sound.

I expect his room to be all preppy. Mallard green and plaids and carpet the color of money. Instead it's surprisingly modern. Chrome and black furniture, stark white walls and a charcoal gray rug.

"What made you think I'd actually—" he says into his cell. "Geoffrey, I never said that. You—"

I wander around his room. There are all the toys I'd expect a rich kid to have, but it's still shocking to see such a large wide-screened TV in a bedroom. In front of the TV are four black leather chairs. Surround-sound speakers hang in the corners. There's also a Wii and a Guitar Hero guitar tossed in the corner. A king-sized bed is at the far corner of the room, beside the two floor-to-ceiling windows. And his laptop, printer and a slew of fancy peripherals are on a glass-topped table.

"No, you stupid bastard," William shouts. "You are seriously deranged." He throws his phone onto his bed and runs his hand through his hair.

"What happened?"

"It's like the whole world's gone mad. He did it out of loyalty. Loyalty. Of all the idiotic…" He grinds his teeth.

"Geoffrey did that to Roger. For you?"

"Not the first roughing up. I don't know anything about that part. I don't know why Mortley felt the need to single me out for that one. Well, actually, I do. It's because I'm a Wallingford. It's like I'm some damned symbol to these people to be worshipped or…" He takes a deep breath. "Look, let me just get this thing and be done with it before I come to my senses. Make yourself at home." He disappears into a walk-in closet.

I sink into a leather chair and worry about my dad. He'd seemed so tired and frail. He barely had the energy to do all the necessary parental things: grounding me until further notice, forbidding me to ever see or even draw Christopher again and threatening to call the doctor if my strange behavior continues. And when I told him I was going to school, he'd said, "Just please come back to me."

Please come back. My dad. Christopher. I feel stretched out like a rope in a game of tug of war.

William returns and sits in the chair beside me. He's wearing jeans and holding a thick pile of papers. "Here are the missing Wallingford Papers."

I glance at the bright white pages. "Ha. Ha."

"See for yourself." He places the stack in my lap. The top page is a color copy of a manuscript page. The original must have been delicate and cracked because the bright white copy paper shows where holes existed in the original. Aside from being on new paper, it looks just like the manuscript under glass in the museum. Yellow-brown parchment and dark-brown calligraphy written in the same sloping manner, in the same illegible ancient writing. I page through the stack. "There must be nearly a hundred sheets."

"I secretly made a copy when my father thought I was reading through them."

"Why secretly?"

He rubs his neck. "Look, these pages aren't supposed to exist. I didn't even know about them until my seventeenth birthday. Knowledge of them is supposed to be a great rite of passage, passed from father to son through the generations. Supposed to make us

Wallingfords humble and, I don't know, bound to each other in some ridiculous way. Of course you probably already know all this."

"Why do you keep saying that I already know?"

"Why do you think?"

"But these really are the missing pages?"

"A copy, yeah. The originals are in my father's safe." He leans back in his chair, cracks his knuckles and gives the door a nervous glance. "If my father knew I'd told anyone, he'd take instant action. At the very least, I'd be disowned on the spot. All of my bank account and my trust fund would disappear."

"You're exaggerating."

"Am I? He's a total bastard when someone goes against him. I've seen it." He bites his pinky nail.

"But these papers are amazingly cool. Why not share them with the world? Scholars should translate them."

"One already has." William takes the pile from my lap and flips to the lower half of the stack. These copies look like pages created on an old manual typewriter. "A historian spent much of his life translating this for my great-grandfather. My ancestors knew the general content of these papers, which had been passed down orally, but with the historian's translation, the family now had every gory detail. The man was sworn to secrecy and paid well for his efforts, but in the end it wasn't enough. My father said the man insisted he publish his work and…"

"And?"

"And he was silenced. Silenced. My father told me the story as if it were a warning to me. Like that's what happens to those who break the Wallingford trust."

"Silenced. You mean…" I swallow. "You're freaking me out."

He raises his brows. "Yeah. Imagine how I feel. I thought if people knew…" He again gnaws on his nail. "Look, I don't know what I was thinking. You can't put any of this in your term paper. Understand?"

"I don't care about the paper. I just need to know what happened to Christopher Newman."

"You're a psychic."

I can't think of a single sensible thing to say.

"Your father confirmed that your mother is psychic."

I can't meet his gaze. "Lots of people tell fortunes."

"You mentioned Christopher Newman. That he was in trouble and needed help. That it was life or death. Why would you bring up that name?"

Now I'm intently focused on William.

"You know things," he's saying. "It was like you were onto me from the start, wasn't it? You knew right away that I was a phony. Always pointing out that I'm not really better than everyone. You knew before I knew it myself. You're the one who's been nagging at my conscience all along. And you know what's in here. You have ESP or something like that."

"I *don't*, okay?"

"Right." He shoves the pile into my lap and stands, his fists clenched. "I really wanted to be honest with you, Michelle."

"So be honest."

"You want honest? Fine." He rubs his neck and paces in front of me, finally stopping. "Here's honest. The Wallingfords. The tremendous, privileged and fortunate Wallingfords. The best win, right?" He gives me a bitter laugh. "And I believed that crap all these years. We are the best and that's why we're so fortunate. My father drilled it into me. Always to be so proud of our family and our status. He belittled me when I did anything he deemed less than perfect. I worked so hard to please him and live up to our family standards. I was one of the best, one of the most deserving. Others, like your mate Roger, they get the crap end of the stick because they aren't as smart or as deserving. But is that the truth? No. The truth is we Wallingfords are no better that the lowest of the low. We're worse, in fact. Because we got ours through lies. Through evil. Through murder."

Christopher. I skim the typed pages in search of his name.

"God, I hate myself now. And all this." William waves his hand around him. "I wish I never had anything to do with this family. I don't want to be like them." He shakes his head. "You couldn't possibly understand." He tears the manuscript from my lap. "I'll make a copy of the translation for you. Then you'd better go."

William sets the pages into the copier feed tray. While the machine whirrs and spits out copies, there's an awkward silence between us.

"You're upset because you have a conscience," I say after a while. "That's a good thing."

"Yeah. Feels great."

I pull out some of the finished pages and start to read:

November 5th, 1460

Dearest Father, you need not interfere. I assure you I am following orders religiously. In addition, I have begun to please my lordship with my punctuality. In contrast, others have disappointed, and so I continue to rise in esteem.

I flip through the other pages in my hand. "Where's December fourth?" I reach for the next few sheets in the copier.

William stops my hand. "How do you know about December fourth?"

"What do you mean? It's just the next date entry. That's all."

He takes the pages from me and looks them over. "No, it isn't. How do you know December fourth was important? How can you stand here and tell me you aren't psychic?"

My palms start to sweat as I think about Christopher sending me home. Saying it was too dangerous for me to stay. "But I don't know what happens. I swear. You have to tell me."

He gives me an odd look. "That's the date one of my ancestors actually tried to show some courage. The courtiers banded together. Percival Wallingford had this idea that really angered…" Tires crunch on gravel outside. William darts to his window, then steps back. "God. My father's car. You'd better get out of here." He takes the newly copied pages from the feed tray and thrusts them into my hands. He stops the machine.

"What about the rest?"

"I've already given you too much." His eyes look wild. "You can't write about this. You can't tell anyone. Ever."

"It's okay. You can trust me." I touch his arm.

"You have to use the back servant's stairs. Then go out through the kitchen door." He takes my hand and pulls me into the hall.

Below, I hear the front door open. William leads me beside the wall and stops with his hand on a glass doorknob. He opens the door, which is cleverly concealed as part of the floral-papered wall. He seems so young and lost all of a sudden, standing there in his jeans, with his messed-up hair and wrinkled Tee. There is definite fear in his face. "Go," he whispers. "Fast."

He pushes me through the door. The panel closes behind me and I hug the pages to me. The copies are still warm.

I go down the steps, escape from the house and don't stop running until I'm in front of the Castle Pub. Panting, I fumble through the pages. Lots of entries for November. I thumb through a few more, find the one for December fourth and start to read as I walk.

December 4th, 1460

Honorable Father,

I sense the spy among us. Day to day existence seems to be a danger to us all. How long before I am charged as well, however falsely? I know that you return soon and I try to trust in your wisdom, yet I feel I must act and am compelled to move forward.

I turn to the next page as I pass St. Paul's graveyard.

The time seemed most favorable for me to take the lead, with the Earl still abattle, along with many a courtier and soldier. Plumson, DeBank, Leeds, Newman and I have banded together to form a secret brotherhood. I know that it will trouble you that Christopher Newman lives yet.

"He lives." I close my eyes. "Be here now. I'm waiting for you. It's okay. It's safe."

A cold gust blows and the papers flutter as if they've come to life. I grip them tightly but find I'm still alone. Maybe I need to be near the castle for him to reach me. I wish I could just go there. I wish I wasn't so worried about leaving my dad right now…

I continue to read while walking toward school.

I felt it certain that we must work together to smoke out the true villain who threatens the Earl. I am full sorry for not telling you thus earlier, but know you shall be full proud as you often chide me for not being more lordly.

Our first quarry was a man known to harbor a suspicious document. This would put Newman to a test, easing even your worries of his loyalties. The fact that I alone knew our direction, enabled a surprise for both Newman and his now-captured servant.

"Thomas," I say in a breath. I'm at the door to the Academic Center and pause, my hand on the glass, as the weight of this sinks in. I open the door and enter the empty hallway.

The man professed his innocence—as they always do. Newman said he would vouchsafe this man's innocence, swearing his life for a servant! Yet as a courtesy, we remanded the servant named Thomas to the dungeon until such treacherous papers could be produced to damn him.

The book. I swallow hard.

Thus I gave my good word that this servant would have a fair trial, although this man spoke most surly unto me ere and is beneath my standing. Father, you may proclaim such action a perceived weakness on my part, yet I believe otherwise. I proved to all we are not bloodthirsty mercenaries but merely instruments of justice. My actions silenced even Newman.

This, I feel, will strengthen mine own standing in the eyes of the Earl. And will strengthen our newly formed brotherhood until together we kill this viper among us.

I stop and look at my cell. It's tea time, so I go to the cafeteria, my mind now lost in the anguish and worry Christopher must be experiencing. And poor Thomas. He's in that dungeon. The one down those small dark steps I'm too claustrophobic to even try to descend.

Inside the cafeteria, William's table seems almost empty without him. But there's Geoffrey, smug and grinning at me. I take a deep breath and glare at him. Constance whispers something to him and he snickers.

I see Guncha and Justine, and nod but go straight to the last table, where Roger sits with his back to the rest of the room.

I drop the stack of papers beside his mug and sink into the seat next to him.

The angry slash across his cheek is raw. He's fiddling with his Walkman. Roger doesn't say hi but he doesn't tell me to go either. For now, it'll have to do.

I flip to the next page of the Wallingford papers. It's the last page I have.

Yet a few mere hours later, all is undone. Father, I know not what to think. Despite my word orders have not been followed and I fear the anarchy that may result. Who has given this order? Who is the viper? There is a true evil among us and our young Brotherhood is now broken. For while Plumson, Leeds,

DeBank and I played at cards for many hours, the servant Thomas was murdered. His bloody head was left resting beside his body.

"De Freccio, what the hell?" Roger tries to push me off of him but I can't let go. All I can do is cling to him, my face buried in his neck, my eyes closed against the horror.

38

Traitor.

Who's the traitor that killed Thomas? That's like the key to everything, including Christopher's peace and happiness.

It's Saturday and I'm pacing in my room trying to think things through. Thomas' killer couldn't have been Plumson. Didn't Percival write that Plumson was with him playing cards at the time? All the courtiers of that brotherhood were. Except Christopher. Where was he?

Thomas knows all of my secrets.

Christopher did say that. What if Thomas knew something...

What's wrong with me? Christopher would never do anything to harm Thomas.

I pick up my cell and dial William again. Again it goes straight to voicemail. I toss the phone onto my bed. I *have* to see the rest of the Wallingford Papers. They'll have the answers I need, I just know it. William can't avoid me forever, even if I am grounded. At the very least, I'll see him Monday at school. And as soon as I see the rest of those papers, I can go to Christopher. I just have to make it through this weekend without freaking out. And I just have to make sure my dad's going to be okay.

I sit cross-legged on the floor and turn my attention back to the linoleum block of the Roman nymph. With careful strokes I carve

away the unwanted areas and remember that statue in the abandoned villa. Its perfect expression of joy. It'll be the right thing to
leave behind for my dad when I go.

When I go… These words sink in and I again try to imagine
what my life will be like. How primitive it will be in some ways.
How dangerous. And will I remain invisible? Will we be able to
kiss…

I'll be with Christopher. That's what counts. Nothing has ever
felt so right for me before. Somehow everything will have work
itself out.

Time passes unnoticed as I continue to work, until finally my
dad calls me down for dinner. I set down the carving tool, stretch
out my stiff fingers and blow on the block, scattering the discarded
brown bits of linoleum onto the newspaper I've spread beneath it.
What remains is a slightly cruder version of the nymph. Somehow
it isn't as animated as the original was, but the nymph is clearly
dancing with elation. I'll ink some prints tonight.

"Coming down, Michelle? It's getting cold," Dad calls.

I find him at the kitchen table with an impressive dish steaming
on a platter. I can tell it's Thai by the curry smell and the shred-
ded coconut sprinkled on top. "More leftovers from your cooking
class?"

"No. This is fresh." He piles noodles and veggies onto my plate.

"You're a quick study." I pick up my fork. "So, you must be like
the only guy in this class. Meet anyone interesting?"

"Oh. Well." He serves himself, dropping most of the noodles
onto the table. "It's just a cooking class, not…just cooking." He
scoops the escaped noodles onto his plate, picking up the last few
with his fingers.

Normally we'd change the subject, start joking about something
in the news, or bring up a fresh concern about school. But suddenly I'm done with all that. I set down my fork. "It's okay, you
know. Meeting other women."

"I don't want to meet—"

"She's gone and she isn't coming back." A soon as I blurt it out, I wish I could take it back.

Dad pushes aside his plate.

"I'm sorry, Dad." I'm pained by his expression.

He rubs his mouth and mumbles, "My fault. Maybe if I were more understanding…"

"And maybe if I were cuter." I tighten my fists. "Or more worthy of her love. Maybe I wouldn't have been so easy to leave. Isn't that right?"

"It wasn't you."

"That's kind of my point. It wasn't you either, was it? It was *her*. She just didn't have the ability to love, did she? Not really." I pick at my food. "Not if really loving someone is about sticking with them no matter what."

"Love is complicated, honey. It's not always so black and white." He squeezes my hand and gives me a gentle smile. "Someday you'll understand."

I clutch my fork. How can he sit here saying to me those very same words that Mom had said to him? I shake my head and calm myself. The last thing I want to do right now is fight with him. If I don't go away sooner, on Friday I'll be allowed to go to the castle for the Ghost Tour. And I don't know if I'll ever return.

We eat for a while, the only sound is the clink of our forks on our plates. "I guess I just want you to be happy, Dad. I don't want you to be alone."

He gives me a meaningful look. "I just felt that way when you were gone and I didn't know—"

"I'm so sorry."

He nods and stares at his food.

"Look, Dad, what I'm trying to say is that you need to make your own life and think of yourself once I leave."

He raises his brows.

"I mean to college and all." I squirm in my seat. "I can't live with you forever."

"No," he smiles. "I don't suppose you can."

I push the mushrooms off to the side and twirl some noodles onto my fork. "I just want you to know that I think you're a great father and I'm lucky to have you."

"Uh oh. How much money do you want?"

"Be serious. I don't want you to worry about me because I'm happy, okay? I'm happy and I'm going to be just fine. I promise you. You do believe me, right?"

He looks at me and nods.

"And I need to know that you'll live your own life and take good care of yourself, and do things that you like to do once I'm, you know, gone. To college. Can you promise me that?"

He tilts his head. "Okay. Deal. But can I miss you just a little bit while I'm having this great new life of mine?"

I try to focus on my noodles. "Just a little bit," I whisper.

• • •

"Wayne De Freccio, please. Yeah. I'll hold." It's early Sunday morning and I'm sitting out back in our tiny walled yard on a rusted metal chair, hugging a thick blanket around me. The sun barely skims the back wall and the corners of the yard are still buried in blue-black shadow.

"Hello, this is Wayne."

"Wayne, hey. It's Michelle."

"Michelle?"

He doesn't sound good. "Your sister. How are you?" I throw this last comment out there as just a formality, but really I hate to ask.

"Who wants to know? You aren't going to tell them, are you?"

I stand and pace the yard. "No. No, of course not," I say, playing along. "I just wanted to hear your voice, you know?"

"Whose voice? You hear it too?"

Those voices in the castle courtyard… "Not really."

"Terrible things. They said mean, cruel things."

"It's okay, Wayne. They can't hurt you. No one will hurt you. Just ignore them."

"But that man, he's always yelling. He's so angry."

"How is your job?" I ask in a cheerful voice.

"I'm the best assembler on the line. They told me that. The supervisors, I mean. It feels good to be doing something useful. And they pay me, too."

There was a time when he'd wanted to be a teacher and coach a school soccer team. "That's great, Wayne. I'm happy for you."

"You're my sister, aren't you?"

"Yes." I'm grateful for his burst of clarity.

"Brothers are trouble. Watch out for brothers."

"Oh. Okay." I twine my finger round and round the branch of a dead rosebush.

"They'll stab you in the back."

"I better go. I love you. Don't ever forget that, Wayne."

"Watch out for Christopher."

"What?" I feel a pinch and notice I've squeezed a thorn. A dot of blood forms on my finger.

"Christopher. He's a brother too. Be careful."

"Wayne, what do you know about Christopher?"

"Only what he tells me. He talks to me. They're brothers. I've heard it. Everyone talks to me. I can't stop it." He sounds panicked.

"It's okay, Wayne. What does Christopher say?"

"That mean man is the one that needs to shut up. He has a knife. He hates everyone."

"Who has a knife?"

A woman tells Wayne to calm down.

"But he's going to kill people," Wayne says. "He's going to ruin everything."

"Who is? Tell me."

"Just relax now, Wayne," a woman says in a soothing voice.

"But the Earl—" he says.

"What about the Earl? Wayne, you have to tell me everything you know."

"I'm sorry," the woman says into the phone. "This is Dr. Bradford. I'm afraid Wayne needs to rest for a while. You're his sister, right?"

"Yes. Is he okay?"

"He's fine. We're just adjusting his medications a bit, so he's in a bit of a rough patch. He should be okay in a few days if you'd like to talk with him then?"

"I have to talk with him now. Just for a minute."

"In a few days," she says. "Goodbye." The line disconnects.

I lick the salty dot of blood from my finger. The sun slips over the garden wall and suddenly it's so dazzling that I can't see. Nothing is clear anymore.

39

I walk through the halls before my first class on Monday and all I can think of is the frantic drawings I secretly sketched last night. My dad would have flipped if he knew I was still drawing Christopher.

With tears blurring my sight, sketch after sketch came to me. Of him holding his head in agony. Of him staring wearily out the window of his room. Of him walking along the ramparts alone, head down. Never looking at me. Christopher in despair over Thomas. Or was it guilt?

Stop thinking that.

As soon as a page was filled, I tore it from the pad and tossed it aside, starting another image in the hopes that this one would find him beyond his misery. Hoping and praying that just maybe he would somehow find his way into my room and my time. Before I ran out of paper, I ran out of images as if someone switched them off in my brain. I tried to sketch another picture but it felt forced and didn't look like him at all.

Finally I accepted that his image wasn't coming anymore that night. So I eagerly went to sleep but only the blank screen of my mind greeted me.

Now bumping through the crowded hallway, I spot Roger; his head towers over the other kids. And I remember the ghost Roger said sometimes appears hanging from the castle rafters. *Suicide.* A chill sweeps through me, as I imagine Christopher…

I quickly push away this thought and push my way forward till I'm beside Roger. "Did you see a doctor?" I ask him. "How's your face?"

"No. And gorgeous, as usual." He turns his cheek to show me his slash, which is now scabbed over. His lip is not as swollen and the bruise around his eye is now tinted yellow at the edges. Better but not gorgeous.

"De Freak-o," someone says. It's Constance. "That's an interesting nickname," she says. "Your brother sounds interesting too." Her smile is extra sweet.

For a second I'm paralyzed. Constance's cousin had finally come through with all the dirt on me. My heart sinks.

"Well, just wanted everyone to know about my cousin's latest update," Constance is saying.

Everyone. She'll tell everyone in the school about me and my family. I know she will.

But really, so what? I'm leaving soon and it won't matter, right? *Soon this name will no longer bother you.*

Huh. So maybe *one* of my mother's predictions came true after all.

"Well, see you in class!" Constance waggles her fingers at me and turns to go.

"Listen Roger," I say, turning my mind to more important things, "we both know who slashed your face. If you won't report him, I will."

"Are you bonkers?" He's about to say more but notices Constance has paused within earshot. He waits for her to move on before saying, "Not satisfied with me being slashed? Want to see me dead as well?"

"Geoffrey's the one that needs to worry. Because his ass is toast."

Roger's eyes grow wide. He grabs my wrist and pulls me off to the side of the hall. "Don't report Geoffrey," he says between his teeth. "Don't you dare. I'm asking you as a friend."

"I thought people like you and I didn't have friends."

"Michelle, come on. This is serious."

"I'll vouch for you. William might too."

"William?" He snorts. "William Wallingford vouching for me? You really are nutty, De Freak-o."

"Don't call me that." Coming from his mouth, these words still sting. I shove his shoulder and hurry past him down the hallway.

"Wait." Roger trots up to me. "Why are *you* getting all angry?"

I stop and sigh. "It's just that Constance knows some stuff I wish she didn't."

"Such as?" He hovers over me with his hands on his hips.

I look around the hall to make sure no one is hanging too close by, and take an extra deep breath. "You've probably already heard through the grapevine that my mom is Madame Florabunda, the supposed psychic." I feel a blush rise on my cheeks.

"I'm not exactly connected to any grapevine."

"Oh." I swallow. Why stop now? "Well, she left us. Just went away. And my brother? He's diagnosed as a schizophrenic. And me? I guess I'm just some freak."

"Wow. This is absolutely brilliant."

"Brilliant?"

"Yeah. Kind of refreshing meeting someone as screwed up as me."

We both break into grins. "You wish," I say.

"I wish you wouldn't rat out Geoffrey. Seriously, just let it go."

"I don't know. It doesn't feel right…"

"Come on. We're mates, right?"

"Maybe. Tell me something first. Why'd you lie about William beating you up?"

Roger stares at me for a long moment, then shrugs. "It seemed a better story than saying me dad did it, you know? And I knew it wouldn't stick anyway. Wallingfords get away with everything."

"God, Roger. You aren't making this friendship thing easy."

"Hey, never said I was a good guy."

"Nope. You never did."

• • •

I walk with my mug of tea across the cafeteria. No sign of William anywhere. This puts me completely on edge. I *need* those missing Wallingford Papers.

Constance obviously hasn't wasted any time spreading her news. People are staring and I can almost hear "De Freak-o" flutter in a whisper around me. I might as well be back at my school in New Jersey.

Someone slams into me and hot tea slops onto my shirt. I gasp and suddenly Geoffrey shoves his face at me. "You'll be sorry you did this, De Freak-o." He points to his cheek and draws an imaginary line there, like a knife cutting a slow gash.

"Some problem here, love?" It's Mrs. Crocker, the sometimes-spitting cafeteria lady. She seems extra-tall and extra-muscular and I'm almost convinced she used to be a man, especially when she drops a large hand onto Geoffrey's shoulder and shoves him toward his table.

Behind her stands Roger, with napkins.

I stick out my hand. "Thanks."

Roger moves the napkins behind his back. "Get your own and piss off." He heads to his lonely table.

Feeling stung, I grab a pile of napkins from the counter and head toward Guncha and Justine. I set my half-empty mug on the table, sit and blot my shirt.

"Michelle," Guncha whispers, "what were you thinking? Turning in William for knifing Roger is crazy. You're seriously playing with fire."

"What? I didn't turn him in. And I wouldn't. William didn't even do it. Geoffrey did."

Guncha glances over her shoulder as if she's uneasy to be seen with me. "Everyone's saying you turned William in. Now he's suspended."

"But it isn't true. This is so messed up." I stand and Guncha seems relieved to see me going.

I swallow hard. When I sit by Roger, he turns his back to me.

"Roger, come on. I told you I—"

He whips around. "I told you not to report Geoffrey, so you report William instead? Oh, that's just grand. And now he's actually suspended. William Wallingford, suspended. You don't think that's going to get back on me somehow?"

"It's all a bunch of lies. I didn't do anything. I swear."

"Then why, when I stopped by the school office before tea, did I overhear the Headmistress talking with Mr. Wallingford about the terms of William's suspension for assaulting one Roger Mortley?"

"What?"

"Crap, De Freccio, only you could bring my reputation here down even lower. Just go."

"Okay." Blinking away the tears that threaten to fall, I reach into my blazer pocket and set my little artist Smurf on the table in front of Roger.

Roger picks it up. "Mint condition." He tries to give it back to me but I stop his hand.

"Keep it."

"But you said it was sentimental and—"

"I want you to have it. You were my friend and I want you to remember…" My throat feels tight. "It's just a crappy little toy."

I stand and Roger grabs my arm. "You need money?" he whispers.

"What?" For a moment I think he wants to pay for the Smurf.

"Money. You're running away, aren't you?"

"Not exactly."

He tilts his head and I rush out of the cafeteria.

40

I go straight to the Headmistress' office. She needs to hear the truth about this whole knifing thing. I know it won't change anyone's opinion of me. Once a freak, always a freak. Still, telling the Headmistress is the right thing to do.

Just before I enter I hear Constance say, "Mother, surely you can do something to help William. Please." Seems Constance has beaten me to the punch. I back up a few steps and wait, leaning against the hallway wall.

"Please?" I hear the Headmistress say. "Do you think that is all it takes to undo rules? You ridiculous child."

The scorn in her voice makes me wince.

There's some mumbling that I can't make out, then the Headmistress says, "Stop that. Right now. How many times do I have to tell you? Weakness is not to be tolerated. A woman must be clever, strong. And I expect nothing less from you. I expect the best. Do you understand? Now go before you embarrass yourself further."

Constance comes rushing out, her eyes red. For a moment we are face to face. For a moment I wish I could console her somehow.

Her expression quickly turns to fury. "What are you looking at?" she demands and she walks away with measured steps as if nothing ever bothered her at all.

With more than a bit of dread, I enter the Headmistress' office. She's sitting, composed, behind an expansive polished desk. I explain that I'm here to talk about William, that he didn't do anything to Roger.

She sighs, glances at her watch and says, "Then why, Miss De Freccio, did William Wallingford turn himself in for punishment?"

"That doesn't make sense. Geoffrey slashed Roger." I look about the room, feeling confused. On a shelf I spot a photo of Constance as a little girl. She's probably only six or seven and sits in her mother's lap, looking up at her as if for attention or approval, but the Headmistress is looking squarely at the camera.

"I appreciate your concern, Miss De Freccio," the Headmistress is saying. "But clearly we have an open and shut case here and you are misinformed." She stands and looks down her nose at me with obvious disdain.

"But—"

"Do try not to overexcite yourself in your state. We wouldn't want an *incident*."

My state? An incident? Seems like the Headmistress has labeled me a freak too.

There's still some time before art class, so I go to the school library and head straight for the stacks. I've already been through all of the books on this subject but maybe I've overlooked something important.

Running my finger across the spines, I stop on one titled *The Earl's Folly* and pull it off the shelf. The cover has a fairly decent pen and ink sketch of the castle. I flip through the pages and start to re-read the chapter titled, "His Demise."

The Earl tangled with danger, being a strong supporter of the Duke of York's opposition to the reigning king. Yet it was the Earl's trusting nature that undid him. His ultimate demise came from his false trust in his courtiers, men who, it is believed, had conspired to steal his fortune. On March 1st, 1461,

*the ringleader, Christopher Newman, is said to have stabbed
the Earl to death in the courtyard of the castle.*

I stop and read this again.

*On March 1st, 1461, the ringleader, Christopher Newman, is
said to have stabbed the Earl to death in the courtyard of the
castle. It is said Newman had long been blackmailing the Earl
over a scandalous document.*

That paper in Christopher's trunk. It was signed and sealed by
the Earl. But this information wasn't in this book before. In fact,
Christopher hadn't been mentioned at all. Somehow this is my
fault. I changed something.

*Once the Earl suddenly refused to pay anything further to the
extortionist, Newman's accomplice, a courtier named Plumson,
held the Earl while Newman plunged his dagger into the man's
back. Thanks to the quick thinking and bravery of Percival
Wallingford, Newman and his cohort were summarily caught
"red-handed," their hands literally dripping with blood.
Wallingford managed to kill Newman, while the other man
was arrested by the Earl's soldiers and beheaded that very night.*

I drop the book and pull out another. In the index I find,
"Christopher Newman, Murderer." I stare at this in disbelief. I
drop that book and pull out another, and another. I glance down
the aisle to see Constance pass by.

With yet another book in my hand, I read this same descrip-
tion: Murderer.

If any of this is true, then March 1st isn't just the day the Earl is
murdered, it's the day Christopher is killed. I was last with him on
December 4th. What day was it there now?

I remember that drawing I did of him a while back. Sword
raised. Murderous expression on his face.

I step back from the pile of books on the floor and simply refuse to believe what I've read. Christopher no more blackmailed and murdered a man than I turned in William. It's a lie. A mix-up. A horrible mistake. I remember Christopher's words...

...Did you bring information I can use to my advantage?

...Who did this to you? Who made it so hard for you to believe?

...You cannot be here now. It isn't safe.

...Trust me and kiss me.

Could he be using me? "Security at all costs," I whisper, a heavy feeling in my gut.

"Miss De Freccio, are you unwell?"

I blink and see Headmistress Hunter looming over me. Constance peers smugly from behind her.

"Such disorder," the Headmistress says between tight lips, taking in the jumble of books at my feet. She's almost trembling with anger. "Horrific. We do not treat reading material so shabbily, Miss De Freccio."

"Yes, ma'am. Sorry."

"The Academy expects appropriate behavior both in school and out. We pride ourselves on being the best." She sniffs as if I clearly don't qualify.

Constance grins.

"Clean this *at once*," the Headmistress is saying. "Understand, this will go on your record. And on your *father's*. This doesn't bode well for his future here."

Constance's grin fades.

"But this isn't his fault," I say and hate the pleading tone in my voice. "Please don't let it affect my dad, Headmistress."

Constance whispers, "Mother, I don't think—"

"Are you criticizing me?"

"No, of course not." Constance looks at the floor.

The Headmistress considers me. "Hm. You'll find I am a reasonable woman. You and your father will have one more chance. But just *one*." She strides away.

Constance silently follows her mother.

41

The next evening, I find myself in my bedroom beside the pile of things I've started to gather for my return to Christopher. There are some toiletries, some first-aid stuff and a few changes of clothes. There's also a picture of my father and my brother from before Wayne was diagnosed. Wayne's holding a soccer ball under his arm and his cheeks are flushed. He'd just scored a goal in the tournament and his eyes are bright with joy. My dad, beaming with pride, has his arm around Wayne's shoulders as if to tell all the world, "This is my son!"

I pick up my cell and dial William. To my surprise, this time he answers.

"William, you idiot. We both know you didn't knife Roger. And everyone thinks I ratted you out. Do you realize what life at the wonderful Wallingford Academy is like for me right now?"

"I did what I had to do, okay? I don't want to talk about it."

"What about Geoffrey?"

Silence.

"William, come on."

More silence.

"Fine. Listen, I really need to see the rest of the Wallingford Papers."

"You didn't tell anyone, did you?"

"No. But I have to see them and this has nothing to do with a term paper. Believe it or not, it may be a matter of life or death."

"Explain." When I remain silent, he says, "Thursday night is the start of the fundraising festival for the Old Roman Grounds. Let me take you there."

"You're suspended. Doesn't that mean you're grounded too?"

"My father thought my confession showed great character. He's allowing me to go. Plus I suspect he wants to make a good show of things for any press that might be there. Anyway, I want to take you. It'll be fun."

"Fun? You're actually talking about a date?" I say in disbelief.

"I'll talk to your dad and convince him. He likes me. And I'll tell you about the Wallingford Papers, but only there. Only if you go with me."

"Blackmail," I whisper.

"What?"

"But that's two days from now."

"Take it or leave it." I hear the steel in his voice. "We'll have plenty of time to talk then."

"We're talking now. *Please.*"

Silence.

• • •

Time spreads out before me. The wait feels nightmarish. I think about sneaking out to the castle but my dad has me on a short leash. If I step into the hallway at night, even if it's just to go to the bathroom, he suddenly leaps out of bed and asks me where I'm going. I could sneak away from school grounds but what if that somehow affects my dad's job? Actually, I have to admit to myself I'm reluctant to go just yet. There are too many questions about Christopher's involvement. Too many doubts keep forming in my brain. I need to know whatever those missing Wallingford Papers say.

Before school, I dial my brother's number hoping he'll be able to tell me more about what he's been hearing, but a nurse picks up saying he is in no condition to come to the phone. At school I avoid Guncha and Justine and Roger by spending tea-time and most of lunch in the library. It's lonely but I know it's better than being where I'm not wanted.

At home I try to draw Christopher but all I come up with is cross-hatching that I fill in more and more until there's nothing but a sheet filled with black.

By Wednesday night I lie in the dark, gnawing my thumbnail and watching the squares of faint streetlight that stretch across my ceiling as doubt gnaws at me.

Was he using me? Now that I've delivered that book and it didn't work out for him, is he done with me?

Did he ever love me, or was he only saying what I wanted to hear?

Is he really the evil blackmailing murderer? Has the day of the murder already come and gone?

I close my eyes tightly. "Trust me and kiss me," I whisper. "Trust me and kiss me." I lie very still, feeling my heart throbbing, till I'm sure he's standing beside my bed in the moonlight. My eyes fly open.

My dad's standing there. "Who are you talking to?"

"No one. It's just a…a song. I'm trying to remember the words."

He leaves and I flick on my lamp. I pull out my sketches from under my bed and I look at one after another. In many, Christopher is looking directly at me. His expression is filled with love. I can't be mistaken.

"I'm trying to trust you," I say, "and to hope." I crawl back into bed for another dreamless night.

42

"Did you bring the pages?" I twist and look into the backseat of William's car but it's too dark to tell.

He shakes his head.

"Seriously?"

"Tell me, why do you need to see them so badly?"

"I just do."

His sky-blue eyes glance at me. "I'll tell you what's in them, as I think of it. You know, throughout the night."

I cross my arms.

He says, "So, do you like roller coasters, because quite frankly they make me a little nauseous."

"William. *Please.*"

He taps the steering wheel. "Fine. After that servant was beheaded, Percival Wallingford was deep in the crapper..."

As he drives, William tells me how Percival's father viciously berated him for acting without waiting for word from him. His father called him the most worthless of creatures to slither about the earth, and said he was traveling back to the castle immediately to fix the mess. "Percival was ordered to abandon his brothers."

"His brothers?"

"That brotherhood he put together," William says. Percival was also told that on no condition was he to take any action or all chances of reaping great financial reward would be lost.

Wallingford's father then asked in detail about Christopher Newman. Percival offered his father little info, just saying that the Earl seemed to again favor Christopher as the suitor for his ward. He was certain the selection was nearly made.

"What?" I sit up straight.

William shrugs. "A ward. It's like some rich orphan heiress."

"I know what a ward is," I snap. I clutch the buttery leather seats and clench my teeth.

The car rumbles off the road and over a grassy field where we park among at least a hundred cars. Beyond the parking area, the sky is lit up in a hazy glow from carnival lights.

"Seems like a good-sized crowd," William says. "But even three days of this won't raise enough money to save the Old Roman Grounds."

"What about those decal things they're selling?"

"The ten-thousand-a-pop Roman General stickers?" He shakes his head. "My father said they'd need to sell at least twenty more of them and by Monday. That's the deadline."

"Oh." I look at my hands. Somehow everything seems to be slipping away.

"You're disappointed?"

I nod. "Your dad must be too."

His expression becomes hard. "Not really." We get out of the car and William takes my arm. "Want some candy floss?"

Mr. Wallingford is at the stand and hands us our food. "Hello, son. Miss De Freccio."

I wave.

"Hello, father," William says. "Making a good show of things?"

Mr. Wallingford gives him a grim look. "That pretty little Constance is looking for you, son."

William glowers as we leave the stand. Thinking about Christopher and the ward, I'm probably glowering too. I pull off a pink tuft of candy floss, which is actually cotton candy, and let it dissolve in my mouth but it doesn't rid me of the bitter taste I have. We walk on, passing ladies wearing sheets pinned like togas over their clothes. They hold out baskets for donations and as William reaches for his wallet, we hear, "Michelle? Yoo-hoo!"

It's Mary wearing a white sheet over a golden tracksuit. She trots up to us. "Isn't this exciting? All these people coming together for a cause. Makes you proud, doesn't it?"

"Hi, Mary. You remember—"

"Oh, William. Your father's been such an inspiration to us all. You must be so proud of him."

William draws his brows together. "You have no idea."

"Don't suppose you'd care to become a 'Roman General'? I've got a few decals in here."

"Sold any yet tonight?" William asks.

"Well, no. Ten thousand pounds per decal is a bit steep. But I also have these badges." She pulls a plastic pin shaped like a scroll from her basket. "Two pounds each."

"I'll take two," William says.

Mary hands them over and takes the money, then gives me a wink. "Enjoy your night!"

I pin on my scroll and William stuffs his into his pocket. We walk along as a local rock band starts to play on a lit stage. "Shall we do some rides?" he shouts over the blaring guitar.

"Tell me more about the papers," I shout back.

"Oh." William seems disappointed. "How about we go on the Ferris wheel then? We can talk on that."

Standing on the line, we finish up the cotton candy. William shouts something but I can't hear over the band, which is now belting out a cover song from the eighties. Roger would approve. William leans closer and says, "I never believed Constance, you know. She's been saying you're crazy."

I nod.

"She's the crazy one," he says in my ear.

The line moves forward. William takes my hand but I pull away. "My fingers are sticky," I say. He crosses his arms.

We're almost at the head of the line, when I notice the guy taking the money. His hand's bandaged and it looks like his thumb is missing. My breath comes in gasps just as it did when I ran from him and his gang.

"Next," he shouts.

William pulls my arm forward. But I pull back. The guy sees me and there's a flash of recognition. I turn and run, pushing through crowds of people. Someone is on my trail. I dodge behind a food cart, then frantically zigzag through a group of teens. Someone grabs my arm and I scream.

"Michelle?" William's holding onto me.

"I tried to warn you about her," a girl says. It's Constance. A cluster of Wallingford Academy students surrounds us. At the center are William's buddies including Geoffrey. Guncha and Justine hang on the perimeter. Constance nods toward me. "Just look. Something about her is not right."

William releases my arm. As I scan the crowd, I realize I'm panting like some wild animal.

Constance places her hand on William's chest. "William, *now* do you believe me? I've been telling you the truth all along. And I've been trying to *protect* you. That's all."

William seems confused.

"Hey, mate," Geoffrey says, grabbing William's hand and shaking hard. "You really stepped up for me. I appreciate it."

Before William can respond, Constance smiles and says, "Come on, William. It's time for things to get back to normal now, don't you think?"

"But I'm with Michelle."

Constance sniffs at me. "Oh, I'm sure she understands." She pulls William's hand around her waist.

William gives me an apologetic look.

I nod. I don't belong. I do understand. My eyes are trained on the trampled grass beneath my feet as I wander away.

"Michelle, you can hang with us," Guncha says, by my side. Her voice is especially kind.

I look up, surprised.

"Forget those twits," she's saying. "Right, Justine?"

Justine, who is now beside me too, casts an evil look at Constance and nods. "Absolutely. We girls should stick together. We can do some rides together, yeah?"

"Thanks," I say with deep feeling. "That means more than you know." I look at the Academy students surrounding us. "Actually, I think I'm just going to call my dad and head home."

Constance says, "Where are you going?"

At first I think she's talking to us but she means William, who is right behind me. He says, "I'm going to be with my girl, if you don't mind."

"Your *girl?*" She laughs as if she can hardly believe what she's hearing. "Maybe you didn't get the message. She's just some freak that—"

That's all I hear because the next second, William grabs me and kisses me hard. And for the briefest of moments I see Christopher.

William lets go, leaving me breathless, my heart throbbing. His eyes glitter in the carnival lights as he turns to Constance. He raises his chin to her and says, "Get the message?"

Christopher. I can't help but smile.

The Wallingford Academy students howl and point. Constance's face burns red. She hugs herself and her eyes well up.

I wish I could enjoy this moment, but I feel bad. How many times have I stood in her shoes with people laughing at me? Too many.

She turns her cat eyes on me. "You," she says, like it's a curse. "You'll be put in your place. You just wait." And she stalks off, with Geoffrey in her wake.

"Yes!" Guncha says, pumping her fist. "Oh, why didn't I think of my mobile's camera to capture that kiss? That was brilliant."

William rubs his neck, looking awkward.

"Uh, we'd better go," Justine says. "Come on, Guncha." As Justine pulls her away, Guncha gives us a cheerful wave.

As the crowd breaks up, William says, "Michelle, why did you run? What happened to you back there?"

I suddenly feel too exposed. I look over my shoulder, then lead him past the twirling teacup ride to a more isolated part of the fair grounds. I look around again, just to make sure the coast is clear.

"Michelle? You okay?"

"No. Yes. I mean, I'm not losing it, if that's what you're afraid of. That money-taker at the ride? He kind of caused these." I hold out my hands, showing him the Band-aids.

"That bastard. I'll kill him."

"No. I just want to go. Please."

"But he should pay for this."

"Please, can we just drop it?"

He looks troubled. "If that's what you want. Look, you're upset. Let's walk a bit. You'll be safe with me. And I still have some things I need to tell you." We walk deeper into the shadows. With his dark leather jacket and jeans and jet-black hair, it's like he disappears into the night.

"William?"

"Right here." He takes my hands. "No moon tonight. No stars either."

I feel a weird mix of emotion and try to remove my hands from his, but he holds onto my fingertips.

"Please," he says. "I'm just feeling a little...lost."

"William, I can't—"

"Sorry about that kiss," he says in a miserable voice. "Listen, I'll tell you everything, Michelle. But can I just say something?" He pauses. "Okay. Here it goes. I think you are one of the first unique people I've ever met in my life. And I'm sorry I'm not, well, whatever..." His voice fades into nothing.

As my vision adjusts to the darkness, I can now see him with his head bent, but it's still too dark to read his expression.

He lets go of my hands. "I'm just pretty confused right now. I'm not sure of who I really am, or who I should become, or what, if anything I can do to make things right again." We stand there in silence with only the disjointed echo of the rock band in the background along with intermittent screams of kids sweeping down the tracks of the roller coaster.

"Listen," he says finally, "I want you to know about me. About what the papers say. My family is where it is because of that scum ancestor Baldwin Wallingford. He was a manipulator that had everyone on strings like a puppet. Percival Wallingford didn't realize what was going on till it was too late. He was set up by his own father as part of a plot to get money from the Earl. It seems like Percival Wallingford wasn't really a bad guy, he was more of a wimp. Did as he was told. Always listened to his father. Always." He rubs his head. "God, I'm such an idiot."

"What are you talking about?"

"Forget it. Percival was forced by his father to betray his friends and this Earl who had always been really nice to him. One by one these friends were set up as traitors, then killed. Percival believed these were real criminals, so he was as much in the dark, in some ways, as the victims. But his own father actually did all the plotting."

Wow. I *knew* Christopher wasn't the traitor.

"Then Baldwin Wallingford made his final move," William says. "Blackmailing the Earl. So the Earl signed over part of his fortune and the hand of the ward to Percival Wallingford."

"Christopher Newman?" I say, my throat dry. "What happened to him?"

"He was brought in front of the Earl for questioning and that's when he stabbed the Earl to death."

"No. The papers didn't say that. You're mixed up." Everything feels like it's spinning. "What were the *exact* words?"

"I don't know. Something like: Newman approached the Earl and the Earl was slain."

I take a staggering step.

William grabs my arms. "You okay?"

"I'm...I'm a little..." I'm a fool... A murderer's fool...

He seats me on the ground and sits beside me. "Better now?"

I give a faint nod.

We sit in silence while he tears blades of grass and tosses them. After a while, he says, "Right after Newman killed the Earl—"

"*Why* would he kill the Earl?" Christopher didn't get to marry the ward... He still needed money for his family... He has a fiery temper...

"The letters never said why. But after that, Percival killed Newman."

Numb, I drop my head to my knees.

William says, "Plumson was captured. And, according to the lost papers, that's when Baldwin Wallingford revealed the truth to Percival. That all the prior attempts on the Earl's life were set-ups by Baldwin, to frame the others."

"Why would Baldwin Wallingford want so many dead?" I whisper, looking up.

"Greed?"

I shake my head. Something is missing here. Somehow, the facts just don't add up. "Why not just blackmail the Earl? And Christopher Newman *was* a murderer. You're sure of that?"

William shrugs and stands, dusting off his pants. "All I know is that Percival had loads of chances to make things right and tell the truth, including at Plumson's trial, before the man was executed. Instead, Percival said nothing. He took the spoils, the money and the prestige that went with it and kept his mouth shut. He even rewrote history with public letters that made him seem like a hero. For centuries, the Wallingfords have continued the tradition of keeping their mouths shut..."

I think about how I've been away from Christopher for an entire week. About William's kiss and of Christopher's face before me for the briefest of moments. So I'm not too late. I'm not. He's still alive but for how long? And why do I care? Hasn't he betrayed me? Lied to me?

William says, "And you know what? Some of the people we screwed over back then still have descendants around here. Because of this evil, we're at the top of the food chain and their lot is poor and miserable. Look at Mortley. He was a distant relative of Plumson."

"Yeah. He told me."

"Well, Mortley's life is a bloody nightmare. Imagine centuries of being loathed and pushed down. And, really, we're still screwing over people to this day." He looks at me. "Come on. I'd better get you home."

Back in the car, we drive on in silence. Then something hits me. "That's why you told the Headmistress you'd hurt Roger, isn't it? To try to make up for things?"

William pulls in front of my house and cuts the engine. "In a way, it was my fault."

"That's stupid, William."

He shrugs. "Guess I'm not very bright, then."

I study his profile in the shadowy streetlights. The perfect outline of his classic nose, his distinctive, strong chin. It's a noble face. "I think you're trying to do the right thing and that says a lot."

"The right thing. What would I know about that?" His voice sounds bitter. "What would a Wallingford know about right and wrong?"

"Your dad's doing this cool fundraising thing to save that land. That's pretty—"

"It's all a lie!" he shouts. "It's just another scam, okay?" He pulls the plastic scroll pin out of his pocket and chucks it onto the dashboard.

At once I remember the rolls of paper in Mr. Wallingford's study. Plans of shops for the Old Roman Grounds. "Your dad. He's the one trying to buy and develop that land?"

William nods. "He's hiding behind a corporation."

"Then why's he helping the community to—"

"I told you, it's all lies. Image. Everyone loves him. Keeps the land price low, too. Who else would bid against the community? Everyone wins, he told me."

"That's so wrong. You have to do something."

He chokes the steering wheel. "There's nothing I can do."

"Talk to him, or tell somebody."

He shakes his head. "I can't. And neither can you. Don't say anything to anyone, Michelle. Swear to me."

"All those people believe in your family."

"Swear to me," he says, this time in a panicked voice.

"You're afraid of him?" When he doesn't answer, I say, "Okay, I swear. But my neighbor Mary and all those ladies at the fair. Your father is making fools of them all. You have to do something about this."

"What do you want me to do? Fight my father, the most powerful man around? Find a way to buy up the land by Monday?"

"Yes. No. I don't know. Do *something*." My throat constricts as I imagine a bulldozer knocking down those ancient trees, flattening all those memories, then burying them forever.

"Look," he says, "you don't understand. I can't. I have to think about my future. Without my family's backing and reputation, I'm nothing."

"You're not, William. You're—"

"I'm *nothing*." He gives me a hard look. "I'm sorry. I know you want me to be all brave and save the day, but I can't. I'm just not that guy."

"No," I say, my face hot with anger as I quickly undo my seatbelt. "Of course you're not. And it looks like you'll never be."

"Michelle, wait. Please."

But I throw open the door and go.

43

Friday night. Finally.

I pull at the zipper on my mother's medieval dress. I must have lost some weight because it fits a little better now and the zipper glides up easily. I'm not crazy about wearing this dress again, but only costumed personnel and ghost hunters will be allowed to access the entire castle tonight. Others will wear Ghost Tour T-shirts and be confined mostly to break rooms.

I shove my things into my backpack and pick up my print of the Roman Nymph. It's rolled like a scroll and tied with a red ribbon. Tucked into the ribbon is a goodbye note to my dad—a note that I hoped would make him understand that I'm going to be okay. Do I leave it for him? Am I actually going away?

I'm a mess.

Gnawing on my thumb, I sit on the edge of my bed and go over the facts. Number one: Christopher has a letter signed by the Earl. Was he blackmailing him? Number two: Christopher made no secret of his goal to gain wealth and power to take care of his family. Three: Now that I have tried but failed to give him the information about the future, he's permanently disappeared from my drawings and my dreams. Four: All the history books now agree that he's a murderer. The missing Wallingford Papers back this up. And fact number five (the most important of all): I feel like I've been royally played.

So that's it, then. I'll tell my dad I'm sick. Not go to the castle for the Ghost Tour. And someday this pain I feel, this awful hollowness, will go away. I'll forget the whole thing.

I twist the dress' maroon fabric round and round my finger.

I'll never be able to forget. I tried to forget about my mom, didn't I? If I could just have one chance to tell my mom off, to really let her know what she did to me and my dad, I'd do it.

Right. So the new plan is I go see Christopher tonight, kick his ass, maybe even try to save that poor Earl, then I come back home. And it's done. I tell myself that going to the castle now has absolutely nothing to do with last chances or wild hopes.

I stand and grab the packed backpack, but if I'm not planning on staying in the past, why take it? So I pick up the scroll and shove it into the pack too and stick it all under my bed. Decision made.

"Michelle?" Dad calls up the steps. "You'd better hurry."

"Okay!" I hesitate. Take this bag or leave it? "I *am* going to kick his ass," I say with determination, but I pull the bag out, throw it over my shoulder and make my way downstairs. Out in the driveway, Mary talks to my dad, who is already in the car with the engine running.

"Oh, here she is now," Mary says. Her pumpkin colored tracksuit matches the car. "Oh, my, my. How very beautiful you look."

"Thanks," I say, feeling awkward.

"Shame we don't always dress like this. So lovely. So stately. Of course, it would get in the way of me aerobic workouts." She jogs in place and jiggles. Mary then takes my hands. "William Wallingford will find you positively irresistible tonight, I dare say."

"He won't be there."

"Oh, well. Shame that." She gives a wink to my dad. "But isn't she a picture?"

"That she is. And she's going to be late."

"Right. Well off with you." She lets go of my hands. "And be well. I mean, keep healthy and happy, and not..." Seeming embarrassed at this reference to my mental health, she says, "Just go on with you," and shoos me away.

I wrap my arms around her, my hands patting the fatty ripples of her back. "Bye, Mary," I whisper just in case.

I pull away and she pats my cheek. "Oh. So sweet. Now go!"

I nod and rush to the car. It takes me a few seconds to stuff my book bag and all of the fabric from my dress around me in the tiny front seat. Soon we're off and in the rearview mirror I watch our house and the orange dot that is Mary fade away like a distant memory. Dad drives like a pro, barely hesitating as he merges into the roundabout and then whisks off the circle onto the road leading to the castle.

"You're quiet tonight," he says. "Everything okay?"

"Yeah. Great."

He gives me a long look before his eyes return to the road. "You do look like Mom in this, you know. You remind me of her in so many ways."

Out the window, tiny semi-detached homes flit by. "I'm sorry."

He's quiet for a while, then says, "Don't be sorry, Shelly. I loved your mother. I always will. I want you to know that."

I glance at him, expecting him to look miserable, but he looks calm and nods at me. It's as if we talk about Mom every day. Maybe the fact that we have talked about her from time to time has been a good thing.

He sweeps some of his thin hair off his forehead. "She was always different. Always a free spirit. I guess we were lucky to have her as long as we did."

"Lucky. Is that what we were?"

Dad sighs and pats my knee. "Lucky. If we weren't, then why would I miss her so much?"

There's a swooping feeling in my stomach, as I remember the night before she left. We were on the sofa watching some old movie. I was nearly asleep when she pulled a blanket over me, pressed her lips to my forehead and whispered, "Love you, baby."

"Dad, don't you wonder where she is? Worry about her? Aren't you *angry* that she never gets in touch? Never once…" *Why am I so easily abandoned?* "I hate them," I whisper.

"Who?"

Christopher. Mom. "I said, I hate this."

"I know. And I do wonder and worry, and I am mad. Sometimes. But she's out there somewhere. Someday she'll be back and it'll all be okay."

We drive the rest of the way in silence and I look out the window wondering if it's foolish or wise to believe in someone just because you love them so very much.

We pull into the parking lot of the castle. And I climb out of the car, yanking out the bag.

"What's in that?" Dad asks walking over to me.

"Change of clothes," I say quickly. "You know, in case I get sick of wearing this thing." I look up at the dark towering castle wall.

"You'd better go."

"Yeah." I swallow hard and grab him in a tight hug.

He wraps his long bony arms around me and kisses my head. "You're going to be late."

I hold onto him a little longer. "Love you, Dad," I whisper and let go.

"Hey, what's not to love? See you in the morning. Six a.m., right?"

"See you," I say in a choked voice. I quickly look away and hurry on. Roger's crappy truck is a few spaces down and I give it an affectionate pat as I pass.

I pick up my skirts and rush along the gravel path and through the castle gate, pausing as I reach the inner courtyard. Scruffy men wearing Ghost Tour Tees are wheeling stacks of electronic equipment on dollies, like roadies at some supernatural rock concert.

Somehow I can't bear to go another step. What am I doing here? Do I really have to put myself into a scenario filled with murder and even more heartbreak, before I can face the truth? *Christopher never loved me.*

Suddenly I want to just forget everything and hide under the duvet in my room and cry until I can't cry anymore. And learn, finally learn for real, not to be so trusting. Not to expect friendship or love.

"De Freccio, come on." Roger, dressed in his Robin Hood-like get up, takes my arm. "If you're any later, they're going to cut you from the roster." He pulls me into the courtyard.

I dig in my heels. "I'm not going. I changed my mind. Anyway, you don't want to hang out with me."

"What are you going on about?" He puts his hands on his hips. "You aren't leaving me stuck all night with the likes of constipated Constance."

"Constance is doing this too?"

"Yeah. Joy, right? At least with you here there'll be a few laughs. Come on."

"I *can't*." I dodge to the right to avoid his outstretched arm, furious with him for interfering. Why can't he just leave me alone? Why can't everyone, once and for all, leave me alone?

A young man's voice says, *"Sir, I am no traitor. You know I have done nothing wrong."*

"I am powerless, son," says a weary man's voice.

"Unhand the Earl!" the young man shouts.

"Silence, and take death like a man." This voice is sharp and cruel.

Then it feels like a bolt of fire sweeps into my back. I involuntarily arch and collapse to the ground in pain.

"Michelle?" Roger kneels beside me. "Michelle, say something."

"There," the cruel man says with satisfaction. "It is done."

"What is done?" Roger says. "What are you talking about?"

I blink at him. "I didn't say that. Did I?" Roger nods and I shiver. "Did I say anything else?"

"No. Just that 'it is done.'" His brows furrow. "Why?"

I can't answer because all I can do is think of that young man's voice. The one pleading for justice. I know that voice. I know it as well as I know his light-green eyes, his strong chin, the gentle touch of his hand on my face. Could I have been wrong? Could history be wrong?

Maybe I am a fool. Maybe Christopher *doesn't* love me. But that doesn't mean I'm not in love with him…

"I have to get in there."

"That's what I've been saying." Roger helps me to my feet. "What just happened to you, anyway? Was that a seizure or something?"

"Cursed spot," I say breathless, as I pick up my bag.

While Roger looks over his shoulder with wide eyes, I race for the door that leads to the Great Hall and the bedroom chambers beyond.

44

"Be prepared to be scared," Roger says in an ominous voice, waggling his eyebrows.

We're in the Great Hall and everyone is holding castle maps and a timetable of events. I had wanted to make a run for the bedroom chambers, but one of the staffers spotted Roger and me on the steps and corralled us with the other workers in the hall.

The helpers have been broken into groups with each led by one of four psychics. I end up with Roger in ancient Miss Colinspot's group. She's so thin and her skin's so translucent she practically looks like a ghost herself.

I spot Constance standing beside the long table, toying with one of the silver candlesticks. To my relief she's in another psychic's group.

Miss Colinspot explains the procedures, while I fidget impatiently, dying to escape. She talks about how we're to blend in and be silent, and to lend a hand if a guest feels sick or nervous. James steps up, now wearing a bright red "Assistant Manager" nametag, and gives us all a stern lecture about "not nicking anything." Then he glares at us from beneath his unibrow.

I study the timetable, which shows a rotation of areas with each group spending approximately an hour in each of the highlighted sections. Before breaking up into groups, though, the visitors start off in two large groups for a tour highlighting the castle's history. That's when I can break off on my own.

"Remember, everyone," Miss Colinspot says, "stay with your group at all times. No wandering off." She glances at me. "And you, remove your bag." She points to a pile of purses and jackets stacked beside a suit of armor.

"But can't I just—"

"No."

So much for planning. I reluctantly set my bag on top of the pile.

At least one hundred visitors, ranging in age from early twenties to senior citizens, are led in. All look excited at the prospect of seeing ghostly activity.

"So the tour begins," Miss Colinspot shouts, her arms waving, her bangles clanging. I follow the crowd out of the Great Hall. On the stairs, the group divides. Half goes out into the courtyard and Miss Colinspot's and Constance's group heads toward the Mating Chair.

"This is the infamous chair," Miss Colinspot says, "so named because it's where the rather charming, rather indiscreet Earl of Blanchley Castle shall we say, 'possessed' many a wench."

The visitors chuckle and nudge each other. Roger whispers in my ear, "*Possessed.* What rubbish. I could have done a better tour."

Miss Colinspot points to the portrait beside the chair. "This is the murderer, Christopher Newman. An ungrateful young man whom the Earl, it is said, doted on." Unlike the painting that hung here before, this one shows a devilish glint in Christopher's eyes, a sneer on his face. The portrait of a villain. It's him but it's not.

I close my eyes. Imagine myself beside Christopher. I try to feel him standing beside me.

Someone bumps into me.

My eyes open. Constance shoots me a sideways glance and steps in front of me.

"But Newman wanted more," Miss Colinspot says. "He wanted money and power. Perhaps tonight our equipment will find evidence of these spirits." She gestures to video cameras trained on the chair. "Now follow me to the Bloody Chapel."

"Oooh Jane, I got goose bumps," a gray-haired woman says to her friend.

I back away while the group moves en masse along the hall, then walks down the stairs. I see Constance's green gown among the people heading that way. I slip into a shadow by a doorway. Once most of the group has gone down, I rush up the stairs to the hall leading to Christopher's room. It's dark here. The electric torches haven't been switched on. I feel my way along the cold stone walls.

My heart thunders in my chest. "Christopher, where are you? Don't leave me here alone."

"What the hell?"

I turn. "Roger?"

"Who were you expecting? The ghost of Blanchley Castle?" There's a click, as he flicks a switch and the torches light up along the walls. "De Freccio, you'll get us both sacked. You can't be here."

"I have to." I stand before Christopher's door. "Just go back and leave me alone, before you wreck everything." In the darkened room I can make out the antique furniture that was never Christopher's. A large bed in the corner, an ornate desk, a spinning wheel.

I close my eyes. *Please come to me,* I think. I trust you. Even if it doesn't make sense. Just help me to understand. *Please.*

I smell smoke. I feel a gush of wind and open my eyes. The torches are now real. His room is chilled, the window unlatched. A pair of black hosiery is strewn on the bed and some papers flutter across the floor. "Christopher?" I step forward.

"Told you. We be too late." A grubby-looking man in a rough brown tunic stands just inside the door, hands on hips, surveying Christopher's things. "Everything's been taken that's worth takin'. We should'a come here straight instead of marching about with the others."

"Maybe so, maybe so," says another man, his hair matted with filth. He paws through some papers in Christopher's wooden chest.

"Ah, but isn't there somethin' fine about seeing a courtier cut to bits? They be no better than the rest of us after all."

My mouth goes dry. "What courtier?" I say in barely a whisper.

"Aye. One traitor's guts be as bloody and foul as another's," the first man says. He picks up the hosiery from the bed and pokes his finger through a hole in its knee. "He'll not be needing these. Not with his legs cut off and his soul rotting in hell." He laughs.

My own legs feel numb. I can hardly breathe. I whirl around, frantic to see something other than what I see. But there is only the ransacked room. And those men leaving with Christopher's hosiery.

My entire body trembles as I go to his bed. It's stripped bare. I touch the lumpy straw-filled mattress and at once I understand. He's not coming to me anymore.

A stab of sorrow cuts into me. It pours from my mouth. My wail shatters the silence.

Arms grab my waist and I'm dragged backward.

Wind swirls. Images quickly flit past me of the two looters. They're walking backwards. Hosiery is placed on the bed as the scene goes into rapid rewind. They quickly back out. Three cloaked men enter backwards, arms filled with bundles of clothing and sheets. They move about the room. Bed sheets unfurl and the bed is remade. Papers from the floor fly back into the chest. The men retreat. A shaft of daylight sweeps from right to left. A giant of a man appears. He drags Christopher. Christopher struggles. A blade is at his neck.

I struggle to reach him. I can't move forward. The grip around my waist is too tight. It tears me back. Away. He's gone.

In the darkened room I can make out the antique furniture that was never Christopher's. A large bed in the corner, an ornate desk, a spinning wheel. An electric torch lights the hallway.

"De Freccio, what the hell was *that?*" Roger releases my waist. He's pale and shaking.

"No. Damn it. NO." I hit Roger. And hit him again. "Why couldn't you leave me alone?"

"Oh, I don't know. I guess when I see my friend start to disappear, I KIND OF FREAK OUT!"

"I was there. He was—" Tears wet my face.

"W-what's going on, De Freccio?" His voice trembles. "If you're messing with my mind, I don't frikken appreciate it."

"I've failed him. And now Christopher…" I wipe my cheeks with the back of my hand. *What's happened is my fault.* Christopher lived because I saved him at the Roman Grounds. Then because of me, he never rode off to protect the ward at the Earl's estate and wasn't killed in that ambush. Greenfeld was instead. Then I saved him from his battle wounds. But somehow my saving him only doomed him to a worse fate. More violent death. A hateful legacy.

I push past Roger.

He grabs my wrist. "Christopher? You mean the guy I saw with the sword. In the drawing you showed me. And in the painting by the Mating Chair?"

"God, don't you understand? He's dead."

"Yeah, for like a few hundred years." He laughs.

A fresh stab of sorrow cuts into me.

"Jesus, De Freccio, I'm sorry." His voice is unusually gentle. "Calm down, okay?" He releases my wrist. "So, if what you say is true… But that's crazy. Then again, what isn't crazy, yeah?" Roger runs his fingers through his hair. "Okay, if you *can* do all that *Back to the Future* rubbish, well you've got all the time in the world to fix things. Just turn your time machine back to an earlier time."

"Time machine. What time machine? Roger, you are such an…" *Idiot.* I'm an idiot for not thinking of this sooner. Roger pulled me back. And time went backwards. At least it looked like it did.

My eyes widen. "If I have time, it's not much." I try to concentrate on Christopher, to pull myself back to his time. I close my eyes and center all my thoughts on him. But before I even open my eyes, I know it didn't work.

Roger crosses his arms. "Time machine busted?"

"He isn't here. Not in this room, anyway. Come on."

"What do you mean, 'come on?'"

"Seems like we're friends, right? I might need your help."

"Like hell," he says but follows me just the same.

45

"Hurry up, De Freccio," Roger says from the hallway just outside the Great Hall. "Someone's coming,"

I scan the bags and coats piled beside the long table in that room, but my bag isn't there.

"Come on," Roger says in a low and urgent voice.

I spot my bag near the wall, far from its original location, take it and run to the door. Roger grabs my arm and pulls me down the stairs and against the wall.

At the top of the landing, James strides into the Great Hall.

Roger exhales. "That was close," he whispers. "Now that James is management, there's no telling what he'll do." His expression grows serious. "At least you've got some first aid supplies with you now."

I swallow hard. "Guess we better go to the cursed spot."

When we arrive, it's clogged with our group and Constance's group still on tour. Miss Colinspot glances in my direction and I push my bag behind me. From the other side of the courtyard, Constance flicks her eyes at me and grins.

Miss Colinspot waves her arms about as she describes how on this very spot the Earl must have tried to fight off his attacker, and how the brave Percival Wallingford struggled with Newman the murderer. "Subduing him with a final deadly strike," she says and dramatically raises her arm high and pretends to stab.

I turn away and shiver. I close my eyes. *Come on, Christopher. Be here. I need you. And you need me.*

After a few minutes, Roger whispers, "You're still here, you know."

"We have to try other parts of the castle. Fast."

Miss Colinspot claps her ancient hands. "Now we shall begin our psychic investigations. My group, off to the dungeon!"

A chill crawls up my back. He's down there. I just know it.

Miss Colinspot disappears down the dungeon stairs at a sprightly pace and the others dutifully follow. Near the top of the stairs I clutch my bag with one hand and cling onto the Ye Olde Instruments of Torture sign with the other.

"You coming or not?" Roger asks.

"Is the dungeon small?"

"It's not huge, if that's what you mean. Come on. Get your arse down there."

"Okay. Right." I let go of the sign and approach the stairs. There's a faint light coming from the bottom. The stairway is narrow. The treads are uneven white stones cemented together. They remind me of giant teeth.

I take a step. Another.

"See? Not bad." Roger says from right behind me.

"Can you back up a bit? Not get so close?" The air feels thin and hot as I take another step down and another. Now I'm so far in that the air is dank and musty.

The stairs turn and I suck in big gulping breaths, convinced I'm suffocating. A few more steps and the dungeon opens before me. But it's small. Too small. One high window crisscrossed with black bars and draped with cobweb provides the only glimpse of freedom. The floor is crowded with Ghost Tour visitors sitting on the packed dirt floor. Rusty chains and cuffs hang from bolts high on the walls. And in one corner beside a tiny desk lamp a technician toys with some equipment.

"There, you made it," Roger says. "That wasn't so bad, was it? Let's sit."

"I'll stay near the steps." I cling to the filthy wall. At least I'll be the first to escape when the air runs out completely.

Roger steps around some of the people on the floor and leans against the wall opposite me. A set of cuffs is right above him.

"A séance is a quiet thing," Miss Colinspot says, her voice soft. She's sitting cross-legged on the floor in the center of the room. "It lets the spirits among us know we are listening to them and that they are welcome to speak. Nevertheless, if you feel at all uncomfortable, our capable staff," she waves to Roger and me and three other people, "are here to assist you. After about a half hour, we will review our equipment readings. Sometimes they are more sensitive than even I am."

A man raises his hand. "Have you captured anything on equipment before?"

"Oh my, yes. At one castle we had quite remarkable results, hearing whispers on the tapes and recording dramatic fluctuations of temperature right when the whispers occurred."

The men and women look at each other. Some smile, others appear nervous.

"But I must caution you, not all tours have these results. So, shall we see? Clear your minds and feel." Her gaze becomes unfocused.

I lean against the wall and feel as if I'm underwater and have just let out my last bit of air. Panicked, I want to run up the stairs, break out of here and fill my lungs again. But I force myself to stay.

A ticking noise comes from the machinery. "Temperature dropping," the technician whispers.

Miss Colinspot doesn't move or react. I almost want to check her for a pulse. Everyone else looks up at the walls as if expecting to see a ghost flit by. The room feels very still.

Suddenly, Miss Colinspot inhales deeply and exhales. A breeze skirts the room, along with a hiss that whispers to me: *Assassin.*

No.

"There!" someone shouts.

Everyone jumps.

"There's the thief. See? I told you," Constance says with great pleasure, as she comes down the stairs with James. His stout form seems to swallow up the entire stairway and, I'm certain, all of the air. I take deep breaths.

He comes straight to me. "Your bag. Show me." He pulls my backpack from my shoulders.

"James," Miss Colinspot says in an imperious voice, "we were about to have an encounter before you so rudely interrupted."

"I'm not tolerating anything being nicked. I'm responsible, you hear?" He paws through my bag and pulls out a candlestick. "Aha!"

"But I didn't do it," I say.

"Tell that to the Constable." James shoves my bag into my hands and holds the candlestick high. People murmur to each other. He grabs my arm and drags me up the stairs.

"No. You can't do this," I say, struggling. "I have to stay." He pulls me up into the courtyard. The fresh air fills my lungs. I'm grateful for the open space, but only for a moment. "You don't understand. I have to get back down there now."

Constance shakes her head and says, "So sad, really."

I yank my arm away from James and face Constance. "I can't believe you're doing this to me. You're actually behind this, aren't you?"

"You think I want this?" she says. "It's your fault this is happening. All your fault. Stealing what isn't yours. Taking what you don't deserve. Ruining everything."

"Enough chatter," James says and nods at me. "You'd best come along."

But I say to Constance, "What about my father? He's innocent. What will this do to him? To his career? To our last chance? You're hurting—" *Christopher.* "Don't do this. Please."

"Please." Constance draws her brows together. "But it's done, isn't it? There's no going back now. Just back to America, I believe." A grin spreads across her face.

"You know what? That's *it*." I throw down my bag and stride toward her, fists clenched.

Alarmed, Constance backpedals a few steps.

"I'm the one," Roger says, popping up between us. "I took the candlestick."

I step back. "You did not."

"I did. You know how I'm always looking to make some money, right? So, I nicked it. Seemed like easy cash. It'd sell much faster and for more than any of that eighties junk I've been collecting. James, you got me. I confess. I stuffed it into her bag."

"Oh." James rubs his mouth. "Roger, this is disappointing."

I whisper to Roger, "Don't cover for me. Your job. Your sister. You can't get arrested."

He whispers back, "Why don't you leave it to me and hurry on off, yeah?" He raises his voice to say, "Couldn't help myself, James. All my fault."

"But it was *her*," Constance says. "She's the one. You said it yourself that she was sneaking around after hours that one night."

"It's all my fault like usual," Roger says. "I've confessed. What more do you want? Can't a bloke do the right thing for once in his life?" His eyes dart at me and there's a glint in them.

"Okay, you," James says. "What's your name again?"

"Constance. Constance Hunter, Mr. *Assistant* Manager," she says in a sarcastic voice.

James' unibrow lowers a fraction. "You did say you just heard about the theft. Not that you actually saw it. You." He picks up my bag and holds it out to me. "You're on the clock. Back to work."

I take the bag and mouth "Thank you" to Roger. When I turn to go, Constance is on my heels.

"This isn't over," she hisses. "I've got all night."

"Now Constance," Roger says, "leave Michelle out of this. If you and me schemed to steal and it failed, you can't go blaming her. It's your jealousy what did us in, love."

"What's this?" James says. "Roger, you and this Constance schemed together?"

"Oops." Roger puts his hand to his mouth.

"What?" Constance says. "Me? I'm the daughter of the Headmistress at Wallingford Academy. And you can't seriously believe what *he* says."

"I can do whatever I like. Because I *am* the assistant manager. The Constable will want more than a word with you."

"No. You can't arrest me," Constance says, panic rising in her voice. "Didn't you hear what I said? I'm the Headmistress' daughter. She'll be furious."

"Sorry, babe," Roger says to Constance. "I just cracked. But the important thing is that we're together now, right? And we'll get through this together like we always do."

"You and me?" Constance says with disgust. "Never, *ever* in this lifetime."

"Now, babe," Roger says, "you know Michelle and I are just friends. I've told you that again and again. Why'd you have to get all jealous and accuse Michelle like that? Hm? In a few more hours we would have smuggled that candlestick out of the castle, cashed it in and been off on our posh lover's holiday just as you planned." He puts his arm around her shoulders.

Constance pushes him off. "Don't you touch me, you mangy low-life."

"But babe, that's not what you said to me last night when we was all cozy. Give us another kiss." Roger puckers up.

"Ugh! Shut your filthy face."

"I know she's not very nice or very bright," Roger tells James, "but what can I do? She's great in—"

"I'll kill him!" Constance shrieks. She dives at Roger but James grabs her arms.

Roger waves at me to go. I nod and hurry down the stairs again, which seem even darker and smaller than before, and when I hit the dirt floor, everyone's looking at me.

"Just a mix up," I say.

"Yes. Thank you for joining us," Miss Colinspot says with a condescending smile. She grows serious. Somebody coughs and a few others move about to get more comfortable. Then silence. Pure silence.

I shift from foot to foot with impatience. The room grows cold. It's as if the walls are made of ice instead of crude stone. The machinery clicks and the technician turns the dials.

Something tickles the back of my neck and I turn, but nothing's there. A breeze gusts down the stairs. The guests exchange meaningful glances.

My sight is drawn to the wall behind Miss Colinspot. There's a crevice cut into it and a small grate set on the floor.

Something stirs there and wraps around the bars of the grate. Then it's gone.

My heart pounds as I step forward.

"Temperature's way, way down," the technician says, his breath fogging the air.

Miss Colinspot sways from side to side. A gust blows a coil of my hair from my brow and I hear the visitors' worried whispers.

I train my vision on that grate and hold my breath. Something wraps around it again. Fingers. *Someone's in there.*

Miss Colinspot's vacant eyes lock on me. Suddenly she's gone. They're all gone. A lone torch fills the room with a smoky light. I step forward slowly, dreading what I'm about to find.

There at my feet, beneath the grate, Christopher lies in a shallow pit. His knees at his chest. His face strained with suffering. His fingers clinging to the bars for dear life.

46

I throw down my bag, fall to my knees and gently touch his hands, which are chafed and bloody.

"Michelle," he whispers. His face is turned to the side and his lips are dry and cracked.

"I'm here. I'll get you out of this." I pull at the grate but it doesn't budge. A huge lock bolts it shut. I tug at it but it's no use. The hole he's in is so small. So much smaller than the dungeon or than any other space I've ever been in. The mere sight of it makes me sweat and pant with terror. "There has to be a key," I say in a breathless voice. I look around but see nothing.

"Go back. I do not want you to see me like this." His voice sounds thin.

"You're in pain. We have to get you out. Where's the key?"

"The jailer."

"Where's the jailer?"

"I do not know."

"What day is it?"

"I have been here one full day." He coughs. "It must be the first of March."

Murder. Today.

I stand and look around the dungeon, hugging myself to hold in my panic. The floor is covered in slimy hay and there's a scritching sound in the corner. "I'm getting you out of here now." I head to the steps, fighting the urge to run up them, and dig at one of the rough white stones until my knuckles bleed. The stone finally starts to loosen. I kick at it with my heel and it comes free.

I grab the rock and return to his side. "Pull in your fingers." I start whacking the lock as hard as I can. The dungeon echoes with the clanging.

"Someone will come," he says between strikes.

"Let them. It's not like they'll see me." I continue hitting the lock. Sparks fly but the lock remains undamaged.

Footsteps pound down the stairs. I pull into the shadows, dropping the stone behind me. It's a man with powerful fists dressed in a dark leather tunic. I cover my nose against his fragrant blend of B.O. and crap. He marches over to Christopher, keys jangling from a ring at his waist. "What in the name of the duke is going on? Well?" He kicks some hay at Christopher, who coughs.

I step close and grab at the keys. But my fingers pass right through him. I pull away as my skin crawls and my mouth is filled with such a foul taste I think I might heave.

He's staring at something on the ground.

I steal myself and try again, this time slowly. My fingers pass through the metal of the keys and into part of the man's hip. My flesh feels as if it's rippling with itchy hives as I yank back my hand. My stomach lurches.

"What is this?" he says, taking a step.

I realize he sees my bag. Quickly I snatch it from the ground.

The man jumps. He looks about the dungeon with wild eyes and turns to Christopher. "There was a sack. Just there. Now it is gone."

Christopher says nothing.

The man casts a nervous glance over his shoulder. "If I hear another bit 'o that noise, I will drop a nice hungry rat between your slats. Got that?" He growls for effect but hurries toward the steps with a fearful expression.

I try to grab at the keys again. Nothing. I follow him and grab again. "No! This has to work." When he reaches the stairs, I grasp once more at nothing. He takes the stairs two at a time while I'm left staring at my empty hand.

"Damn it!" I pound my fist against the stone wall. Tears of frustration sting my eyes as I spit out the disgusting taste left burning on my tongue.

"Please. Do not torture yourself."

"I can't do it," I say in a choked voice. "I can't help you at all."

"It is enough I got to be with you one more time."

"Don't talk like that." I go to the pit and kneel beside him. Reaching my fingertips through the bars, I touch his cheek. He closes his eyes.

"We must face reality," he says.

"No. There has to be something I can do. Tell me what's going on. You have to be totally honest. What was in that note in your wooden chest? The document signed by the Earl."

"How do you know of it?"

"I know."

"It was a letter from the Earl, inviting me to this castle."

"Not something you could use against the Earl?"

His hands tighten on the bars. "I am no blackmailer. I serve the Earl and the House of York."

I hear the conviction in his voice and can't help but believe in him.

"Christopher, Wallingford's father is behind it all. He's been blackmailing the Earl. He set up all the supposed traitors, who were falsely accused. It's all his doing."

"Thomas," he says in a very small voice.

"I know." I stroke his hair. "I'm so sorry. You *are* innocent, aren't you? I should have had more faith."

"And I should have been wiser and seen through Wallingford's schemes, instead of being trapped like some dog. Go. Leave me to die in my shame."

There's a nasty rustle in the straw not far from us. Terror squeezes my throat. "No. I won't leave you. And you have nothing to be ashamed of. You have always lived honorably and brought pride to your family name." I lean over and kiss his forehead between the bars. Then I sit up straight. "Christopher, you wouldn't happen to be wearing your bear pin, would you?"

"My pendant? Yes. Yes, of course. I will give it to you now as a token of my unending love." He struggles and groans, trying to move his hand within the tight pit. At last, with his fingertips barely reaching through the bars, he offers up the pin. "Remember me always."

I take it and grab the lock on the grate. Stick the sharp pin tip into the keyhole. "Come on." I jab the pin around. "It can't be that complicated."

"What are you doing?"

"What am I doing?" I say, frantically poking at the lock. At once there's a click and the lock opens. "I'm getting you the hell out."

47

I toss the lock, quickly pin the pendant on my dress and lift the heavy grate, dropping it off to the side.

Christopher moans as he tries to unfold his body from the hole.

"Gently," I say, helping him to straighten his arms. Then I wrap my arms around his back and slowly pull him upright.

He seems so weak and there's dried blood around his nose, but he's smiling. "My dear lady."

I rest my cheek against his for a delicious moment. "Can you walk? We have to get out of here fast." I pick up my bag, wrap his arm over my shoulder and guide him as he limps toward the narrow stairs.

When we finally reach the top, we peer out into the courtyard where the night is lit by a partial moon. I barely have a second to swallow a great gulp of fresh air. Christopher's jailor is several yards away, flirting with a woman. And a cluster of men swaps stories in the center of the courtyard.

Christopher nods to the right. I support him as we manage to hurry unnoticed into a doorway of a small room. He pulls the door shut behind us. My heart is thundering in my chest.

"Shh now," he whispers. "Do not look so terrified. I am here. Now I will always be here right by your side." He tugs on one of my curls and smiles as it springs back. Taking my hands, he says, "Let me look at you. I thought I would never see you again. Dressed like a lady as well." He touches his pin. "This suits you."

"Christopher, this trouble. It's not over yet."

"No, it is not," he says with a low but determined voice. "There are some people I have to kill first." Anger flares in his eyes and for a moment I believe he could be capable of murder.

"You're not a killer."

"Honor has been compromised. First I must kill Percival Wallingford, then his vile father." He grits his teeth.

"No." I put my hand against his chest. "You have to think this through. Percival is innocent."

"Hang innocent. He tossed me into that infernal hellhole. Said I was plotting to kill the Earl."

"He thought you were a traitor. He was following orders. He doesn't know about his father's involvement yet."

"Ignorance is no excuse."

"Didn't you follow orders, too?"

"I hunted up Craigston." He hangs his head and slumps against the wall. "And assisted with other apprehensions. Perhaps I deserve to be executed."

"No. Look at me." I lift his chin. "You're not a blackmailer, or a traitor, or a murderer. We have to get you away from here. The Earl is about to be killed and you and Plumson are to take the blame, and…" I can't bear to tell him anything more.

"Wait. You know this for a fact?"

"It's going to happen in the courtyard."

"The courtyard? Murder and betrayal in such an open location where so many folk can bear witness?"

"Thomas is dead because of me and that stupid book. If I hadn't brought it, he wouldn't have been accused of spying. And I can't take you also…" Hot tears fill my eyes.

Christopher brushes a teardrop from my cheek. "No. It is not your fault. The fault lies with Wallingford and his father."

"We'd better get you some food and water, and clean up your cuts."

"I am fine." He wipes the dried blood from beneath his nose.

"You look weak. Is your old injury bothering you?" I touch his side.

"Long healed. There is no time for your fussing. We must move." Christopher opens the door a crack.

"Find him, idiot!" a man shouts. "Alert the guards."

Another man yells, "Close the castle gate!"

"How could this have happened?" It's Percival Wallingford and he's just outside our door. Through the crack I can see the jailer beside him.

"I do not know, sir," the jailer says. "I checked on him only a minute earlier and he was secured."

"Idiot!" Percival says, his hands on the hips of his rich blue tunic. "Do you have any idea what my fa—, what the Earl will do when he discovers this? He's expecting the prisoner to be brought before him in the chapel now."

"The gate is secured, sir."

"Then the traitor is here yet. But there are too many holes where a rat can hide." Percival looks about. "Order your men to begin searching every possible location. Plumson has also been implicated for treachery. Have your men arrest him and bring him to me at the chapel. Perhaps that will distract my father for a while."

"You mean the Earl," the guard says. "Distract the Earl."

"Just find Newman at once, or I promise you will be the one locked in the pit."

They stride off in opposite directions.

Christopher pulls the door shut. "We are trapped." He touches my hair. "I want you to go. There is no need for you to see…" He leans forward to kiss me and I step back.

"Stop it. Don't you dare give up. You forget that I'm part of your fate now. And I think I have an idea. I'll divert everyone's attention while you run off to a hiding place. Somewhere we can lay low for a while." I reach for the door.

"Michelle, wait. If you can secret me out of this room, I must go directly to the chapel."

"But it's the Bloody Chapel."

"Yes, it bloody well is."

"No. You don't understand. People are going to die. You…" I swallow hard. "We have to go somewhere safe."

He holds my hands. "The Earl will be at the chapel and soon so will Plumson. I shall not abandon them."

"Don't go all noble on me. You have to stay away from the Earl. You won't be helping anyone if you're dead. Don't you understand?"

He pulls away his hands. "I am to die today."

I look at the ground and whisper, "In the courtyard."

"Oh." He takes a step back and touches the coin hanging around his neck. "I see." There's a long silence. "Then we best get away from the courtyard and to the chapel at once."

"You can't go near the Earl. What they'll do to you…" I shut my eyes.

"I well know what torture a traitor must endure. I have seen it."

When I glance up at him, his brow is furrowed.

He gives me a determined look. "I am sworn to protect the Earl."

"Christopher, please."

He raises his chin.

I clench my fists. "Why must you be so damned noble and so damned stubborn?"

"I shall not waver."

"Okay, then," I say. "If that's the way it's got to be, then let's do this thing." I open my bag and pull out my weapon of choice—my red Chuck. "When the time is right, you run like hell, you got that?"

48

Christopher kisses my cheek for luck and I step into the moonlit courtyard, leaving the door ajar behind me. Shoe in hand, I edge closer to the small crowd milling about the center.

Among the men stands the woman the guard was flirting with earlier. She's short and curvy with long red hair. A spindly man with a greasy moustache clasps his hands behind his back and says, "These men are most coarse for a delicate creature as yourself, Milady. May I escort you into more private surroundings?" He licks his lips and peers down the top of her dress.

"You may not, sir. I came only to hear what news is about." She turns from him with obvious distaste.

I aim for the woman's ass and throw my Chuck.

Direct hit. She jumps.

I pick up the shoe before anyone notices it.

"What do you think I am?" she shouts, her cheeks now as red as her hair. She slaps Mr. Moustache.

Some other men turn, point, laugh.

He frowns. "Why you haughty little—"

"Speak not so of me!" She slaps him again, this time so hard he staggers back.

Furious, he lunges for her. I back away as several men leap to stop him. Others jump into the fray. Fists fly. The crowd encircles them, hooting with delight.

I scream, "Christopher, run!" He bolts from the door and dashes across the courtyard. Hiking up my long skirt, I race after him. He runs through an archway and I follow, meeting him just inside.

"You are quite the mischief-maker," he says with the hint of a smile on his face. I stow my Chuck in my bag and he takes my hand and pulls me down a stairway. This opens into an expansive torch-lit cellar with a low-beamed ceiling, casks stacked against the walls and tables spread with tools. He picks up an axe and we run to the opposite side.

He pushes open a heavy door. We climb more stairs, go down a long hallway and stop at the closed arched doorway to the chapel.

He grips the axe tight. "Stay here," he whispers.

"No way. I'm coming with you."

"Michelle."

"You're not the only one who can be stubborn."

He tightens his jaw. "Stay behind me, then. Out of harm's way."

"Wait. What's the plan?"

"I shall tell the Earl the truth and Baldwin Wallingford shall be locked away."

"But what if it doesn't work. What if—"

"Shh, Mother Hen." He rubs my cheek, then pushes open the door and strides up the aisle. I hurry behind him.

The tiny chapel is aglow from candles set along the walls. There are a mere ten rows of pews filling part of the room. Arched stained glass windows are along the left wall and a painted carving of a praying Madonna is on the right wall.

At the head of the chapel is an open space before a wooden altar. There stands Baldwin Wallingford with his beastly furred cloak and a self-satisfied smile. Next to him is a jittery Percival. A guy with a savage face and a hulk-like build is by the front pew standing guard beside the Earl, who turns as we enter. He's still handsome but seems much less merry than he had the last time I'd seen him.

"I hear tell you seek me," Christopher says as he nears them.

"Traitor! Release your weapon," Percival says, drawing his sword.

"If you release yours."

"Do I look a fool?"

"You have been played as one." Christopher halts before the Earl and his guard.

"Son," the Earl says, "you surely have no need of a weapon here."

"Sire, I am ever your servant." Christopher kneels before the Earl and sets the axe at his feet.

The guard grabs the axe and tosses it. It whirls toward the wooden altar, where it lodges with a solid thunk.

Christopher rises, fists clenched.

Baldwin laughs. "Well done, Hurly," he says to the guard.

"Don't worry," I say. "I'll get the axe." I hike up my bag and rush for the altar.

"No. Stay behind me. Out of harm's way," Christopher says, his voice growing angry.

"The Earl is quite safe, Newman," Baldwin says.

"Me too," I say over my shoulder as I pull on the rough axe handle. But the blade is deeply embedded in the altar.

"Yes," Baldwin says, crossing his arms, "quite safe, despite you plotting his death. So how did you escape?"

Now I'm pulling the axe so hard my hands sting, but it doesn't budge.

"Bars cannot hold an innocent man," Christopher says and kneels again before the Earl. He shakes his hair from his eyes. "Sir, I am no traitor. You know I have done nothing wrong."

At least the Earl's bodyguard can fight on our side once the Earl learns the truth. But Christopher looks too vulnerable kneeling there, weaponless. I rub my hands on my dress and look for something he can use. On the altar are a giant Bible, a lit candelabra and a huge golden cross on a stand. I spin around. Candles by the windows. That's it.

"The real traitor is Baldwin Wallingford," Christopher is saying in a strong voice. "Sire, I know that he is blackmailing you. But there are far greater evils afoot."

The Earl shoots an embarrassed glance at his blackmailer.

"How dare you speak so of my father," Percival says. His blue eyes seem to spark with anger. "He is a great and honorable man."

"Easy," Baldwin says, grinning. "Your loyalty is admirable, but mere words cannot harm."

Percival beams at his father. He *is* loyal. Like a dog. If he had a tail, it'd be wagging like crazy right now.

"Son," the Earl says to Christopher in a kindly voice, "I would hear all you know."

"My Lord, every assassination attempt on your life came from Baldwin Wallingford. He has set up every supposed assassin who has been executed." Christopher rises to his feet, his pale green eyes full of intensity. "And now he aims to kill you."

The Earl studies Christopher for a long moment and I can't tell what he's thinking. I bite my lip hard.

"Baldwin Wallingford," the Earl says at last, his expression fierce. "You animal. If this is true I shall see you dead." He lunges toward Baldwin, who stumbles backward in surprise, nearly tripping on his cloak.

I'm about to cheer when Hurly grabs the Earl's shoulder and pulls.

"Unhand the Earl!" Christopher shouts.

The Earl struggles to free himself. "Wallingford, make your thug release me."

Wallingford's thug? The odds quickly shift out of our favor.

Hurly yanks the Earl back another step.

Christopher looks stunned. "My Lord, what is the meaning of this?"

"It seems I am powerless, son," the Earl says in a weary voice.

The words I'd heard at the cursed spot. A chill sweeps up my neck.

"Father," Percival says, "I know you said Hurly is here to keep the Earl safe, but is this use of force really necessary?"

"Do not question me," Baldwin says. "Ever. This is all for the Earl's benefit."

"Yes, Father. Of course."

"Wallingford, you monster," the Earl says, as he continues to struggle. "If what Newman says is true, I shall make you pay. I shall haunt you till you are brought to your doom."

"I am not the villain here." Baldwin tucks his hands into his cloak sleeves as if he were a holy monk. "Do you honestly think I want everyone dead, my Lord? Even you? How in God's name would I profit from that?"

How *would* he profit? Again, something about all this just doesn't add up. Maybe Baldwin Wallingford is simply insane.

But he looks serene standing here and he's speaking in a calm voice. "I merely want justice to be served," he says. "And this criminal is the one who must pay." Baldwin pulls a dagger from his sleeve.

I freeze. *The murder weapon.* Its sharp blade glints in the candlelight.

With weapons drawn, Baldwin and Percival swiftly advance on Christopher who crouches in a defensive position, fists raised.

I grab the crucifix from the altar. It's surprisingly heavy—perfect for bashing skulls. As I race toward Christopher, Percival swings. Christopher jumps backward. The sword whips through me with a zing. An electric-like jolt shoots through my waist. I double over.

"No!" Christopher shouts.

An unbearable itch radiates along my torso and a bitter metallic taste overwhelms my mouth. I force myself upright. "I…I'm okay."

"My God," Christopher says, "I thought—"

"Silence, and take death like a man," Baldwin Wallingford says with a sneer. "Percival, you may do the honors."

Percival nods and steps forward.

I hand the crucifix to Christopher. He grabs it and whispers to me, "Step away." Then, with a fierce growl, he swings the cross like a bat.

Percival staggers backwards, nearly dropping his sword. "H-how did that get there?"

I realize the cross must have appeared before his eyes as soon as I let go of it. They all look rattled. Even Hurly crosses himself again and again.

At once I remember my mother's psychic shop. Sitting under her table, pretending I was a ghost from the great beyond. "Christopher, say the name of the first guy who was killed." I rummage through my bag.

"Craigston?"

"W-where?" Percival says, backing up another step.

I pull out my red Chucks and toss my bag onto the first pew. Hurley spots the bag and takes a step back.

I say, "Tell them 'Craigston is coming for the murderer.'"

Christopher gives me a knowing grin. As he says his line, I set the shoes on the ground before the Wallingfords. Hurly squeals.

I move one shoe forward and let go, then the other, and let go. Percival retreats. "I did nothing. I swear!"

Baldwin backs up, as my Chucks seem to march steadily toward them both.

"Baldwin Wallingford," Christopher says in a ghostly voice, "why did you kill me?"

"Work of the devil," Hurly says, gruffly. He shifts from foot to foot.

"Hurly," Baldwin says in a warning voice, pointing at him, "remain where you are."

I jump the shoes to right in front of Baldwin and Percival. They fling their backs against the chapel wall and a whimper escapes from Baldwin. Percival's sword is shaking in his hand.

"Work of the devil!" Hurly shouts. He pushes aside the Earl, then dodges Christopher, tears down the aisle and is gone.

"How dare you, Wallingford," the Earl says, crossing himself. He moves to Christopher's side. "Even thinking of such unholy deeds in such hallowed surroundings. No wonder the spirits have been roused."

"Drop your weapons," Christopher orders. "Now!"

With a clang, Percival's sword hits the ground beside my Chucks.

Christopher drops the crucifix. Grabs for the sword. His fingers close on the hilt. Baldwin's heavy boot smashes down, trapping Christopher's hand.

Christopher grits his teeth. The Earl leaps to help, but Baldwin's dagger flashes before the Earl's handsome face.

I try to push away Baldwin's foot, but my hands fly right through it. My fingers writhe with itch and my tongue is coated with the flavor of rotted food.

"Now you must surrender, Newman," Percival says, sounding almost relieved.

"There is no surrender for a traitor," Baldwin says. He rocks his full weight onto his foot. I hear the sound of cracking bones.

Christopher cries out.

"Stop torturing him!" I scream.

"Go. Now," Christopher says to me, his voice tight with pain. "Go to safer times."

"I'm not leaving you."

"Ah, but you are not going anywhere Newman," Baldwin says. "Your sword, Percival. Get it." He lifts his foot and Percival snatches his sword from Christopher's damaged hand.

I help Christopher to his feet. He's breathing hard. Already two of his fingers balloon from swelling.

Baldwin says, "Now you finish this, Percival," and he wedges his dagger beneath the Earl's jaw. "Watch closely, my Lord."

"But father," Percival says, "the spirits—"

"What do I care of spirits? Of damnation? And I see mere shoes." With disdain, he kicks one of the Chucks. "Newman has studied sleight of hand from the traveling magician, no doubt."

I retrieve the crucifix and Christopher takes it, holding it mainly with his uninjured left hand.

Baldwin looks startled at the crucifix's sudden reappearance. "A deft magician, indeed."

With a deep breath, Christopher swings.

Percival dodges then bounds forward.

Christopher steps back, avoiding Percival's blade. And with a crash, his cross parries Percival's sword. Percival staggers back.

Christopher moves again, slicing. The tip of the cross slashes Percival's cheek and he cries out. A line of blood appears and drips.

Then, with angry force, Percival strikes. His sword knocks the crucifix out of Christopher's injured hand. The crucifix skitters across the floor. The sharp tip of Percival's blade touches Christopher's throat. The two are panting, nearly chin to chin.

I draw in my breath.

And for a flash, it's like everything stops. My eyes trace the curve of Christopher's neck, the squared edge of his jaw. And, like a reflection, Percival's neck and jaw. The same curve. The same squared edge. I turn to the Earl. See his jaw…

In my mind I hear Wayne again saying, *"Watch out for brothers."* And William, telling me, *"Percival was ordered to abandon his brothers."* And Percival, talking about the Earl's careless wenching, saying, *"Perhaps what they say is true…"*

And everything makes sense.

Suddenly all is back in motion.

"Be done with this," Baldwin urges. "Why do you hesitate?"

My words tumble out fast as I say, "Ask Percival if he's loyal to his father and his family."

Christopher's eyes look down at Percival's sword. "Wallingford, are you loyal to your father and family?"

"Am I not doing my father's bidding? My family is everything to me."

"Tell him he's wrong," I say. "Make the Earl explain."

"You are mistaken. You are not loyal to your family or your father." He swallows and his Adam's apple skims the blade tip. "Can you explain this, my Lord?"

"He stalls," Baldwin says. "Strike him and—"

"I meant to care for you, Percival," the Earl says.

Percival's brow furrows with confusion.

"I meant to care for all of you," the Earl continues. "To share my wealth with you, and none of my shame. I meant to see each of you well set in life. You are my—"

"Son," Christopher says, looking shaken. "You are the Earl's son. As am I. Is that not so, my Lord?"

The Earl hangs his head.

"I do not understand," Percival says, his blade lowering a fraction.

"Percival," the Earl begins, "I—"

"Do not speak," Baldwin says, waving the dagger. "What this filth means to say is that he defiled your mother under the excuses of wit and charm. I only learned of this horror when the Countess told me. She knew about the other sons as well and was disgusted they were paraded under her very nose. And the Earl *will* care for us, only us. That is why I have done what I have."

"What have you done?" Percival says, his voice full of accusation.

"Just listen to me and do as I say and you will have all the riches and power and success. As I have urged you before, you must put your bias for Newman aside. Percival," Baldwin says, his voice becoming oily, "we shall finally live a grand life. The sort of life you have always wanted. Do this and you will have everyone's respect. Even mine. You shall finally be a great man. You want to be the best, remember? It is your dream."

An eerie smile grows on Percival's face.

Terror grips me.

"There will be no witnesses," Baldwin says, his voice now a seductive whisper. "All shall bend to you. We will be a great family. Can you not imagine it? Honor *and* justice. Now, Percival, my *son*, prove your worth. It is time."

Christopher says in an even voice, "Yes, it is time, my *brother*."

Percival stares at Christopher. Beads of sweat form on his brow. Very slowly, he brings his sword to Christopher's stomach. He pauses.

I can't breathe. Can't move. Time stretches out painfully.

Christopher's ghostly-green eyes shift to me, and soften. A tender expression of goodbye.

Baldwin roars, "Do it, you spineless—"

Percival pulls back his arm. He strikes fast.

"No!" I scream. My eyes close. There is a horrible moist sound. The thud of a body landing.

My shaking hands cover my face. And I am falling into nothing...

49

Darkness. I freefall into an abyss. But I can't escape the scorching burn of anguish that engulfs me.

Someone catches me, shakes me.

No. Let me be.

"Shh," a voice murmurs in a breath warm against my ear. "All is well."

My eyes flutter open. I'm in his arms. His solid arms. This is no dream. No delusion. I run my hands over his face. "How?"

"My brother chose the path of honor and justice." He nods to the body of Baldwin Wallingford in a heap on the ground. Percival's sword is plunged into Baldwin's gut.

Percival stands over the corpse, shivering so badly his teeth chatter. The Earl removes his cape. "Here, son," he says and drapes it around Percival's shoulders.

My eyes return to the corpse. Blood soaks its mangy cloak and pools around the body.

I hide my face in Christopher's chest. He kisses my hair and sets me onto the pew. His arms surround me protectively.

"I have done nothing," someone is saying. There is a struggle at the door as Plumson is finally dragged into the chapel. He says, "I swear. Whatever it is, it is not my fault."

Christopher pulls away. "I shall be right back. I promise."

He joins the Earl and it takes but a little explaining before Plumson is released and the story shared. Though disappointed to learn that he is not one of the Earl's sons, Plumson is relieved to be free, and talk soon turns toward celebration. A raucous evening of song, drink and card play.

Christopher says, "Sorry, my good fellows. I have other plans." He scoops up my Chucks from the floor and walks to me dangling them from a finger of his left hand. "Your elegant footwear, I believe? Not terribly attractive but apparently quite useful."

I snatch them from him. And I gently lift his right hand. The injured fingers have swollen even more. "This must hurt."

"I feel nought but joy now." His face breaks into a huge smile. He takes my hand, I grab my bag from the pew and he leads me out of the chapel into the hall. "Do you know what would bring me the greatest joy of all?" He brings his lips to my ear and whispers, "Wed me."

50

"Are you sure you will not join me? The water is quite warm."

"Maybe after we exchange vows."

"Ah, but after vows, I believe I will be in the bed." He smiles at me over his shoulder.

I feel a blush rise on my cheeks. I force my view away from him and try to focus on putting Band-Aids on cuts I'd gotten from digging out the stone in the dungeon. I've been trying to do this for the past twenty minutes or so, but it's difficult to concentrate on anything other than Christopher splashing around naked in an enormous tub he had servants leave in his bedroom. It's filled with steaming water and herbs, making the air moist and minty.

"When you get out of there, you have to let me put a brace on those fingers," I say. I already have some kindling twigs set on the side table for this purpose.

"Yes, Milady." He briefly dips his head beneath the water, then shakes it like a dog, spraying me with drops.

"Hey!"

He laughs. His shoulders relax and he sinks lower into the water, sighing. "I feel almost human again."

"That's good. I don't want to marry some grungy animal." I'm amazed at his resiliency. After being kept in that torturous pit for an entire day, then facing near-death, he is now light-hearted and ready to move on with our life together. I am not quite as strong. Putting the Band-Aid wrappers into my bag, my arms still shake as images flit through my mind of Christopher in that dungeon, of the sword raised against him, of the bloody corpse on the chapel floor.

And I can't forget that horrible hatred Baldwin Wallingford emanated. Or the joy he had crushing Christopher's hand. And torturing the Earl by forcing him to think each of his sons were traitors. Making him watch them die until only Percival was left.

And to think that the Countess wanted all of this to occur. After the stabbing, the Earl retrieved the blackmail documents from Baldwin's quarters. He found them sealed with the Earl's own official signet ring. The Countess must have snuck the ring from the Earl's chamber while he had slept. So much hatred.

I tilt my head and study Christopher's back and the way his elbows rest with casual confidence on the rim of the wooden tub. Reaching into my bag for my pencils and sketchpad, I can already picture the lines I will set down to capture his gesture. But I realize I didn't pack a single art supply. "You'd better be able to get me lots of paints and canvases and paper and pencils. I'll be lost without being able to draw and paint."

"And carve. You can easily do wood cuttings like the one you did in the Roman villa. We will decorate the walls of our manor with your glorious art."

"Sounds like a plan." I reach into my bag and pull out the rolled-up print of the nymph, which has gotten squished and bent. From beneath the ribbon, I slide out the note I'd written for my dad, unfold it and read it.

I wish I'd left it for him. Now he'll think I went away without saying goodbye. I unroll the print and marvel at the unbridled joy of the Roman nymph, wishing that my own joy didn't have this edge of sadness to it. I sigh and set the print and note on Christopher's bedside table.

I take out the photo of my dad and Wayne and realize I'm losing my brother for good at the same time that Christopher has discovered his half-brother. "How will your mother react when she hears you're the Earl's son?"

"In truth, she must be well aware."

"Oh, right. Sorry. That was dumb of me."

There's a slosh of water, as he turns and leans his chin on the edge of the tub. "I do not know how to confront her with this without implying…"

"Maybe she'll be relieved that you finally know. That's a pretty big secret to keep, and that can't have been easy." I think about how hard it's been to keep my own big secrets.

"Perhaps. She loved my father. The man I knew as my father. Of that I'm certain. And he loved me like his own son." Christopher considers this for a minute. "It is remarkable, when you think about it."

"You're a loveable guy. I should know."

He laughs. "And now I have a brother." He runs his fingers through his hair. "Strange how much a life can change in a day."

"Yeah. Strange." I again look at the photo. "You know what I don't understand? The history books all said that the Earl was stabbed in the courtyard."

"But you also said the history books declared the Wallingfords, including Baldwin, as heroes of the day, and stated that honorable men were actually traitors. Perhaps you should not believe everything you read."

"True. But in the courtyard was where the cursed spot was. That's where the Earl's anger could be felt and where, in my time, I could actually hear the murders. Why would that be if it all actually happened in the chapel?"

"I think I know why. Where do all go to gossip and share news of the day but to the courtyard? Naturally that is where his spirit would go. Get me my towel." He suddenly stands. His damp body shimmers in the firelight.

"R-right." I drop the photo, take the linen cloth from the chair and walk it to him.

He grabs my arms with his wet hands and pulls me forward. "Join my bath."

"You'll ruin the dress," I say, ready to jump in.

He chuckles and grabs the towel, rubbing his hair with it. "A lovely dress it is." He wraps the cloth around his middle and steps out. "Your wedding dress. We shall have many sumptuous dresses made for you now that the Earl has pledged his support."

"But I kind of like the things I usually wear. Jeans and stuff. I brought a few."

"And those elegant shoes?" He tugs one of my curls and smiles. "My bride shall have whatever she wants."

I make a brace for his two fingers with the twigs and tape them with several Band-Aids.

Christopher smiles and reaches for his green tunic that he'd laid out on the bed. It's the same one he wore when we'd first met. Before he picks it up, he notices the photo lying beside it. "What manner of painting is this?" He turns it over and over.

"It's not a painting. It's a photograph. An image that's captured on film and then printed."

"But it looks so realistic. It must have been created by a very talented artist."

"Actually anyone can make one."

"Really? Make one of you, then, for me to carry."

"You need a camera and I didn't bring one. Sorry."

"That is a shame. Who are these people?"

"That's my dad and that's my brother Wayne."

"You said he was unwell. Yet he looks hale and hardy enough."

I take the photo and set it on the table. "Not in his mind. He hears voices all the time that aren't there."

"Like you heard voices in the cursed spot?"

"It's not the same. He's been under a doctor's care and taking tons of medications but he never gets better."

Christopher takes my hand with his good one and squeezes. "Actually, he says he's heard you. And he knew about the Earl. He talked about someone who wanted to kill everyone."

"Baldwin Wallingford. He is not ill, then. He's a witch like yourself."

"I'm not a witch and it isn't the same. The doctors are certain he has a mental illness called schizophrenia. Most of what he hears is bizarre and unreal." I furrow my brows. "It's so sad. It's like the real him is in there, in his mind, but trapped."

"I wish I could help your brother. If only it were in my power, I would see you without a care. What can I do?"

"Never mind. Even if you were far in the future, were filthy rich and could give all your money to scientific research for studying just this illness, it would probably take like a century to find a cure. Otherwise they probably would have found one by now." I sigh. "It's hopeless."

"Someone very wise once told me that believing in something is the first step toward making it come true."

"*I* said that."

"Yes." He smiles. "When we were at the Roman ruins."

"It's *still* hopeless," I say, tearfully.

He rubs my temple. "Shh, now. Do not be sad. Not today."

I give him a gentle smile and hand him his green tunic, which he slips over his head.

Christopher's light-green eyes glow, as he touches the bear pin on my dress, then takes my hand. "Ready?"

51

"You sure you would not rather say our vows in a more sumptuous location?" he asks. "Or outside the door of the church, as is customary?"

I shake my head. "I can't think of a more perfect spot than this." We stand hand in hand on top of the tower where he had once found me sketching and where he had drawn his dagger on me. It seems to have been so long ago, though really it's only been a matter of weeks. Not for Christopher, I remind myself. For him it has been months. The early March air feels mild and the moon is high now, bathing us in golden light.

"Alright then." He straightens his tunic and adjusts his hair, trying to look his best for me.

But he always looks his best to me. Strong and beautiful and passionate and caring. "I love you," I whisper.

He holds me tight. "And I love you."

I pull back and our faces are close. "Are we married yet?"

"Not yet." He kisses the tip of my nose with such tenderness, I can't help but think of how kind and loving a husband he'll be, how gentle and caring a father. He steps back and takes both of my hands in his. "Michelle De Freccio, lady of my heart, I can barely speak of all I feel. I pledge my heart, my body, my mind and my very soul unto you, hereby binding myself unto you for all eternity. Take me to thee and thee to me. Be my wife." His face is solemn.

"Christopher Newman, you are...my soul mate." I stroke his injured hand. "We belong to each other." This last part comes out in barely a whisper. I swallow hard and say in a firm and clear voice, "Be my husband." I touch his face. "Are we married now?"

"Nearly." He leans into me. "First we must seal our promise with a kiss." His arms wrap around me and my lips feel drawn to his, but I pull back.

"We can't. I'll disappear and what if I can't come back?"

"I shall kiss your cheek then, and you mine."

"No." I step away. Something feels wrong. Very wrong. "This is a sign."

"It is merely a roadblock. We have faced other obstacles and we can bypass this one as well."

"I'm not meant to be here, Christopher. Just like the information in that book I tried to bring was never meant to be here. I thought everything would work out somehow, but don't you get it? If we can't kiss, we can't marry."

"Michelle, stop. This is merely a case of nerves. We shall be fine." He takes my hand.

"But how can we be fine? I shouldn't be here. You said it yourself. My news of the future has brought evil here. Because of me, Thomas is dead."

"He was a good man." Christopher looks at his feet.

"He was and he loved you, and it is all my fault—"

"Hush now." He gives me a long look. "You forget that because of you I am alive. And Plumson. And the Earl. And a truly horrible evil has been terminated."

"Look, there's a print back in your room and a note. I want you to have them. The note, well, I mean the words in it."

"Stop this. We shall be fine."

I rush into his arms and hold him tightly. "But what if I hurt you even more?"

"Nonsense. You bring me naught but joy and bliss."

I inhale the scent of him. The mint from his bath, the dab of cinnamon oil at his neck. I shake my head. "And no children," I say with certainty. Not being able to kiss is just the start of our problems. "I can't do this to you."

He grabs my arms hard and holds me before him. "What do you mean?"

"I've been selfish. I love you *so* much. That's why I have to go back."

"No. You are being ridiculous. Emotional."

"I'm not." I grab his arms as well. "I'm being realistic. I need you to have a real life now. A normal life."

"Normal is overrated. These are your words."

I shake my head. "You need a life where you have a companion in every way. You should have children. Lots of children. Remember all the things that you wanted to teach them? You'll be such an amazing father, Christopher. And you should have a wife who can be a real wife to you, not invisible and absent. I want this for you."

"Stop that." He shakes me. "You are all that I want. You are bound to me and I to you and that is all that matters."

I touch his cheeks. "Yes. All that matters is that I love you."

He breathes a sigh of relief. "Good. I thought—"

"So trust me and kiss me."

"Michelle."

"Trust me and kiss me, Christopher. If I'm meant to stay here, then nothing will happen, right?"

He touches his forehead to mine. "No. I dare not risk it."

"Please. Trust me and kiss me."

He shakes his head.

"You know in your heart I'm right. Please, Christopher." I rub my nose against his. "Please."

He nuzzles his nose against mine and his lips are so close I can feel their heat. He hesitates, then his lips touch mine. I pull him close and we kiss deeply. My arms encircle his neck, his arms draw my waist close. He pulls back and we look at each other, incredulous.

"It works," I say.

"Yes," he says in a breathless voice. "I love you, Lady Newman." We laugh and he pulls me even closer. Our lips touch again and caress and devour. My fingers twine into his hair, which suddenly feels cold and thin and Christopher's lips against mine are saying, "No."

The last I see are his eyes. His beautiful light-green eyes, filled with sorrow…

I am alone on top of the tower and shivering from a bitter October wind and from my own sorrow. I stand at the tower's edge, looking down through the gray early dawn onto the cars in the parking lot. And I am sure my life is over.

52

I don't know how long I stay up on that tower, more alone that I have ever felt in my life. It hurts even more to know that Christopher is here as well, separated by time.

Eventually birds begin to sing. Car doors slam in the lot below. And the tower seems too desolate.

I stumble down the circular stairs, tripping on the dress, wishing I could rip it off and be done with it. I wander along, passing a few Ghost Tour guests holding pastries and paper cups of steaming coffee. "That was certainly well worth the money," an elderly woman says. "When the wind started blowing in that dungeon it nearly took off my wig."

"I know," the other woman says in an earnest voice. "You can't fake things like that. And how about that recording of the voice, saying 'I'll get you out of here.'"

"I thought it said, 'Get out of here.' Nearly jumped out of my skin when they played it back."

I push past them and find myself in the sitting room, where the crew is packing up their recording equipment beside the Mating Chair. Christopher's eyes in the portrait stop me. They're a soft green, paler than I remember them, and his hair is sandy with gray. The artist included the faintest tracing of laugh lines around his eyes. Christopher's an old man. And joyful. My lip trembles as I study every wave of his hair and the twist of his mouth so ready to smile. He's holding a small-framed picture—my print of the dancing nymph. I want to laugh and cry at once as I imagine him reading my note. Words that were first meant for my dad:

> *Please don't worry about me. I'm where I need to be and happier than you can ever imagine. I am so fortunate to have had you in my life. I want you to be happy too. Find new love and live your life well, and remember that wherever I am, I will always, always love you.*

"Alright, everybody clear out now," James says as he hurries past. "We've got to get ready to open the castle to the public, you know."

"De Freccio, there you are. Your ride's waiting," Roger says.

Reluctantly, I leave Christopher's picture.

"Hey," he grabs my arm. "You okay? You don't look so good."

My lip starts to tremble again. "I'm fine."

"You sure?"

My eyes are swimming. "Just really tired. What happened with the police?"

"What police?"

I focus on him. "Roger, your face."

"What? Is it dirty?"

"No. It's perfect" The scab from the knife wound has disappeared completely and his skin color isn't as pale as usual. Plus, I notice with astonishment, his cheeks are no longer gaunt.

"Thanks, De Freccio. Didn't know you cared." He grins. "Come on. Wayne is waiting for you."

"*Wayne?*"

"Wayne. Your brother?"

I push past him and rush down the stairs and into the courtyard. The first beams of daylight have started to fill the sky and some of the sleepy workers stagger through the main gate. I pause and look at every face. When Roger catches up to me, I say, "Wayne's not here."

"He's in the car park, you silly arse. What's your hurry? I'm sure he'll—"

I never hear what Wayne will or won't do because I pick up my skirt and race through the gate and along the gravel path. Ahead in the parking lot, people are putting things into trunks of their cars and engines start up. And at the edge of the lot is the gaudy Clockwork Orange with someone leaning against the hood, arms crossed.

My heart does a swoop, because it *is* Wayne. I run to him and throw my arms around him.

"Ooph," he says. "You trying to kill me?"

"Wayne? What are you doing here?"

"Picking you up, dummy." His eyes are clear and focused. He smiles and then his left shoulder jerks as if he's startled.

"But where's Dad?"

"Back at the house. I told you I'd pick you up, didn't I?"

"I don't understand. You can drive?"

"Come on, Michelle. I've been driving these crazy English roads for the past two months now. I think you can trust me." His shoulder jerks again.

"But you were back in Philly."

"Why would I be in Philly? You know I have to stick close to the Newman Institute as long as I'm taking part in that trial of their new drug."

"The Newman Institute?"

"Yeah, the Newman Institute. The place doing all the groundbreaking schizophrenia research? Ring any bells?"

I open my mouth.

"Earth to Michelle?" Wayne snaps his fingers. "Wow, you really need some sleep. Let's go." He swings his key ring on his finger.

"Wayne, wait. Does this Newman Institute have anything to do with Christopher Newman?"

"Of course." His shoulder twitches yet again. "He was the philanthropist dude who started the Institute like a few hundred years ago or something. Now enough with the twenty questions. Get in."

I close my eyes and whisper, "Thank you." When I open my eyes, I stare at my brother, stunned. Mom had predicted I'd take care of Wayne. "God. She was right. About everything."

"Who was right?"

I'll always be there for you. Hope surges through me. "Wayne, where's Mom?"

Wayne's face clouds over. "Come on, Michelle. You know none of us have heard from her. What's wrong with you?"

"I...I'm just really tired, like you said."

He nods and opens the car door.

A silver compact car pulls up beside us and Roger powers down the window.

"Whoa," I say, "what happened to your rusty truck?"

"Me? In a rusty truck?" He snorts. "De Freccio, give me credit for having *some* class. Listen, must have been some mix up because Christopher's come to pick you up too."

"Christopher?" My heart lunges. "Where? How?"

"Relax, De Freccio. There he is now." Roger nods his head toward a crowd of people tromping to their cars.

I search every face for him but the only person I recognize is William, who smiles and waves, striding up to Roger's car. They shake hands. "How's it going, mate?" William says.

Mate? Since when?

"Not bad." Roger says. "We still on for tonight?"

"Yeah. Guitar Hero play-offs."

"I hope you got some decent eighties tunes this time."

William laughs. "You wish. See you then."

Roger nods and drives off. William's saying something to me but I'm too busy looking around for Christopher. I stand on my tiptoes and peer around but the lot has cleared and the last few cars are now driving out.

Wayne waves to William. "Hey, how you doing?"

"Good. We must have gotten our signals crossed. I thought I was picking up Michelle."

Him too? Who's going to show up next? Mary on a bicycle?

"That works out okay for me," Wayne says. "I've got to stop in at the Newman Institute anyway. Later." He waves and the Clockwork Orange zooms off.

Now it is only me, William and a small powder-blue car with a rusty bumper. He says, "Shall we go?"

"Actually, someone else is here to give me a ride."

"Really?" William looks around. "Who?"

I twirl around, confused. "He should be here."

"He who?"

I raise my shoulders. "Would you believe, Christopher?"

"Would I believe what?"

"Christopher."

"Yes?"

"William, what's wrong with you?"

"Christopher." He narrows his eyes at me. "The name's Christopher."

"Excuse me? William, you can't—"

"Why do you keep calling me by my middle name?"

"Christopher. *You're* Christopher."

"Yes. Christopher. Named after my great, great, great and so forth uncle, Christopher Newman. And?"

"Christopher Newman of the Newman Institute?"

"Michelle, you know all this. You get hit in the head or something?"

My thoughts swirl around in confusion. "Could you tell me just one more time, just to clarify things? I...I really like history."

He shrugs. "Sure. There's a tradition in the Wallingford family that honors Christopher Newman, the famous half-brother from long ago who co-founded the Academy and—"

"Really? He co-founded it?"

"Yes, though he's best known for endowing the Institute. He was quite important. Anyway, since he never had children—"

"Wait. He never had kids? Are you sure?"

William (or is it Christopher?) gives me a sideways glance. "Yeah. I'm pretty sure. He and my ancestor Percival Wallingford were very close, and since Newman never married and had children, every generation of Wallingfords has had a son named Christopher."

"But I don't understand. That can't—"

"Michelle? What's wrong?"

"No." I shake my head. "It's all wrong. Everything."

"Shh now." He steps close. "Do not look so terrified. Whatever is wrong, I am here. I will always be here right by your side." He tugs on one of my curls and smiles when it springs back.

Stunned, I glance up at his sky-blue eyes.

For a moment he seems stunned, too. He takes a step back and rubs his neck.

I turn toward the castle.

And I realize that Christopher did live on. He's everywhere. In the better life for Roger. In the better health for Wayne and who knows how many other poor souls. He's even involved in the school I attend.

Christopher William Wallingford walks to the passenger side door of the rusty blue car, holding it open for me.

"What happened to your Porsche?"

"I kind of sold it. I sold quite a few things, actually." He gives me a sheepish grin.

I notice the back of his windshield is dotted with at least a dozen decals declaring "I'm a Roman General," each one representing ten thousand pounds given for the Old Roman Grounds. I wonder if it's enough to preserve the land.

In the middle of all the decals is a green sticker that reads *"Lute Academy—Making Each Day Better."* A smile quivers around the edges of my mouth. "But your father…"

"He's furious and ready to destroy me any way he can. So, are you coming?" He raises his chin and I know with certainty that the spirit of my Christopher is within this young man standing before me right now.

"Yeah. I'm coming," I say, knowing he will also always live within my heart. And I climb into the rusty car, ready to see where we'll go from here.

Also by
Marie Lamba

Over My Head

Sang Jumnal jumps into summer with big plans, but she didn't plan on falling for a college-aged lifeguard. Is he the love of her life or just a player out to break her heart?

Available where books are sold

What I Meant...

Ever feel misunderstood? Ever have people tell lies about you? Ever try to do the right thing only to have it turn out so very wrong? *What I Meant...* is the hilarious and touching story about one girl who fights back hard...and sort of wins.

Available where books are sold

Acknowledgments

Jennifer DeChiara for always being in my corner. My daughters Adria and Cari, and Janice Bashman for their brilliant guidance and edits. Jacqueline Busterna for her help with Britishisms and Steve Busterna for being a great first reader. Santo and Louisa Busterna for being the best and most supportive parents a kid could ask for. Gregory Frost for his wonderful graphic art skills and for going above and beyond in helping me come up with an amazing book cover. My fantastic writers group the Rebel Writers for insightful critiques and meaningful friendship: Jeanne Denault, Damian McNicholl, David Jarret, Chris Bauer, John Wirebach and Russ Allen. My poor family, especially my husband, who suffered through a messy house and plenty of lousy dinners while this book was written. My glorious Liars Club who are always there to share advice, to laugh with and to lean on: Kelly Simmons, Merry Jones, Solomon Jones, Jonathan Maberry, Gregory Frost, Don Lafferty, Ed Pettit, Keith Strunk, Keith DeCandido, Jon McGoran, Dennis Tafoya and especially Leslie Banks who inspired me to go indie and who we all miss very much. The book *The Center Cannot Hold* by Elyn R. Saks, for personal insights into schizophrenia. Merry Sue Baum for having Christopher's eye color! Coldplay for their *Viva La Vida or Death and All of His Friends* album, which played like a soundtrack in my mind while I wrote scenes for this novel, and inspired me to no end. And to Vi Booker, who gave me my first taste of British hospitality.

About the Author

Marie Lamba is a full-time writer and author of young adult novels including *What I Meant...* (Random House) and *Over My Head*. Her work also appears in many national magazines, in the fiction anthology *Liar Liar* (Mendacity Press) and in *Call Me Okaasan: Adventures in Multicultural Mothering* (Wyatt MacKenzie Publishing). In a perfect world, Marie would spend half the year lounging in a village in Italy, sketching and eating dark chocolate. The other half of the year she'd spend cloistered in her studio writing novels, while also eating dark chocolate. Marie lives in Pennsylvania with her husband, their two remarkable daughters and a wacky poodle. To keep up with Marie's new books, to contact her, get book club guides, or to plan an author visit, stop by www.marelamba.com.